KILLHER

THE AKIRA FILES **BOOK 1**

A NOVEL

VALERIO VENTURA

VENTURA EXIT BOOKS

VENTURA EXIT

Joshua Tree, California USA

KILLHER. Copyright © 2022 by Valerio Ventura.
Based on the short story from the short film WINTER,
Copyright © 1997 by Valerio Ventura.
written and directed by Valerio Ventura,
with characters created by Valerio Ventura
with executive producer Gay Lawrence.

A few chapters of this book
based on the full-length script, WINTER
by Valerio Ventura and Larry D. Edwards Jr.,
Characters and story by Valerio Ventura.

www.ValerioVentura.com

First edition July 2023

ISBN: 979-8-9996920-0-9

Cover art direction by Gay Lawrence
Cover art © 2022 by Valerio Ventura

To my wife, Gay, you're my supernova.

KILLHER

THE AKIRA FILES BOOK 1

"*Hell is empty and all the devils are here.*"

Ariel, the magic spirit.

The Tempest, by William Shakespeare.

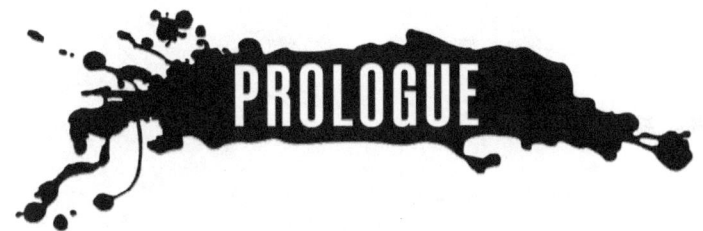

PROLOGUE

In 2019, in an exposé in the *Los Angeles Tribunal*, journalist Lori Hill reported that thirty-six professional assassins had operated out of California during the 1990s. The article was based on files given to her by an unnamed source and were used as the building blocks for her story.

During the better part of two years, Hill met with her secret informant and was able to piece together a tale of conspiracy, murder for hire, and human trafficking that spans the globe all the way to the highest of places.

This grim account was based solely on one small section of those findings and from a series of folders labeled The Akira Files.

In her article, Hill stated that twelve assassins had worked in the Los Angeles County alone, four of them women.

This is the story of one of those women—codename HER.

CHAPTER 1

Sir Charles

WEDNESDAY, NOVEMBER 18, 1998
ARRIVALS, TOM BRADLEY INTERNATIONAL TERMINAL, LAX
LOS ANGELES, CALIFORNIA

A murmuration of glittering birds dotted the skies above a concrete spider-ship as angels spewed from bellies of steel.

But harbingers of death, dark wolves, walked among the angels.

Calamities that brought agony and destruction to all innocents.

But she held a sword sharpened by the sun, with a promise to avenge and kill, to end all that was unjust.

———

Sir Charles Barton stepped through the automatic doors of the busy terminal. At sixty, he was still in good shape but for his slight limp. And as usual, he was turned out impeccably—a tailored three-piece suit and short, perfectly coiffed afro.

He leaned on his cane and shielded his obsidian-like irises from the assaulting sunlight, then pulled a pair of Ray-Bans from his vest pocket and put them on. It was November, yet this city, a dry desert turd, was still bright and sunny all the fucking time.

Outside the terminal, traffic was at a standstill. Too many cars were trying to leave at the same time and couldn't maneuver their way out; incoming vehicles fought over the few available parking spots. A driver complained of unfair treatment to the traffic cop who'd just issued him a ticket. An airport worker steered a yellow burden-carrier towing dozens of luggage carts back to their rental hub.

Sir Charles's eyes searched the sidewalk. A patrol car passed him, and the police officer in the passenger seat stared at him as if he recognized him, then turned away as if embarrassed to have made eye contact.

"Excuse me!" a woman's voice yelled out.

Sir Charles ignored the voice and continued onward, scanning the curb for his awaiting car. A thick White woman in her fifties approached him.

"Oh my goodness, I love your show, Mr. Cosby! Can I have an autograph?"

The woman held out a pen and a piece of paper the size of a business card. Sir Charles grimaced and put his arm out, deflecting her.

"Nonsense. Fuck off, woman," he hissed.

She was left shocked, frozen in place. *What a dick.*

A fan dream had come crashing down like a ton of bricks. Oh, the sadness.

Sir Charles's family were immigrants from British-colonized Sudan, where they'd experienced the conflict between north and south. His father, Ibrahim, had been in the Republican Guard during the start of the Sudanese Civil War in 1956, and when Sir Charles's mother had been murdered, Ibrahim had been left with no choice but to arrange for new identities and escape the country. Young Charles had grown up within the culture he'd been assimilated into in southern Sudan. Ibrahim had secured a job as an administrator at Oxford University, giving Charles the chance to earn a degree in economics.

Growing up as a British citizen with a fake identity, there'd been so much at stake. Being mistaken for the Hollywood actor sparked feelings of shame and vulnerability. Yet another assault to his identity, and one of the few things that could trigger his narcissistic rage.

In front of the terminal, a black Lincoln

Town Car idled at the curb. The driver was Robert Banks, a mid-thirties ex-heavyweight boxer who'd recently turned security. His fair hair was unkept and the suit over his black Lacoste inexpensive. He'd been hired for only three days but was being paid handsomely.

Sir Charles walked over to the Lincoln, followed at a short distance by his towering bodyguard. Early forties, ex-military type. James Craw, or Jimmy as he was known, was missing two fingers on his left hand. A scar threaded from the side of his face down to his neck and disappeared under his Valentino suit.

"Sorry, about that, sir. That bird came out of nowhere," Jimmy said.

"No worries, Jimmy. Glad she didn't have a gun, for fuck's sake. It is the US after all. Everyone carries, apparently. Although I'd prefer to be shot than mistaken for that Hollywood cunt."

Bobby held the door for him.

"Thank you, Robert," Sir Charles said.

"It's Bobby, boss,"

Sir Charles stepped into the back seat. "Very well, Bobby. Let's drive."

————

THE CONCOURSE HOTEL
LOS ANGELES, CALIFORNIA

Christmas garlands and lights framed the driveway up to the Concourse Hotel. A regiment of red poinsettias bordered the island, and two huge red-and-white harlequin deer welcomed guests to the valet area.

The Lincoln parked by the curb. Bobby popped the trunk and a valet approached the car with a luggage trolley.

Jimmy got out and scanned the area, walked up to a second valet in a booth and handed him the car keys. Bobby hurried around the Lincoln and opened the rear passenger door. Sir Charles wedged his cane against Bobby's foot, held on to the door with his left hand, and pulled himself out. He scrutinized the entry and looked up at the building. More shitty American architecture. Then he pulled a small glass vial out of his chest pocket and handed it to Bobby.

Micro-dosing on PCP was Sir Charles's addiction, and the onset of withdrawal had begun to slice through his gut like a bag of razor blades.

"Need more blow, boss?" Bobby asked.

"You said Bobby, right?"

"Yes, boss."

"Sure, Bobby. Well, we are in Los Angeles. I'm not looking for a 'White girl,' if you catch my drift. More of a dusty ... Angeleno. You understand, Bobby? The priest, the cardinal, and the pope, all in one special little vial."

Bobby's face lit up. "Ha! Gotcha. For sure, boss. No problemo. I'll get on that."

Sir Charles returned an empty stare that turned Bobby's smile into a dry cough. The driver pulled out his cell phone and punched in a number.

Sir Charles made his way through the turnstile and met with his bodyguard in the lobby.

"All good, sir?" Jimmy asked as they headed for a bank of elevators.

"Where did you find that imbecile?"

"Well, sir, last-minute thing, you know? And we are in California. They grow them cunts like oranges."

Sir Charles cracked a smile. "They do, my boy. They do."

Jimmy scanned the area, then pressed the elevator button. Sir Charles looked through the lobby and out into the driveway. A tourist bus had just pulled up. The doors opened with a loud hiss of compressed air. Two giggling young Asian women wearing tight short dresses and platform booties climbed out. Behind them, a thin man in his early thirties and wearing mirrored Ray-Bans began to flirt with them.

Sir Charles watched the girls, his tongue peeking from his narrow lips.

The man said something to one of the girls. She smiled, bobbing her head. He whispered something in her ear and handed her his camera. She giggled, and the other girl joined in, putting her hand in front of her mouth, trying to contain her laugh. The man posed for a few pictures, then the girls handed the camera back to him and walked to the rear of the bus, where the driver was unloading luggage for a dozen waiting passengers. As the girls leaned down to pick up their cases, Sir Charles caught a glimpse of their underwear.

His eyes trailed back to the man, who had turned the camera toward him and Jimmy, and was adjusting the focus. Was he taking pictures of them?

Bobby was near the bus, still glued to his cell phone. The man pointed the camera at Bobby and maneuvered the zoom lens.

What the fuck?

Again, the man turned his attention back to Jimmy and Sir Charles at the bank of elevators, and snapped more pictures.

"Sir," Jimmy said.

"What?" Sir Charles snapped, and turned toward Jimmy.

His bodyguard gestured toward the waiting elevator.

Sir Charles stepped through the open doors. "Fucking cunt."

A middle-aged woman hovered nearby, seemingly startled by the profanity. Sir Charles looked right past her, still watching the man with the camera.

"You are coming in, luv?" Jimmy asked.

Sir Charles jammed his cane across the door frame, blocking the woman's entry. She stepped back, shook her head, and walked off muttering.

Jimmy pressed floor ten and the door closed.

"That fucking cunt just snapped a picture of me."

"Who? That bird, sir? Are you sure? I didn't see a camera?"

"No, some tourist outside. A fucking bloke just took a picture of us."

"Are you sure, sir? A bloke?"

"Yes. And I saw him take a picture of Bobby too. They know, Jimmy. These fucking cunts, they know where we are."

"Calm down, sir. I'm good at what I do. Nobody knows you're here. Let's get the room all sorted out and make you comfortable. Trust me when I tell you that no one knows we're here."

———————

As Jimmy said it, the details crept back to him. The people looking for his boss wouldn't take too long to find him. Fuck, maybe they were already here. Jimmy pulled a .45 SIG-Sauer from his concealed holster and twisted a suppressor into the barrel. It wouldn't completely eliminate the noise but it would do. At least people wouldn't be calling the cops or running out of their rooms in a panic if they heard that muffled sound. And it would give Jimmy enough time to react, figure out his next move.

He pulled the SIG's slide back and loaded the chamber.

"What's wrong, Jimmy?" Sir Charles asked.

"Just in case, sir. Better to be on the alert. Stay behind me."

Sir Charles stepped back. A worried look washed over his face.

Jimmy gave his boss a reassuring nod. Yes, he felt threatened, but that didn't mean he couldn't keep his calm. Fearless, that's what he was. It came with the turf. Just one of the benefits of being a high-functioning psychopath.

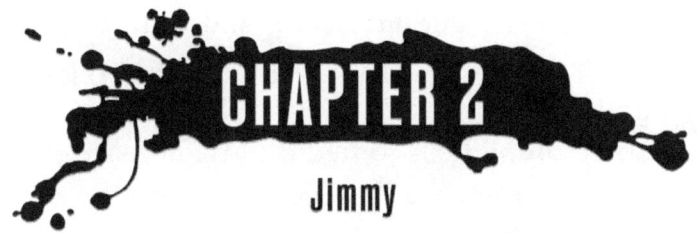

CHAPTER 2

Jimmy

Jimmy had been born in the East End of London, grown up during a period of economic reorganization that had affected every inch of the industrial infrastructure around him and led to one of the darkest stretches of unemployment in UK history. His childhood had been bleak, wrought with violence. He'd joined a gang at only fourteen, and because of his size, the crime bosses hadn't hesitated to use him as an enforcer. By the age of sixteen, he'd already made a name for himself by murdering two rival gangsters with a small axe.

Landing a cozy bodyguard job with Sir Charles had come later. First, he'd been a mercenary, working in the late eighties for a private military company that shipped soldiers out to the world's most dangerous war zones. Early on in his career, he'd spent two years in Somalia, where he'd taken part in at least one massacre, and four years in Sudan, where he'd fought the good guys supporting the corrupt regime.

Some individuals joined a PMC because they could commit murder and get away with it.

Jimmy was one of them.

In the 1980s, a British soldier was paid £500 per month but served under the limitations of the law. Jimmy had made double that per day in the private sector, and with no legal restrictions. By using hundreds of mercenaries like him, private military contractors had helped governments conquer and control territory with a level of covert and lethal authority unmatched by any state-sanctioned body.

The political struggle and violence in the Horn of Africa had allowed corporations to exploit the atrocities occurring there. Jimmy had fitted right into that chaos. He'd made friends with local gangs, and had occasionally partnered with them outside his PMC contract, selling weapons and dealing drugs.

During one of his most notorious missions back in Somalia in 1989, when a single-party military dictatorship had been in charge, his group had been commissioned to stop a small army of rebels outside Burco, the country's second largest city.

The rebels had been holed up in a gas energy plant, but Jimmy's squad had made a grave error with coordinates. Instead, an elementary school five miles away had become the target. After firing at the school for two hours, the soldiers realized their mistake and went in.

It was too late. Most of the teachers and children had been killed. In one of the classrooms they'd been having a party, and many of the children's faces were painted blue to celebrate peace.

It was as if a bomb had gone off in Jimmy's mind, and he went ballistic, killing the survivors, injuring himself in the process.

He was extracted, and the rest of the squad was left to deal with the aftermath—and the ensuing coverup.

A year after the massacre, his mercenary friends would quote Jimmy as having said: "We ended twenty-eight Smurfs, six Papa Smurfs, and four Smurfettes."

Ironically, it was the little blue comic-book character stories he'd enjoyed the most as a child.

He and his younger brother Tommy would read comics together after school. One day, their father had come home to find that both boys had painted their faces blue. He beat them both savagely.

The man's brutality had injured Jimmy and

killed Tommy.

Rather than face a prison sentence, his father had buried his little brother in the backyard, his face still painted blue.

That horrific day changed Jimmy forever. He'd been only ten years old. From then on the blue face of his dead brother would haunt him.

As would that day at the school. A child had come out of nowhere, grabbed his military vest, and pulled a pin right out of one of his flash-bang explosives. He'd tried to dispose of the flash-bang. It killed the child and cost Jimmy two of his fingers.

After two decades of fighting in Somalia, there was no shortage of offensive nicknames for people with war injuries. Jimmy's first had been Infidel. After the school incident, he'd been granted a less favorable moniker—Faroole, or No Fingers. He flew back to London for his new job, leaving his fingers and nickname back in Somalia. Still, even the simple task of pressing an elevator button reminded him of his missing extremities and the name Faroole. Every single time. *That fucking Smurf.*

———————

THE CONCOURSE HOTEL
LOS ANGELES, CALIFORNIA

Jimmy's jaw tensed as his neck spasmed, the vertebrae cracking loudly. Sir Charles winced. They'd known each other for years, but his boss had never got used to Jimmy's tic.

The elevator came to a slow stop. The doors chimed and opened with a whisper.

Jimmy peeked into the corridor. Looked left and right. Hid the pistol inside his jacket and stepped out into the hallway. He checked the room signage and followed the right-pointing arrow, Sir Charles in his wake.

They stopped in front of room 1405.

Further ahead, plastic sheeting blocked the path to the rest of the suites. A large sign read *Remodel in Progress—Keep Out—Authorized Personnel Only*.

Jimmy opened the door with a keycard, and he and Sir Charles stepped in. The door swung back and locked behind them. His boss headed for a small bar without giving the room so much as a glance, grabbed a tumbler, and put it on the counter. His hands were shaking.

Jimmy scanned the room.

"Jimmy, just pour me a fucking drink," Sir Charles said, and walked over to a window. He pulled the curtain across, leaving just a sliver open, and peered through it.

"Of course, sir," Jimmy said. "The usual, coming up."

Jimmy placed his pistol on the counter and grabbed an unopened bottle of Macallan single malt from the shelf. Examined it, twisted the cap off, poured a double shot. He walked it over to Sir Charles, who slammed it down and handed back the glass.

Jimmy repeated the process, this time with two glasses and plenty of ice. Sir Charles brought the tumbler up to his nose and sniffed the malt. Jimmy lit a cigarette, pulled a long drag and offered it to Sir Charles. His boss began to toke on it while they both peeked through the curtains.

Traffic on Century Boulevard was at a standstill, and the sky was turning orange and lavender thanks to the setting sun and the smog polluting the city air. They continued the ritual, passing each other the cigarette, sipping the whiskey, as if they'd done this for a hundred years. When the cigarette was down to the butt end, Jimmy crushed it in an ashtray and lit another.

CHAPTER 3

Bobby

"I can't hear you," Bobby said, cell phone pressed to his ear. "Hang on, I'll go outside."

He stepped out of the restrooms, headed along a long hallway and quickened his pace until he'd reached the Concourse's lobby.

It was late afternoon and a group of business-people conversed around a large coffee table. Others read newspapers or tapped on laptops. Bobby pulled up the antenna on his Motorola StarTAC and headed for the exit.

"Raffi! Can you hear me?"

"You're muffled but, yeah, I can hear you."

"Fucking phone," Bobby said. "Come meet me with that refill. I got cash for you. I need this now. These people I'm working with, they're fucking weird. They want it now. Where are you?"

"I'll be there, bro, like twenty minutes."

"Twenty? From Beverly Hills?" The phone line crackled with static. "What? I can't hear you. Fucking AT&T."

"Yo, can you hear me now? I said I got a crotch rocket."

"Cool! What did you get?"

The phone went silent. Bobby looked at it, then put it back to his ear. "Raffi? Can you hear me?"

The piece-of-shit phone was dead.

He went to the reception desk, held out a charging cable, and waved it toward an outlet on the wall behind a young woman with a long blond ponytail. Her name was printed on a tag pinned to her sharp gray suit. *Lisa*.

"Do you need to charge your cell phone, sir?"

Bobby nodded.

"See those comfy chairs?" She pointed. "There are—"

"I don't need to sit down, Lisa. What I need is right there behind you. That outlet. To plug it in and charge it. You fucking get it?"

The receptionist took a slight step back, her default smile turning into a gasp.

"I'm sorry. Yes, sir, right next to those chairs over there, on the wall. There are dedicated outlets just for cell phones."

Lisa pointed again. Bobby turned and looked toward a concierge lounge with sectionals and low tables.

"You could have said that in the first place. What the fuck is wrong with you?"

He stormed into the lounge, fumbled the charging cord into outlet, and sunk into a large chair with soft cushions. He placed the cell phone on the coffee table next to a recent copy of *Car and Driver*. The cover image featured a beautiful red 1969 Mustang Boss 429, the epitome of hot rods. Bobby opened the magazine toward the middle, flipped a few more pages and stopped at the cover story. The headline read: *1969 FORD MUSTANG BOSS 429, A LEGENDARY BEAST*. This was his number-one favorite car in the entire world. And when this job was done, he'd have enough cash to buy one. So hot in that candy apple red color, too.

"Ha! That's Larry Shinoda, right?"

Bobby looked up. A Lufthansa pilot stood next to him, looking down at the magazine.

"What?" Bobby asked, making a sour face. Who the fuck was this guy?

"The Boss. Larry Shinoda was the designer. He headed the project at Ford in 1968. He made that car." The pilot smiled, leaned over and cocked his head, looking at the story again. Then he extended his arm. "Name's Stan. Stan Winston."

Bobby ignored the hand. Stan hovered for a few seconds, then aborted the handshake.

The guy had a big smile, friendly. And though he was in his forties, balding and stocky, he had that kind of confidence that would give him an edge over anybody younger, better looking, and physically fitter. The kind of guy who had no problem getting laid.

"I saw you at the airport getting into a Town-Car," Stan said.

"Yeah? Are you the pilot that brought my boss over?" Bobby gave away a smirk.

"I don't know, maybe. I flew a Lufthansa Airbus, flight one-nine-three-nine."

"Guess not. He was on a Virgin. Virgin Atlantic, I mean."

Jokes formed in his head, going a hundred miles per hour.

Stan smirked. "Was he on top, or was she?"

They both cracked up. Instant connection. This guy was hilarious.

"I'm Bobby. So, you like Mustangs?"

Stan extended his hand again. This time Bobby shook it.

As Stan sat down on a small ottoman, Bobby checked his cell phone and turned it on. It beeped once.

"I do like Mustangs," Stan said. "I have one—a 302. The thing is a beast, more than I can handle."

"Get outta here. You can handle a plane, you can handle anything."

"Nah, planes are easy." Stan pointed at the picture of the Mustang's interior. "You have to love what Larry did with the steering wheel. Iconic right?"

"Larry?" Bobby asked.

"Shinoda, Larry Shinoda. He designed the Boss and the first steering wheel with three holes in its spokes. Classic race-car design, straight out of NASCAR."

Bobby examined the photo. A beautiful black leather interior with clean wood trim and red leather piping. "Wow. Yeah, that's one of my favorite parts of that interior."

"You know what happened to Larry, right?" Stan asked.

"No, I don't. So he designed the Boss, uh?"

"Yes, siree. And that was after they interned him and his family."

Interned? What the fuck did that mean?

"You know," Stan said. "What they did to Japanese Americans during World War Two."

Bobby shook his head.

"Well, after the Japanese attacked Pearl Harbor, there was a rash of fear about national security. So, if you were Japanese, or of Japanese descent, you were pretty much under arrest and taken to a camp far away from your home. And, to be fair, the government did that to the Italians and Germans too, but they hit the Japanese people hardest."

"Really? That's fucked up. How many did they arrest?" Bobby asked.

This historic fact disturbed him. He'd grown up in Little Tokyo, Downtown LA. And most of his childhood friends, people who were still friends to this day, were Japanese. And yet he'd never heard of internment camps.

"This is crazy. Why was I not told this? Never mind, go on."

"Well, they moved more than a 100,000 people to prison camps. In places like Colorado and whatnot. That's what interned means."

"And this Larry guy?"

"Well, like most people affected, after the war was over, his family stayed in Colorado. Larry moved to California and served in the Korean War. When he returned, he became a successful race-car driver, winning the NHRA nationals with a Ford. And after that, Chevy hired him to design cars. I mean, can you believe it? Larry designed the Corvette Stingray. Genius."

"Really? What a comeback story. I love this guy!"

Bobby turned the page.

"Anyway," Stan said, "the rest is history. He moved to Ford a few years later and designed the

Mustang Boss. And you know, he put a NASCAR engine in—"

Bobby's cell phone rang. Raffi's name popped up on the screen. He flipped it open and put his hand over the mic. "Hey, Stan, gotta take this."

Stan nodded. "Until we meet again, Bobby."

Once the pilot was out of earshot, Bobby pulled up the antenna with his teeth. "What's up?"

"Where the fuck are you? I'm here, bro."

Bobby looked over to the entryway. Beyond the glass was a motorcyclist on a black Ducati Monster talking into a cell phone.

"That's a sweet ride," Bobby said, and headed toward the doors.

The lobby was busier now, people everywhere. Like there was a special event going on. Pretty much everyone was holding a briefcase. A woman in a business suit stood near the reception desk, handing out pamphlets to arriving guests as the buses outside spewed out a sea of people all at once.

Seemed like he was the only person going toward the exit, and the throng of the crowd pressed in on him. He cut between a decorative palm tree and a line of people by a kiosk, but someone had the same idea and bumped hard into him. Something dropped on the floor. Bobby picked it up, thinking it was his.

It was a makeup compact.

"Sorry about that," a woman said.

He looked up, and caught his breath. Another Lufthansa employee, wearing a flight-attendant uniform, sheer stockings, and dark-purple heels. And she was gorgeous.

"Can I have it back?" The woman spoke with a sultry voice, and reminded him of his favorite Victoria's Secret's model, Tyra Banks.

Oh, man, keep those catalogues coming.

Bobby tried to respond with words, but instead a squeak emerged from his mouth from God knows where.

Way to go you, idiot.

"May I?" She extended her hand.

Bobby handed her the compact. "Here."

She thanked him, smiled, spun around, and walked away.

Bobby couldn't keep his eyes off those dark-purple stilettos, and the mile-long bare legs making their way up to a magnificent behind, swinging right under the smallest waist. As she walked away, Bobby swore he could hear the sound of necks snapping from every man in the lobby.

His mobile rang. Fuck, Raffi again.

Bobby headed through the turnstile and walked over to Raffi.

"What the fuck, dude?" Raffi said, and lifted

his visor.

"Back off. I got busy, alright?"

Raffi handed him a pack of Marlboro. Bobby opened the top and peeked in. There were a few cigarettes and four small glass vials full of white powder.

"Good man. This is the best shit, right?" Bobby stuffed a wad of cash in Raffi's jacket pocket.

"Best phencyclidine in the country, bro. Angel dust, baby. Are we good?"

"Sweet. Yeah, we're good. Probably going to need more in a couple of days."

"Just bring the cash and I'll bring the dust."

CHAPTER 4

Akira

The villa, resplendent with Christmas trimmings, intermittently lit up the night sky of one of the city's wealthiest neighborhoods on South Oak Knoll Avenue. Two black Mercedes-Benzes were parked in the driveway. In front of them, a life-size cast of Santa Claus, complete with sleigh and reindeer, welcomed passersby.

A collection of swords and a samurai suit of armor stood guard by a grand staircase that led up to a landing. A large Gustave Doré print hung on the wall. The etching depicted Satan raping an angel, its shimmering silver wings staked to the ground and drenched with blood as it stabbed at Satan's throat with a knife.

On the upper foyer, a shaft of moonlight

sliced the parquet floor through an open bedroom door.

There, on a four-poster bed, was the shadowy
figure of an Asian woman in her late twenties with
long black hair and a small muscular frame. Akira
was making love to her boyfriend, Kyle—a California native. Similar age, tall, handsome, wiry. A
Kenpo champion, former US Special Forces and
ex-CIA operative.

Kyle was the only man she'd said "I love you"
to. Three simple words she'd thought she'd never say. Before Kyle, she'd vowed never to fall in
love, but then he'd come, and the words had risen
to her lips without thought or effort. But *why?*
Every time she saw his face on these sheets, she
asked herself the same question.

She straddled him and traced her fingernails
over his face, his mouth, his eyebrows. He'd
looked so beautiful as he'd mouthed back those
three words.

The external Christmas lights flickered over
her shimmering skin in a kaleidoscope of colors,
accentuating the muscles already enhanced by the
elaborate tattoo of a phoenix wrapped around
her body. The sign of a yakuza upbringing.

Kyle held her hips as he thrust into her. Then
his fingers traced the long scar on the side of her
torso. Her back arched, rousing the phoenix's
feathers. Akira moaned, told him she loved him

once more, then craned her neck back up toward the slow-spinning ceiling fan and its strobing blades.

Until Kyle, all men had looked like her mom's boyfriend, the man she'd been told to call Uncle William. The monster who'd killed her mother.

She looked down at her right hand, the knuckles white from her grip.

That she was clutching a pair of scissors came as a surprise. They were large, black and sharp. Tailor's scissors. The thought of killing Kyle was ever-present and instinctive. Strangely, it might have been what kept them together.

She tensed and moaned louder as Kyle thrust harder into her.

They locked eyes.

Akira raised the scissors.

And plunged the twin blades toward his face.

Kyle grabbed her wrist, holding the scissors halfway between them. Akira bore down, using her momentum and the full weight of her slender frame.

Kyle's eyes widened. "Why?" he spluttered.

"Uncle William?"

Akira's skin was slippery with body lotion and sweat, and Kyle began to lose his grip. He fumbled with her wrist but it slipped from his grasp and the scissors sank into his neck.

It was as if she'd opened a faucet.

Blood sprayed everywhere. Kyle's hands flew to his neck but Akira raised the scissors again and stabbed at the gushing wound. Then, using both hands now, she pounded the flashing blades into his chest and shoulders as Kyle's strangled screams became a gurgle—

Akira's eyes snapped open, her heart racing, the sheets beneath her pooled with her own sweat.

The cruel nightmare was a recurring one.

She stared up at the ceiling fan. Kyle's sleeping form was reflected in the blades. She bolted into the bathroom and braced herself in front of the mirror. She was ashen, her expression tense, raw. She cupped her hands under the running water and splashed her face. Went to dry up, but vomited into the sink instead.

She wiped her mouth with a towel and took a deep, slow breath. Just great—the nightmare that kept on giving.

Kyle pulled on his boxer shorts and went to the kitchen. The coffee pot was hot; he poured himself a cup and inhaled the rich aroma.

Akira's black Nokia Vertu vibrated on the marble countertop behind him. Kyle looked at it. *Fuck that*. He headed for the study, sat down behind a large wooden desk, and powered up his computer. The Vertu vibrated again back in the kitchen.

Why the fuck was it that a four-thousand-dollar phone, one with a paid "special" service that cost way more than the phone itself, vibrated louder than any other Nokia model? The damn thing was two rooms away yet it felt like a trip hammer hitting a metal plate in his brain.

Kyle opened a Word document—"Book Draft One"—and began to type. He stopped, sipped coffee while he contemplated the next sentence, typed again, stopped again, hit delete. This was his second book and he'd been at it for two years now. The first had been written just after he'd retired, but he'd abandoned it. He thought of it as a kind of casualty of his new endeavor to become a writer.

And this was a ritual—type, back up, erase. Type, back up, erase less. Over time, he'd gotten to writing more than he was deleting. And coffee always helped him get into his rhythm.

Again the Vertu vibrated. Stopped. Started again.

Kyle stormed into the kitchen, picked it up, and went into the living room. Akira was asleep on the sofa, wearing headphones connected to an MP3 player, arm thrown over her eyes. The usual routine after a nightmare—come downstairs, eat carbs, fall asleep listening to music.

She wore a large black robe over a red sweat-shirt, loose white silk pajama pants, and a pair of reindeer slippers. An empty pizza box lay across her lap, and an open carton of eggnog stood on the nearby coffee table.

Her eyes were closed and there was a smile on her face. Kyle heard the muffled sound of "Before It's Too Late" by the Goo Goo Dolls.

He turned up the volume on the phone as it rang again with the iconic Nokia ringtone of "Sandpiper" by Italian composer Dario Marianelli, designed exclusively for the Vertu. High pitched. Extremely invasive.

Akira jolted up.

"Fuck! Is that my phone?"

Kyle tossed the Vertu into the pizza box. Akira's forehead crumpled as she grabbed it. Then she tossed the pizza box to the side and stood up. The headset dragged the MP3 player before disconnecting. She ripped off the headphones and tossed them on the floor.

Kyle followed her out of the room and across the foyer. Halfway up the staircase, Akira picked up the call. He listened to her side of the conversation.

"Yes?" She stopped on the stairs. "Today?" A pause. "Not really. Fine, send the gear."

The doorbell rang. Akira turned and glanced

down to the bottom of the staircase where Kyle was waiting.

"It's here," she said, and covered the mobile with her hand. "Could you get that for me, Kye? It's my gear."

"Sure thing."

He swung the door open hard, like he was punching an invisible opponent.

No one was there.

He scanned the front yard. Nothing, not even the sound of a car taking off, just the large double gate at the end of the driveway closing.

He looked down.

A large red bowling-ball bag sat on the mat. An agent working for Wilshire, the company Akira was employed by had dropped it off. For some reason, these people always felt they had to act like ghosts. Probably wanting to convey their superiority, remind you that they could enter your property, your home, without you noticing.

Kyle didn't buy into it, wasn't impressed by their stealth, didn't give a shit what they thought. In the end, only one thing counted. Survival.

Kyle took the bag up the bedroom and laid it at the foot of the bed.

He looked over at the window where Akira stood topless, wearing black panties and matching socks. He was momentarily paralyzed, feeling like he was sixteen again. *Wow*. Every time he looked at her felt like the first time. Turned out that Akira was the only woman who could give his life any sense of meaning. No, more than that— any sense of redemption.

She pulled back the slide and loaded a magazine into the chamber of a Walther PPK. Then she took a tiny holster from the bowling bag and slipped it, and the gun, into her black clutch.

As she slid into a pair of black skinny jeans, Kyle checked out her stomach. It sported an awe-inspiring set of abs that could handle a punch from Mike Tyson.

Akira stared at Kyle indignantly, as if anticipating a disapproving speech.

More items came out of the bowling bag and onto the bed—black leather jacket, bulletproof vest, black sweater.

"You said we were going out," Kyle said, "and that you wouldn't take another gig for a while."

Akira zipped up the jeans. "You're being silly. I've never said that."

"What do you mean? I thought we were going to see the Bergman flick."

"I don't book jobs, they book me. You know that."

Fuck, not this again. "I disagree," Kyle said. "Don't you see the problem here?" He'd tried to have this conversation since the day he'd gone on his writing sabbatical, had thought she'd understood, that she'd consider slowing down, maybe even quitting. Had he misunderstood? Was this all in his head?

"No, I don't. As I said, I've never said that," Akira said.

"Bullshit."

"Sorry."

"It's all twisted now. You can't give up the rush, right?"

"You should know. Same monsters, different demons," Akira said.

"Exactly. That's how I know where you're at. The adrenaline rush isn't even there anymore. You don't even feel it, do you? What drives you? Do you even know?"

"Stop psychoanalyzing me. You know this tone of yours will eventually piss me off. That's all you're going to get if you're condescending. You're no fucking different, Kyle. End of story." She sat on the bed and pulled a pair of black ankle-high tactical boots out of the bag, then slipped the left one over her foot. "You really think I'm an assassin because I love killing? Really?"

"Yes, really."

"You really think you were able to quit?"

"I made a choice. Yes, I'm done," Kyle said.

Akira raised her chin. "Wake the fuck up, Kyle. You can't just say 'I'm through.' This thing here, it fucking clings to you."

"I'm fucking done. I've been out for two years."

"You think they're ever going to let you stop? You're just on a sabbatical, on leave, on vacation. One day you'll get the call, and you won't be able to say no."

Akira pulled on the other boot and secured its Velcro straps.

"That's more bullshit," Kyle said. "They signed off, and it's been cool since. You can choose not to play the game, right?" He spoke firmly but his conviction had been rattled.

"I need this," she said. "This has always been who I am."

"You don't get it, do you? We can walk away anytime. We've got plenty of money."

Akira stood up. "You're alive because I'm still on payroll, that's why. You do understand that, right?"

"Bullshit," Kyle said.

Akira zipped the vest over her bare torso and pulled the black sweater over the top. "You know it's not about money with me. It never was."

"We'll close the shop here," Kyle said. "We'll move to the beach where no one can touch us. No one knows us there. We always said we'd start a new life."

"No, you always said that. We are what we are. Accept it and move on."

"That's more bullshit. Do you think you're living in a Bergman film? The difference between us is that I know I can't play chess with death forever. Death is inevitable. We all die. Life is about what you do before that."

The Vertu beeped twice. Akira picked it up and looked at it, then put it in the clutch. "Time to go."

"Look, I know—"

She glared at him, slipped into the leather jacket, and placed the suppressor from the bowling bag in an inside pocket.

"Do you love me?" Kyle asked.

Akira moved close, her face inches from his.

"Yes. I love you to death."

"Death can be claustrophobic," Kyle said. Even he could hear the frustration that had crept into his voice. Too much like a whine.

Akira smiled slightly. He moved his lips to hers.

She pulled away and put her hand over his mouth. "Not now."

She grabbed the black clutch and the car keys from the nightstand, and walked out of the bedroom. Kyle stood there, defeated, then sank into a chair by the window and watched her slide behind the wheel of a the blacked-out C43 AMG Merc.

The gate opened. The highly tuned V8 engine rumbled. And Akira drove through the gates and took a right into Oak Knoll Avenue.

CHAPTER 5

Priest Cardinal Pope

Sir Charles had chosen a fine black suit, black tie, and vest over a perfectly ironed white shirt. The blue sky was marred only by contrail streaks from a passing jet. He sipped a cup of English tea, mouth pressed into a hard line, then sighed heavily as he stared down at the heavy Century Boulevard traffic. Why the fuck call it a boulevard? Perhaps it made these idiots feel like they were stepping up in the world. Boulevard sounded classy. *Lipstick on a pig.*

A young woman, partially covered by the bed sheets, lay motionless behind him. Next to her was his cane with its wolf's-head grip. The pillows were spattered with blood.

How fragile life was. In the twinkle of an eye,

one passed from blue skies, through the smoke of hell, and plunged into the fires below.

He placed the teacup on the nightstand and lifted the sheets. *And there you are.*

A young Asian girl, early twenties but probably carded frequently for looking fifteen. Shoulder-length dyed platinum-blond hair. Skin flawless—except for the strangulation marks around her neck. Eyes, bloodshot, bulging from the sheer force Sir Charles had used to choke her.

She'd been dead for hours.

Sir Charles smiled and picked up the cane just as Jimmy walked in.

"You all right, sir?"

"I feel better, Jimmy, much better."

"I'll take care of this. You should have some food, sir. You must be famished. I'll get room service."

"I'm all right, Jimmy. You do your thing. Just find another one. And I need more dust, too."

Sir Charles pulled out a small glass vial from his pocket and handed it to his bodyguard.

"More magic, sir?"

"Yes, more dust for the angels."

"You used it all, sir?" Jimmy asked.

"No, no. You know, I need only a little to get to one thousand percent. It was the girl—she thought it was cocaine, just as expected. It just makes it more fun." He grinned. "They take so much longer to expire."

Sir Charles loved to kill, and it was a pleasure he'd been denied since being on the run from the UK. Now, a furious urge was building inside him, and it was time to feed it. He and Jimmy had enjoyed sharing these moments many times in the past, and Sir Charles wanted more.

"I'll fetch some of that plastic. There's some in the hallway," Jimmy said, his neck twitching left to right with the usual crack as he exited the room.

Sir Charles took a long sip of his tea, then used a crisp white handkerchief from his vest pocket to wipe the blood off the cane. He turned back to the window. *Ah, Los Angeles, look at you, blood everywhere. Blood in the buildings, blood in the cars, and blood in the streets. I'd paint the town red if only you'd let me.*

Fucking losers. He folded his handkerchief, pocketed it, adjusted his tie, and went into the living room. Jimmy was on the couch, holding a copy of *The Telegraph*.

"Anything from the old country?" Sir Charles asked.

"Not about you, sir, but one of your chaps got fucked."

"Who now?"

"Michael Davies. You know him?"

"I do indeed. The cunt owes me money. He's

from the left. Did they find out he's homosexual?"

"Yeah. He was cruising by a gay club. Got mugged at knifepoint. The police showed up, and that's how the papers got hold of the story." Jimmy turned to the next page. "I guess he lied when asked about it, and Tony didn't like that, sir. They aren't talking either."

"The poor fucker," Sir Charles said. "So, nothing about us and the church?"

"No, sir. Like I said, nothing. Like Santa Claus, sir. I've checked twice." A smirk slipped from the side of his mouth as he flipped through the last pages.

Sir Charles tapped his cane on three newspapers lying on the coffee table. "And these?"

"Yes, sir. Checked all those, too. Same thing. Just more Michael Davies stories." Jimmy placed the newspaper on top of the others.

Sir Charles walked over to the bar and tapped a cigarette out of a pack of Pall Mall. He lit up and took a long drag. Jimmy picked up a snow dome from the coffee table and wound it. "Auld Lang Syne" played as he examined the sparkles falling over a Los Angeles skyline.

Jimmy's Nokia rang. Sir Charles nodded—a signal that Jimmy should engage the speaker button—and adjusted his necktie.

"You called with a request. S&M HC level 2,

blond Asian in her twenties," a female voice said.

"Yes, that's right. Hardcore."

"We've got you covered, Mr. Craw."

"She better be a nice bitch, if you know what I mean."

Satisfied with the way his tie looked, Sir Charles filled a tumbler with ice and a shot of the Macallan.

"Don't forget the rules," the caller said in a clipped tone. "We take care of our girls. Understood?"

"Don't worry, luv. We're not going to break her."

"Mr. Craw, I need you to say it, sir."

"Understood, of course. The rules." Jimmy's neck twitched and cracked.

"I can confirm that we received cash-in-hand last night. I see in the notes you want extra service," she said matter-of-factly.

"Yes, luv, and cash is not a problem, but we prefer to negotiate the extra here if you don't fucking mind. That's how my boss wants it. You can check with the source if you must. We gave you the reference. You get me, sweetie?"

"Yes, sir, we've informed her."

"Fucking cheers then." Jimmy placed the phone on the coffee table. "It's like pizza, sir. I just ordered a bitch with extra cheese."

"Where's Bobby?" Sir Charles asked.

"He delivered the cash last night and went to sleep. He should be here soon."

"Just check on him."

Jimmy dialed and tapped the speaker button again. The phone rang a few times, then Bobby picked up.

"Hey, Jimmy, what's up?" Bobby slurred.

"Good morning, sunshine. Where the fuck are you?"

"What? I can't hear you."

Jimmy stood up and walked over to the window. "That better? You need to come back, got it?"

"Yeah, bro. Chill, I got it. I'm on my way. It's Beverly Hills and traffic is shit. Will take like forty-five minutes."

"Beverly Hills? I thought you went to eat upstairs. You sound drunk. Don't crash the fucking Lincoln, you hear me?"

"I'm in a cab. I left the Lincoln at the hotel."

Jimmy's forehead crumpled awkwardly. "What the fuck are you doing in Beverly Hills? We need you here, just in case."

"Yeah, it's cool. Just had a late night. I'll be right over."

The line went dead.

"I'll fucking kill that Yankee cunt," Jimmy said as another crack came from his spasming neck.

Sir Charles chuckled. "Settle down, Jimmy.

Hassan is coming, and we're off to the Saudis where your old team's waiting for us. And then we are fucking done. No one can touch us."

"Yes, sir. I'll take care of the body in the bedroom; it'll calm me down."

"You don't trust Bobby with that matter?"

"No, sir. Bobby doesn't know about the dead girl, and doesn't have to. He's not a killer. Besides, all we need him for is the drugs. We don't want to attract attention by buying PCP from an unknown. Bobby comes recommended, and he's got connections. But he's another loose end we'll have to fix before we leave. I'll take care of that when it's time."

Sir Charles nodded. "I'm sure you will, my boy. I'm sure you will."

CHAPTER 6

Uncle Bu

Akira switched to the car waiting for her at a shopping mall courtesy of Wilshire. Most jobs that required a vehicle were prepped by them. She turned the silver Porsche Carrera Turbo into a narrow street and drove to the end of the block. The crosswalk ahead was clear so she nudged the gas.

The roller-skater came out of nowhere—a young girl wearing headsets and a Walkman.

Akira slammed on the brakes.

The girl stumbled to the other side of the street, oblivious to the fact that a car had missed her by few inches. In that moment, Akira felt a longing for the young girl she'd once been. Maybe there was some truth to the idea that the past made us who we are, and that was the reason she was here right now. But she still missed that girl, the one she'd been before.

She crossed the intersection, continued south on Vermont Avenue for half a mile and stopped at a red light on Olympic Boulevard.

The restaurant just over the way served the best food in Koreatown. Could she smell it from here or was that just a trick her mind was playing on her?

She'd grown up in K-Town with her mom but hadn't been back since her Uncle Bunsei— Uncle Bu as she called him—had died three years earlier. Being the executor of his estate had proven tedious, but she'd have done anything for him. He'd been a jovial and loving man, like a father to her. What she'd not known until his death was that he'd amassed a fortune.

Uncle Bu had been born in Japan. Then his father had moved the family to South Korea, transplanting his ancient weapons restoration business there. Akira's grandfather had overseen a family tradition going back to the Heian period, but Uncle Bu's vision had been different, one that involved reaching out to the American market. And so he'd moved to Los Angeles. Weapons restoration had been put aside. Instead, he'd learned to repair rare, expensive watches, his true passion. After years honing his craft with Cartier, Patek Philippe and Rolex, he'd earned a reputation and gone on to establish his own business in Koreatown.

Akira's dad had died before she was born. Her mother, Sung-soo, had already been pregnant when she'd moved to Korea. When Akira was ten, they'd followed Uncle Bu to LA. Her mom's life had taken a somewhat different turn to her brother's; she'd given into drug addiction and gotten mixed up with the wrong men. The worst was William, an ex-con and drug dealer who'd had been convicted for rape and attempted murder. He'd controlled every aspect of their lives.

Then Uncle Bu had died and left all he had to Akira. Her uncle's words flashed through her mind. *Hello, my little Aki-Aki, teriyaki. Where's your red motorbikey?* The memory always made her smile. It was a ritual she'd endured every time they'd met. He'd make his joke, then follow through with a big infectious guffaw. They'd both laugh, then play KenKen, her uncle's favorite pastime. Akira would joke about his name, and call him Uncle Boo-boo. More laughter would fill their spirits.

Uncle Bu had often showed Akira how he repaired watches. She'd been fascinated by the mechanisms, the intricate repairs he worked on, and the stories about his eccentric mega-rich clients.

It had been six years since the LA riots in which

looters had burned down her uncle's shop. Those events had reshaped Koreatown and changed most people's lives forever. The riots and looting had depleted the neighborhood of their only sources of income. It had taken a terrible toll on the Korean community, but Uncle Bu had gotten himself out there, helping afflicted shop owners with all he could give. With little-to-no aid from the city, K-Town continued to struggle with poverty and major crime. The Los Angeles city government had been too busy with the Rampart CRASH scandal involving police corruption that culminated in lawsuits costing the city over one hundred million in settlements. Politicians couldn't care less about anything else when the issue of gangs and cops conspiring together in murder and billion-dollar drug deals was nipping at their ankles. What a clusterfuck.

Akira crossed Olympic and parked in front of the restaurant. The same old neon sign from when she was a kid flickered. She'd help Uncle Bu around the house, then they'd come here and she'd order fried fish cakes—kind of spongy, a little sweet, and slightly reminiscent of the sea. Just the way she liked them. She'd follow with a good dose of doenjang jjigae stew—heaven in a bowl.

Then her life had taken a turn, and heaven was no more. *Fucking memories*.

Akira's forehead tightened as the memories

threatened to overwhelm her. She inhaled one more breath of that heavenly aroma, let an old lady cross in front of her, then went inside. The door chimed as she entered.

The restaurant was an authentic hole-in-the-wall, with just ten tables. Akira was glad it was winter because the only way to chill this place down in summer was a swamp cooler right above the entrance, which for as long as she could remember had never accomplished the job. There was one free table, next to the bathroom. A teenage boy with the name tag *Jin-ho* hurried over to her.

"How many?" the server asked.

"It's to go, thank you," she said in Korean.

He handed her a stained paper menu.

Akira ignored it. "I'll have one eomuk bokkeum and the doenjang jjigae. Make that spicy." She handed him a twenty-dollar bill. "Keep the change, but can you bring it to me? I'm parked by the curb." She added another ten dollars.

Jin-ho thanked her, punched a smile out of his mouth, and bobbed his head. Akira picked up a toothpick from a small box by the register and flipped through the menus until she found a clean one. She folded it and slipped it in her jacket pocket.

The door chimed. Akira spun around and found herself at eye level with a police-officer's badge that read *Chavez, Rampart Division, LAPD.*

Officer Chavez was a six-five Hispanic man with dark handlebars and long sideburns. A veritable human refrigerator. He wore a tight, impeccably clean LAPD uniform and red-mirrored Oakley shades.

At first, Akira smelled starch and body odor. Then an overpowering minty aftershave took over.

"Sorry, ma'am," Chavez said in a strong raspy voice.

He looked over her head toward the bathroom. A smile slipped through his handlebars, and he moved over. As Akira squeezed past him toward the door, her pocket caught on Chavez's holster. The officer pulled his revolver—a .357 Taurus—toward himself, freeing Akira.

Jin-ho emerged from the kitchen and turned white as a sheet as he spotted Chavez. He came over, head bobbing, and stammered a welcome.

"O-o-o Gin. O-o-o bring the usual." Chavez's mockery turned into a cruel cackle.

"Y-y-yes, s-sir."

The officer headed for the empty table and sat down, blocking the path to the restrooms. Like it was his table. Akira suspected that Jin-ho kept it available for the cop at all times.

Chavez grabbed a Budweiser from a small fridge next to him and sipped from it.

Jin-ho hurried over, chin down, visibly upset. "Is my g-g-girlfriend okay? When she c-c-coming back?"

"Ha! Gin! Always worried about your girl. She's fine. Don't worry. You'll have her back before you know it. So, where's my fucking food?"

"But it's been two m-months!" Jin-ho blurted out.

The whole place went quiet, Jin-ho's despair hanging in the air, naked and vulnerable.

Chavez stood up. The table rattled as he shoved it against the teenage boy and stood towering over him. Two tables emptied immediately, and the patrons hurried out of the restaurant. Those remaining resumed their meals, chins down. No one wanted to mess with Officer Chavez.

Akira went through the door, stepped outside, and looked back through the glass. Chavez grabbed Jin-ho by the collar and lifted him over to the bathroom like a rag doll.

The boy's feet never touched the ground.

———

Chavez slammed Jin-ho onto the sink and against the mirror. "Listen carefully, you little fu-fu-fuck. You raise your voice at me again and I'll sell that little bitch to the Mexican mafia, you fucking hear me?" Chavez snarled, revealing two gold teeth.

Chavez's giant hands wrapped around Jin-ho's throat. The boy's eyes filled with tears as he gasped for air.

"Now, shut the fuck up and bring me my food." Chavez said, and walked over to the toilet. He unzipped his pants and unloaded a stream of urine that sounded like it was coming from a Clydesdale.

Jin-ho took deep breaths, trying to control his trembling muscles and the urge to puke. Chavez had terrorized him for months, but there was nothing he could do. He slid down from the sink and vomited into it, gagging as he gasped for more air while Chavez was pissing into the bowl, one hand braced against the wall.

Jin-ho wiped his mouth with a paper towel and ducked out of the bathroom. He collected two to-go Styrofoam containers from the kitchen and bagged them, then fumbled with the cash register until it finally spat out a receipt. Then the stapler wouldn't work so he stuffed the receipt inside the paper bag. *Done*.

The toilet began to flush just as he folded the top of the bag over twice.

Jin-ho's father emerged from the kitchen with a plate overfilled with appetizers. A Chavez special. He placed the plate in the center, then came over to his son, grabbing napkins and cutlery from a nearby cart on the way. At the cash register, he bent down, took a handful of small spice packets from a shelf, and handed them to Jin-ho.

"Go," he hissed. "Take the food to the lady outside. I'll take care of this."

Jin-ho wiped his face with a sleeve and nodded.

In front of Chavez's patrol car was a silver Porsche. The passenger window lowered. Jin-ho eyed the woman and placed the paper bag on the passenger seat by a black clutch.

"Thank you. Hey, are you alright?" she asked.

Jin-ho stammered a response but she didn't look convinced.

As he hurried back into the restaurant, the Porsche's engine fired up and took off with a scream, leaving tire rubber in its wake. Jin-ho could only wish he was with her.

CHAPTER 7
Purple Stilettos

Ambient music piped through high-fidelity speakers hidden in the ceiling. Sounded to Bobby like "Santa Baby" covered by Madonna. He strolled through the lobby and ducked into the restrooms.

He eyed the third sink across from the stalls. What the hell? A black lacey G-string hung from a faucet. He heard a clap, followed by a moan. A woman's moan. *What the fuck?* The clap came again. No, a slap. The woman moaned again, this time louder.

Bobby sneaked over to the stall and peeked through the space between the door and the post. And there was his new friend Stan, hand raised, ready to connect with the woman's buttocks again.

The woman wore a flight-attendant uniform and—whaddya know?—dark-purple stilettos. *Hello again!* This time her skirt was pulled up, revealing her naked ass cheeks. Both her arms were braced against the partition with the neighboring stall, her fingers grasping the top.

Stan began to finger her, and she groaned louder.

"Fuck me, Stan. Fuck me from behind."

Stan pushed his finger deeper. "Not yet, Jo. You need to beg a little more."

Bobby snuck into the next stall and moved his face close to Jo's hands, smelling her while Stan continued to finger her.

Bobby unzipped his pants and looked down at himself, then at Jo's hands on the partition.

"Please fuck me," Jo said.

The partition began to shake as the pilot got down to business. For the next few minutes, Bobby masturbated until Stan reached his climax with a loud, exhausted grunt.

Then for a whole sixty seconds there was silence.

"Now then, Jo. Let's see you do it for yourself," Stan said.

There was a squeak as Stan's door opened. Had he come out?

One of the woman's hands remained on the partition. Bobby had to assume she was pleasuring herself with the other. He continued getting off as he moved his mouth close to her hand and flicked his tongue over her fingers.

"Yes. Atta boy," she whispered.

The partition shook gently, and she groaned as Bobby continued to lick her fingers and pleasure himself. One of her fingers found its way into his mouth. It sent him over the edge, and he finished all over the floor.

Then, remembering why he'd come in the bathroom in the first place, he began urinating. Meanwhile, Jo moaned, groaned, then screamed as she climaxed.

Bobby zipped up and walked out of the stall.

Stan was at the sink, drying his hands with a small hand towel. Bobby wiped beads of sweat from his forehead, cleared his throat, and spat into the sink. Both men's eyes locked in the mirror, then they laughed.

"Hey, buddy," Stan said.

In the stall, Jo reached a second orgasm and groaned loudly as she finished.

"Jo likes to finish alone. Loves it that way, pal. Freaky, but she's a cool cat."

"She's hot."

"Yeah, but you're more her type—tall, strong, good-looking. And you're big. I bet you fuck like a horse."

Bobby puffed out his chest, feeling proud.

Stan pointed at the stall and shrugged. "I think Her Majesty is done."

The lock clicked and Jo stepped out of the stall, looking glorious. Her high heels clicked on the hard floors as her chin came up and she made eye contact with him. Bobby's mouth dried up just looking at her ... she was so fucking hot.

Jo bit her lip and said, "Who's the big dawg, Stanley?"

CHAPTER 8

Rhino

Akira took the ramp on South Hoover Street, and the Porsche's engine roared as the speedometer climbed to eighty in a blink. The rush was short-lived; as she merged with the Santa Monica Freeway South, bumper-to-bumper traffic forced her to slow down.

She glanced at the food bag on the passenger seat. It smelled so good. *Come on people, move it!*

A biker on a yellow Ducati sped by, splitting the lanes, inches from the vehicles either side. She smiled, knowing exactly how that felt when she did the same on her own Italian crotch rocket.

She took a healthy bite of a fish cake and moaned. Oh my God, this was so good. *I miss you,*

Uncle Bu. She took another bite and licked her fingers. Exit 15A appeared ahead; the East Seventeenth Street ramp. She turned into it, made a right on Hooper, drove through an intersection, and made a left on Washington. The road was clear. She sped up, allowing the Turbo to breathe. *Ah, that sound*. Slowed down again and made a right on Compton Avenue.

A young Korean girl driving a Porsche; she'd stick out like a sore thumb on this street. This was South Central LA and she'd need to keep an eye out. Patrol cars were a rare sight, and the gang bangers who owned this territory enforced their rules viciously.

She drove a few blocks to Jefferson High School and pulled up by the curb. The front of the school was on East Forty-First Street, about half a mile away, but it was closed. Students in after-school programs exited from a large gate operated by a security guard.

Akira parked a hundred feet from the gate and killed the engine. She turned on the Blaupunkt and was treated to "No Diggity" by Blackstreet. The clock on the dashboard read 4:12 p.m. The gate wouldn't open until 4:30. Time for a heavenly slice of Korea.

She opened the bag and pulled out a spoon, napkins, and the steaming soup cup. *Hot, but not too hot*. As a kid, she'd always burned the top of her mouth. The hearty and comforting aromas of soybean paste, pork, and vegetables filled the car. She abandoned the spoon and drank straight from the cup until it was empty.

She scanned the streets, got out of the Porsche, and walked up to a trash can. As she dumped the bag, a patrol car turned onto Compton Avenue and headed for the side gate.

Officer Chavez. Right on time.

She slipped behind the wheel of the Porsche and turned the stereo off, then parked in front of the side gate and lowered the window. Chavez stepped out of his car, leaving the engine running as the security guard greeted him.

At 4:32, a few dozen students spilled from two trailers behind the chain-link fence. One was a young Korean girl with long black hair. She was short and looked frail, almost undernourished. She wore sneakers, black leggings, a black sweater, and a pink beany, and held a Hello Kitty backpack. Next to her was a Black woman in her fifties.

"Making our neighborhood safer, Officer Chavez?" the woman said.

"Trying my best, Mrs. Diggs. Trying my best," Chavez said with a crooked smile.

The girl kept her chin down and, without looking at Chavez, opened the patrol car's door and got in.

"Soo did great today. It's an honorable thing you've done, taking care of her after her parents died. I don't know what would have happened to her, all alone like that at fifteen. She's lucky to have you, Officer."

"Nah, Mrs. Diggs. Just doing what my heart tells me to. She's a good girl, and she deserves a chance."

Chavez got in his car, made a three-point turn, and drove south on Compton Avenue.

Akira waited a few seconds, then followed him.

———

SOUTH GATE, LOS ANGELES, CALIFORNIA

Fifteen minutes later, Chavez made a left on Tweedy Boulevard and drove a couple of miles. He pulled up in front of a barbershop and barked, "Get out."

Soo did as instructed and went inside, Chavez behind her. Two barbers were busy with clients. One, a Latino man whose face and neck were inked with gang tattoos, nodded to Chavez as he walked through the shop and into the backroom. The shop owner was playing Solitaire at a table. He looked up from his game and appraised Soo.

Chavez nodded. "Castillo."

"Chavez, my man."

"Got the money?"

"Is this the merchandise?" He stood up and walked up to Soo.

Soo looked down at the floor. Castillo pulled a wad of cash the size of a beer can from his jeans pocked and handed it to Chavez, then touched Soo's hair and felt her arms.

Chavez handed a key to Castillo.

"This is for the storage locker. Not tonight. She needs to rest first. Tomorrow, when you're done, bring the key to my house. Put it in the mail slot at my front door."

Castillo pulled Soo closer, sniffed the top of her head and grinned. "See you tomorrow, chica."

The cop pulled into the driveway of a house. Akira parked a few houses back behind a truck, and kept the engine idling.

According to the file Akira had reviewed, the neighborhood was in terrible shape. Crime was rife. Drug dealers hung out on street corners. Graffiti marking the various gangs' territories defaced the walls of businesses and fences. Trash sat on sidewalks for weeks.

The perfect place for Chavez's profiteering. All approved by his bosses in the Rampart Division. This territory was his, and for years he'd been raking it in.

But now someone, somewhere, wanted him gone. Who and why were questions Akira would never ask—a job was a job. End of.

Chavez and the girl walked across the street to the back wall of the South Gate Self Storage facility. They stopped by a door marked *Employees Only*. Chavez pulled a brass key from his front pocket, opened the door and shoved the girl inside.

The file stated that the job had been on standby for a month. That's why Wilshire didn't know about the storage unit, Soo, or what Chavez was up to right now.

Which meant Soo was a loose end. And loose ends couldn't be allowed to exist.

An hour later, Chavez emerged alone from the storage facility and pulled a duffle bag and shotgun from the trunk. The alarm beeped twice as he walked up to the front door and went into the house.

Akira pulled on black latex gloves and took the Walther from her clutch. She popped the magazine and checked the chamber. Both loaded. She scanned the sidewalk and the street behind her.

No one in sight. Then she twisted the suppressor onto the muzzle. Not great but it would muffle the sound of a .38 to a tiny *thunk*, enough to ensure the sound didn't leave the room. Safety off, she exited the car and walked to the front door.

First she removed her boots and placed them on the stoop. Then she used a short switchblade to work the lock.

The interior was dark, heavy curtains blocking any light coming through the windows. Chavez's uniform and gun belt were on a chair by a sofa. The shotgun was propped against a corner wall. Akira crept over the old floors and stopped as a muffled groan came from a hallway.

She went toward it. The bathroom door was open, and silhouetted by two light sconces either side of the vanity mirror was Chavez. He was naked, masturbating over the sink with one hand, holding a polaroid in the other. He looked huge, even bigger than Akira knew he was. Like a rhino.

Akira held her breath and inched stealth-like toward him over the vinyl floor, almost gliding, the Walther aimed straight at his head. She stopped six feet away from him.

The floor creaked loudly beneath her feet.

Chavez spun around, right hand still holding his erection. He dropped the polaroid and flipped the hallway light switch.

"Hola, motherfucker," Akira said.

Chavez's eyes widened, and for a moment he looked perplexed. Then his forehead crumpled like a crushed beer can. "You!"

"Yeah, me," she hissed.

There were two muffled pops. Then twin holes appeared in the center of Chavez's forehead. Blood and brain matter spattered on the vanity mirror behind him. Akira landed a powerful sidekick under his chin, and Chavez collapsed backward. The back of his head connected with the sink. The porcelain shattered, exposing the cast-iron plumbing beneath. As he fell to the floor, his throat was impaled by the end of a broken pipe. The rhino twitched for a few seconds, then stilled.

Akira stepped closer and looked down at him. "I know, you're an organ donor. LAPD-fundraiser shit, right? Blah, blah, blah and donated your heart. However, I cannot fucking imagine letting anybody walk around with your ham inside them, you piece of shit."

And she put two shots in his chest just to be sure.

A search of his pockets produced two keys—the brass one he'd used to access the storage complex, and a silver key with the number 208 stamped on it.

Akira went to the kitchen, opened the fridge, and took a long pull from a bottle of water, then eyed a wad a cash sitting on the counter. Grabbed it and headed outside.

Still quiet; no one around. She slipped her pistol in her belt and put her boots on, then walked to the storage facility. The brass key got her into the parking area. To her right was the building itself, with a door similar to the previous one. She tried the brass key again. It worked.

She stepped into a corridor brightly illuminated by ceiling lights. A sign pointed her toward units 200–300. Akira followed the arrow, stopped outside 208, and slid the silver key into the lock.

The stench of human feces and urine assaulted her nose and throat. She coughed and felt along the wall until she found and flipped a switch. A bright neon light flickered on the ceiling.

Lying unconscious on several flattened cardboard boxes, and covered with nothing but a dirty blanket, was Soo. It looked like Chavez had raped her. Her thighs, breasts and neck were black and blue. Her clothes lay beside her, the leggings ripped.

The room was filthy. A large cardboard box doubled as a trashcan, and it was full to the rim. Chavez had left a bag of toilet rolls next to a five-gallon plastic container being used as a toilet.

This was fucked up.

Akira lifted the girl over her shoulders and

carried her back to the car. As she drove off, the Virtu rang.

"It's done," Akira said before the caller could say a word.

"Perfect. Anything else?" the male voice asked.

"No. Just driving away."

"Great. You're cleared, but we have an issue. Another job came up. Tonight, at the Concourse Hotel by the airport."

"Why me?"

"They want an Asian girl. You need to cut your hair and dye it platinum blond."

"Lucky me. Maybe I should play the fucking lottery," Akira said.

"Stay focused. This is sensitive. We want the best, and it's at the highest international level. I'll leave the details at the front desk. A room at the Concourse has been booked for you."

The line went dead. Akira placed the phone back in her jacket and looked over at Soo.

Fuck.

CHAPTER 9

Undone

Later that evening, Bobby, Stan, and Jo shared drinks in the rooftop bar. "Come Undone" by Duran Duran played in the background. Empty long-neck beer bottles and shot glasses littered the table. The ashtray was full.

Jo took a long drag from a cigarette and ran her fingers through Bobby's unkept hair. "I think you should get a haircut!"

Bobby grinned. "Fuck off."

She laughed and flicked cigarette ash over the railing. "I'm good with the scissors, you know."

Bobby laughed and sipped his Michelob. Jo lifted her shot glass and slammed back tequila.

Stan chuckled, a cigarette smoldering from the corner of his mouth. "Don't listen to her,

Bobby. She's always trying to give me a haircut, even though there isn't much left up here."

Below the balcony, Century Boulevard traffic flowed like red lava toward the airport terminals. As a similar trail of headlights headed away from the arrival ramp.

Bobby was used to women hitting on him; he just didn't like relationships. He'd never dated and didn't hook up with any girl, no matter who she was. Sex was something he paid for. Usually. But Jo Purple Stilettos was an exception to an unbreakable rule. Had to be. She was a fantasy come true.

Bobby thought about Tyra Banks again. He had a few posters of her back at his place, including her Playboy centerfold. He'd turned the backroom into a small shrine to her and a few American hot rods. That's where he'd bring prostitutes – and have sex looking straight into his favorite Victoria's Secret model and that Mustang he'd be able to afford soon enough.

Jo smiled and continued to fuss with Bobby's hair. "I'm serious. You'll look even sexier."

Stan sipped his whiskey and pointed at the traffic below. "Look at all these people, going about their day, not knowing that tonight or tomorrow we'll spend their money."

What the fuck did that mean? "How? What money?" Bobby asked.

"Their money is our money," Stan said, and began to hum the Mission Impossible theme.

"What the fuck money are you talking about?" Bobby asked, irritated. "Seriously, why did you say that?"

"Calm down, brother," Stan said as Jo waved at a passing server and ordered another round.

"Don't be saying shit like that and then go silent on me, bro," Bobby said, his words slurred.

Stan shot a look at Jo and said, "You bet. No need to get upset."

Jo tapped her long fingers on the railing, then leant into Bobby's ear and whispered, "Can you keep a secret?"

"Yeah, sure I can. What's up?" Bobby turned to Stan, who looked at Jo. She nodded. "Well?"

The server brought their drinks and scurried off. Jo slammed down her shot and licked her lips. Bobby loved a woman who could drink.

"Okay," Stan said finally. "Jo here has a sister who works in a bank. She's a supervisor, a customer accounts manager."

"How fucking exciting," Bobby said.

Jo wagged a finger. "Let him finish."

"Jo worked at the same bank for about a year," Stan said. "Three years ago, the bank sent Jo on a training course to learn the ins and outs of digital banking."

"Yeah, I know computers," Bobby said, and

belched. "I don't use them, but my new boss does. I mean, he's not my boss. This is just a job I'm doing."

"That's what we are talking about," Jo said. "Your guy probably uses a laptop, right?"

"Yeah. He's got the latest, a G3."

"Wow, that's outstanding. That's it!" Stan said and pointed at the traffic. "See that car over there leaving the airport? And that one there coming in? What if these cars were all computers, sending money to each other? And what if you could intercept that money and take just a little of it before it gets to the recipient, such a small amount that they wouldn't notice that it's missing? You follow?"

"I think so."

"And what if we could do it without taking money from actual customer accounts?"

"You what? You lost me," Bobby said.

"So the thing is this: we're taking money that belongs to someone. The question is, how do we hide that transaction? So what we do is use people's passwords to log into thousands of accounts. That gives us a gateway to the bank's network. You with me?"

Bobby nodded, not sure he was with Stan at all.

"Of course, we need those passwords, but once we're in, we position ourselves in the middle of the transactions and take five bucks here, ten bucks there from each of them," Stan said.

"How many transactions?" Bobby asked.

"How many cars do you see, Bobby?" Stan pointed at the street below.

The stream of vehicles seemed endless, and moved rhythmically in both directions like glowing ants. Their lights poured into side streets, parking structures, hotel driveways, and freeway ramps. Now he was getting the point, loud and clear.

"Now," Stan said, "when we started, we made a mistake. We got greedy and took too much directly from customer accounts."

"Exactly. Can't land in Indonesia anymore." Jo chuckled and sipped a Michelob.

"Right, no *ambulance*," Stan said. "We only take all the money from some people, but we plan it very carefully. That's what we call the ambulance."

Bobby felt confused all over again. Why the fuck couldn't these people just keep it simple?

"Think about it," Stan said. "How often do you see an ambulance, Bobby? Not so often. And in just the same way, it's not often that we take everything from an account. And when we do, we do it in a country we don't like to go to. Because if the authorities discover our scheme, we won't be able to land there anymore. Once you're made, you're made." Stan looked at Jo.

"And we don't want to get caught," Jo said. "We have a degree of protection, but we're not the big fish. Let the big-time hackers siphon money from banks and commit credit-card fraud. Let them get caught."

"So, places like the US and England, you don't take from the person logging in?" Bobby said.

Stan nodded. "You got it. We like being here. And we don't want them becoming suspicious and changing their passwords or alerting the institutions, right? If that happens we'll have the FBI after our asses."

"We need the gateway every time they log in," Jo said. "Then we attach what's missing to the bank fee, using it like a Trojan horse. Pretty fucking brilliant, right? Our money is hidden until we take it. The bank doesn't see that; only the bank's customer sees that additional charge, as if the charge is coming from the bank."

"They can't tell?" Bobby Asked.

"Nope, because the charge is spread across their bank statements. It's too small for them to notice it."

"And since we fly," Stan said, "we have connections all over, so we take a little bit from Japan, a little bit from Italy, a little bit from Germany, Malaysia, Saudi Arabia, Mozambique, you name it."

"Mozambique?" Bobby asked.

"Mozambique, Bobby!" Jo said.

Bobby laughed, and they clinked their bottles. "Mozambique!"

"We're together on this. Bobby, you want in?" Jo inched closer to Bobby, slipped her hand under the table and stroked his thigh. "What do you say?"

"Fuck, yeah, I want in," Bobby said.

"To get a piece of this, you've got to bring something to the table," Stan said.

"It's only fair, right?" Jo said. "We can teach you how to get these passwords."

"Who says I don't have one already?" Bobby said.

Jo leant forward. "If you've got something, bring it to the table. If you have nothing, well, let's finish up here and go back to my room and fuck."

"Okay okay," Bobby said. "I have a password, but this is just ten dollars here, twenty dollars there, plus your cut. I mean, how much money are we talking about?"

Jo shook her head. "Thing is, Bobby, once we're in, we're in the *bank*. Which means we can access the transactions of every single costumer." She grinned, showing off her perfectly bleached teeth.

Finally, the sheer scope of the scheme was

revealing itself in Bobby's head. He took a long look at both of them. "See, my boss has done something bad. Something he's running from. He's a Brit and he's got all this cash stashed away in a Swiss bank account."

"Do you know why? What he did?" Stan asked.

"No, but I know he has something they want, and it's not just the money."

"It's always the money," Jo said.

"Let him finish." Stan turned to Bobby. "So how did you get the password?"

"See, he was accessing his account and had just entered his password when his laptop froze up. He was all pissed and slammed it shut. He'd been recharging it at the time and unplugged the power cord, but he left the phone cable in."

"Sounds like your boss has a temper," Stan said.

"He's scary when he gets mad. He goes off like a stick of dynamite."

"I thought the Brits were always so calm," Jo said.

"Anyway," Bobby said, "the next minute he gets a phone call from the bank. He was supposed to transfer some of his money to the vice president's account—our hook-up there. He gets special treatment. They go way back, those two."

"You're killing me, man," Stan said.

"And he asked me to reboot the PowerBook,

then went into the other room and got on his cell phone." Bobby took another sip from his beer.

"And?" Jo said.

"I went to reboot it. The computer had gone into battery mode when he pulled out the power cord. It was still connected to the outlet so the screen was still on. And there it was—the log-in window, and the password right there in the middle of the screen. The funny thing is, I didn't even need a pen to write it down. Who wouldn't remember that?"

"Why?" Stan said.

"Pussy1Pussy2Pussy3," Bobby said. "That's the password!"

"You're awesome." Jo grabbed Bobby's face with both hands and planted a juicy kiss on his mouth.

Bobby reached under her blouse. She recoiled playfully, laughed, and bit his ear.

"You just made yourself a very rich man, Bobby," Stan said, and cracked a smile that would freak out a Rottweiler.

"Now let's play, shall we?" Jo said.

Bobby chuckled, trying to keep his composure, though the booze was making it hard. Jo shoved a small silver canister with a smiley face sticker on it in front of his face. He stared at it, puzzled, and looked at Jo for a clue.

She popped the top off, revealing a spray tip.

Then she spun the canister around, pointing the tip at him. On the other side was another sticker, this one a frown. "Are you smiley or sad?"

"You're fucking crazy," Bobby said.

Jo pressed the nozzle. Bobby's world began to blur. Then the lights went out.

CHAPTER 10

Platinum

It was closing time at Jeon Ju restaurant. Akira turned into a back alley and killed the headlights. Soo was still groggy—it would be a good few hours before the drugs were out of her system. Akira grabbed a water bottle from the backseat, twisted the cap, and handed it to the girl.

"Who are you?" Soo asked, and took a long pull from the bottle. She took a deep breath and slugged on the water again until the bottle was empty.

"I'm a friend of Jin-ho's," Akira said.

"You are? Oh my God, where is he?"

Akira pointed at the restaurant's back door.

Soo shook her head and began to tremble, her arms flailing. "No no no. What have you done?

He'll kill us all. Chavez is crazy. Please take me back to him. You have to take—"

"Chavez is dead, Soo. I know this because I was there."

"What?" Soo grabbed at Akira with both hands. "Are you serious?"

"Yes, he had a heart attack. He's dead. Won't bother you again, I promise."

"Oh my God. I can go?" Soo began to sob.

"Yeah, but you have to promise me something."

"Yes, anything."

"I was never here."

Soo nodded, and more tears streamed down her bruised face.

"I need you to say it. It's very important. I was never here. Do you understand?"

Soo wiped her face. "Yes. You were never here. I don't know you. I don't even know your name … And thank you."

Akira pulled the wad of cash she'd taken from Chavez and handed it to her..

"Take this and go," Akira said.

"Oh my God. You're serious?"

"Go."

Soo stumbled out of the car, wrapped in that dirty blanket, and headed toward the restaurant. She braced herself against a brick wall, and staggered up a few steps to the back door.

The loose end had walked.

It was the first time Akira had allowed such a thing. Even a month ago, she'd not have hesitated to kill Soo. There was no way of knowing if she could trust the girl, so why had she done it?

Because Akira had seen herself in Soo.

Right after her own fucking world had gone to hell.

Just as someone had been there for Akira, so she would be there for Soo. That bastard Chavez had been right on one thing at least. She deserved a chance.

———————

Akira had picked up a dress and high heels at a stripper shop in Downtown, then stopped at a beauty supply store for the hair-coloring paraphernalia. Now she was in a bathroom at a Union 76 gas station in Inglewood. An hour later she'd cut and dyed her hair as per the agency's instructions. The scissors and colorant kit went into the trash can. She dried her hair with some paper towels and used her fingers to comb her bangs right over her eyebrows. *Yeah, that's it.*

Then she doubled over and vomited.

She wiped her mouth and took one last look in the mirror. *Time to roll.*

It was a short drive to Century Boulevard. The

dash clock read 11:05 p.m. An enormous neon sign behind a line of palm trees announced her arrival. Akira drove into the guest parking lot and took a spot between a box truck and a cargo van.

Her Vertu beeped. It was Kyle.

"Hey."

"What's up, babe?"

"Yeah, I know. I'm late."

"You are. What's going on?"

"Have to take care of one more thing. Be home later."

"Wilshire?"

"Yes, they need this."

"Of course, they do. They always fucking do." Kyle inhaled sharply. "You need anything?"

"No, I'm good."

"All right, babe. I'll wait up."

He hung up. Akira dumped the phone in the clutch, and grabbed the leather jacket from the back seat. It was cold outside, even by California standards, and her breath formed clouds of vapor as she walked toward the entrance. She pulled her collar up and quickened her pace. Hundreds of poinsettias lined the driveway, like beacons directing people to the hotel's turnstile. Valet attendants greeted guests as they stepped out of their vehicles.

Akira went into the hotel. An elegantly decorated Christmas tree stood proudly in the lobby, reminding Akira of holidays with Uncle Bu. Nothing made her happier than those holiday memories.

Back to business. She clocked the concierge lounge and approached the reception desk.

A woman greeted her with a smile. "Good evening. I'm Lisa. Welcome to the Concourse Hotel. How can I help you?"

"I have a reservation under Winter." Akira placed her driver's license on the counter.

Lisa checked it and smiled. "Love your hair," she said, and handed a keycard to Akira. "You're in Room 1411. Thank you for choosing the Concourse, Ms. Winter."

"Is there a message for me?" Akira asked.

Lisa tapped at her keyboard, and nodded. A printer beeped twice and spat out a sheet of paper. "Is there anything else I can do for you?"

Akira ordered a cup of coffee.

"Certainly," Lisa said. "Do you want it in your room?"

"No, thank you. I'll be sitting right there," Akira said, and gestured toward the lounge.

She found a seat and read the printout. It was in Korean and coded. Akira had learned decoding at fourteen when she'd had to move back to Japan temporarily. The message read:

Room 1405. Two adjuncts: One, US-born, Robert Banks, ex-boxer, dangerous, Level 5. Two, James

Craw, ex-Special Ops, sadist, dangerous, Level 10. One mark: Sir Charles Barton, British diplomat, sadist, dangerous, Level 9. Mission: Eliminate all at all costs. Secure all electronics and one compact disc, and stand by for cleaning crew.

Akira folded the paper and put it inside her jacket pocket. A clean-cut server scurried over. She tipped him, dismissed him, and spent a full minute stirring two sugar cubes into her coffee, enjoying the aroma of the Robusta bean from sub-Saharan Africa. Just what she liked.

Finally, the tension in her forehead released, and for a moment she was at peace.

She thought about Soo and Jin-ho. Was her secret safe? Would Wilshire find out?

The Vertu beeped twice. The signal she was waiting for.

Time to meet the mark.

Akira set the coffee cup back on the tray and headed for the elevator.

CHAPTER 11

Tokyo

Sir Charles leant against the bar counter, cell phone to his ear, trying not to lose patience with Helger Janss, the vice president of a Swiss bank. The imbecile driver, Bobby, sat slumped on the sofa, a defeated look on his face.

Helger and Sir Charles went way back, having worked side by side in UK's financial market during the 1980s—a period of growth and expansion. Both had started in the insurance industry, cooking up schemes to defraud companies of millions.

Sir Charles had gone into politics, and in a short time had created an unusual bond with the Vatican. Meanwhile, Helger had gone to Switzerland, where he'd became the money-laundering to-go man for a Colombian cartel. His status didn't intimidate Sir Charles, but right now Helger had the upper hand. He controlled all Sir Charles's accounts. Money Sir Charles had accumulated during a lifetime of embezzlement, bribes, and human trafficking operations in Europe and Saudi Arabia.

Each man knew exactly how to push the other's buttons.

"No. You listen here!"

"Do not yell at me, Charles," Helger said.

"My apologies, my friend, but leaving all I have and the club in these circumstances wasn't easy, you know."

"No, Charles, I don't know. What you did, if the chatter I hear is true, is something I cannot be part of."

"I know what they're saying," Sir Charles said, "but it's not exactly the whole truth, is it? There's always more to it as you well know. They don't have a shred of proof. If they did, I'd be all over the papers."

"Was it the Vatican? Was it *him*?"

"Yes, it was. Whatever you hear, it's him, not me."

"This *is* about you, Charles. It's what you did to what we've built this past forty years."

Sir Charles, Helger, and a member of the Vatican whose identity was known only to Sir Charles had formed a club that operated a money-laundering business between London, Rome, and Geneva. Then Sir Charles and his Vatican partner had used the connections for their own addiction to sex and murder, and stolen millions that the Vatican was supposed to launder for an Italian enterprise.

"The Triangle is still on, Helger."

Sir Charles loved the moniker—a nod to the one in the Bermudas. Like the myth, their operation made things disappear.

"Oh, for fuck's sake, Charles, stop calling it that. Your Vatican ghost hasn't done shit for us. Might as well call it the Bi-angle. It's you and I that did everything."

"Well, I guess that's it then," Sir Charles said.

"No, that's not it. They want you, and they're hell-bent on getting your money. I don't know how much longer I can hide it from them."

"Helger, listen, we have this thing and it goes way back. It's you and me, and they don't know what we've got."

"Like I said, they want the money. They want you."

"They don't know where I am. They don't know about you. And they don't know where the money is."

Sir Charles's forehead pounded—his blood pressure had gone through the roof. His face was hot, and a vein began to throb at his temple.

"I know," Helger said, "but this is a delicate maneuver. If I do this, I'll need to protect myself and my family. Do you hear me? Wait for my signal, and log in as usual. No more phone calls. I'll message the hotel."

"Thank you, Helger. You won't regret this."

The line went dead.

Sir Charles slammed his fist on the counter. "I don't trust that fucking cunt!"

"What's happening, boss?" Bobby asked.

"Nothing that concerns you. Where's Jimmy?" Sir Charles said, and began to pace around the room.

"He's in the shitter. I think he's taking a shower."

Bobby looked away and slurped water from a glass, both legs jiggling. Sir Charles glared at him. The stupid fuck was a fidget as well as an idiot.

The phone on the wet bar rang, and Sir Charles answered.

"I have a message for you, Mr. Barton," the concierge said. "You're to wait thirty minutes before completing your bank transaction."

Sir Charles hung up.

"Bobby, get my laptop from the bedroom."

———

The laptop and the phone cable were on a large chest with a mirror on top, but the charger was missing. Bobby looked around the room and spotted the plug in an outlet on the far wall.

He picked up the laptop and cable, and walked around the bed.

And wished he hadn't.

A large roll of plastic sheeting lay on the floor, tucked halfway under the bed. Inside was the body of a young Asian girl.

He squinted and breathed hard, trying to make sense of what he was seeing. For a moment, everything seemed to go a little hazy, like time had slowed. He felt lightheaded and wondered if he was going to faint. Sweat beaded on his forehead, and his heart began to thump faster.

Fuck me. Fuck fuck fuck.

Bobby was not a killer. Sure, he'd killed a man in the ring during a boxing match. Yes, he'd been diagnosed at a young age with antisocial personality disorder. And one or two assholes had told him over the years that he had sociopathic tendencies. But this? This was off the scale. This was horrifying and tragic.

He blinked, trying to suppress the sensation of something utterly foreign to him—panic.

Fuck fuck fuck.

He leaned over the body and inspected it.

Blood had pooled under the girl. Her eyes were still open, and bloodshot. And—

Wait a minute.

He looked closer at her face, and his stomach tightened.

He knew this woman. No, more than knew her. This was Lily. His childhood best friend.

They'd grown up in the same neighborhood. Bobby had attended middle school with her and her brother. She'd had a tragic childhood. Her brother had died in a freak accident while playing on the train tracks near Downtown. And Lily had gotten really close to Bobby, who'd been there for her when she'd needed a friend and a brother. The whole family had practically adopted him after his parents died.

Lily and Bobby had remained best friends, meeting for drinks when she'd worked her clients at the Westin Bonaventure Hotel in Downtown while he washed cars in the underground garage. The money wasn't good, but the tips had been remarkable. Now and then he'd make a duplicate set of a client's car keys and sell them to a crew in North Hollywood. That's when he'd made real good money. Lily had used her connection with the hotel's initial investors, men from a subsidiary of the Japanese corporation that owned the hotel. That's the reason she'd worked at the Westin. From then on, she'd been known as Tokyo.

Of course, it didn't take long for Lily to get a duplicate room key, which they'd use to stay in the owners' suite when vacant. They'd bring their own booze and watch movies with a couple of other friends they'd grown up with. Lily had been fun. They'd looked after each other. And—

Bobby's breathing became ragged.

And Lily had saved his life.

They'd loved getting together in the hours when few people were using the bar. One day, Bobby had been eating a shrimp cocktail and enjoying the slow-passing view from the revolving restaurant on the top floor. The place had emptied, and they'd had it all to themselves. The bartender had gone in the back to grab a case of beer.

Lily had just returned from the bathroom. She found Bobby standing frozen, wide-eyed, water trickling out of his nose. His eyes had been bulging out of their sockets she'd later told him, as he'd been gasping for air, choking on a shrimp lodged in his throat. She'd gotten behind him and carried out the Heimlich maneuver she'd seen on some random TV show. It hadn't worked. He'd turned blue, suffocating, dying right there in front of her. That's when Lily got back around him and punched him in the middle of his chest. Once. Twice. Three was a charm. A large shrimp had shot out of Bobby's mouth like a cannonball had been fired.

Bobby had never forgotten that, and even though he wasn't a spiritual man, Lily had become sacred to him. It was why they'd never been intimate. He'd loved her too much as a friend.

And now it had come to this. What the fuck were these psychos doing here? His mind raced. *Focus, get the cord, and get back out there.*

He unplugged the charger, then realized there was a problem. The charger was near the body. They'd know he'd seen her. He plugged it back into the outlet, wiped the sweat from his forehead, and went back into the living room.

Stay cool.

"You took your sweet time," Sir Charles spat.

"I'm sorry, boss."

"Leave it on the counter."

"Should I turn it on?"

"No, just connect it and go sit."

The man spoke like a psycho, like he was completely devoid of humanity, as if he, Bobby, was some sort of insect.

Bobby connected the G3 to a phone line and checked the battery level. It was halfway. Then he picked up a magazine from the coffee table and slumped back in the sofa. It was the same one he'd looked at in the lobby. He turned immediately to the Mustang Boss article and came to the bit about Larry Shinoda. Perfect. He'd wanted a distraction from thinking about his friend Lily, and now the first thing that had come to mind was Stan and Jo, and how they'd tricked him into giving up the password for Sir Charles's bank account.

Right now, though, all of that was secondary. Larry was Asian. That reminded him of the internment camps, and the injustices borne by the Japanese people after the war. And now Lily, his best friend. In the next room. Dead.

Motherfuckers.

Bobby bit his lip so hard it began to bleed. Several drops of blood fell onto the magazine page, highlighting the words *Japanese American*.

Calm down, you fucking idiot, or you'll never get out of this room alive.

Hatred gripped him. He wiped his lip. He needed to stay focused on the job so he could get out of here without raising suspicion. Head straight to Little Tokyo, get twenty friends from the local gym, most of them yakuza, then come back here and kill both these psychos. He would do it for Lily.

"Flow like water in between obstacles and even the sharpest blade can't hurt you," Lily would say when things weren't going well. That's what he needed to do right now.

The G3 booted up and Sir Charles began typing. "What the hell? Fucking screen's frozen."

punched the keyboard, then slammed the laptop shut. "Shit. Bobby!"

"Yes, boss."

A cold wave of panic rose from Bobby's gut. He looked at the door, then checked himself. Running was not the safest option. These people weren't fucking around. He'd be dead in minutes. *Flow like water, Bobby*.

"Find Jimmy for fuck's sake," Sir Charles barked.

Bobby punched a redial key on his cell phone. Jimmy picked up. "Yes?"

"The boss needs you."

"I'm here. Coming up the elevator right now."

The line went dead.

CHAPTER 12

Van Halen

It was a hot summer's day, about an hour's drive up the coast from Santa Monica. Kyle, sporting nothing but a sleeveless white shirt and swimming trunks, was at the wheel of a topless red Jeep CJ7—no doors, monster tires. The leash holding the surfboard to the roll bar fluttered in the wind as Van Halen's "When It's Love" blasted out of large speakers. His ponytail bopped as he sang along.

Another Jeep, this one black, pulled up alongside. The driver was a stunning Asian girl and the same song came from her stereo. A mane of long black hair, tossed by the wind, caressed her face as if it were a sheet of silk. A short gust caught her short yellow summer dress, revealing her thighs and—for a moment—just a little bit more.

Kyle offered her a stupid grin and leaned over to the side, still ogling her thighs. "Hi. I'm lost. Looking for California Street."

The woman pointed ahead, and one of the spaghetti straps fell off her shoulder.

"That way?" Kyle asked.

She shook her head and pointed again, more urgently now, then braked and downshifted.

Kyle glanced forward. The light ahead had turned red and the traffic had come to a stop.

Shit.

He slammed on the brakes. The Jeep screeched and shuddered to a stop, oversized tires smoking, the massive bumper now just inches from a police car. Kyle gripped the wheel. Thank fuck he'd strapped down the surfboard this time.

The woman pulled up next to him. "Great reflex!"

A police officer emerged from the black-and-white and approached the Jeep. The turning light went green, and the woman drove off, laughing.

Kyle killed the radio and forced a smile.

"Hello, Officer."

"License and registration, please."

———

It was right after lunch time, and Lassen's grocery store in Ventura was practically empty. Akira was feeling playful and energetic—nothing like a morning swim to jump start her metabolism. She swerved past an old woman, who gave her a dirty look, and barreled her shopping cart over to check-out three.

The college boy whose name tag read *Chad* cracked an infectious smile, all teeth, and eyed the two pizzas, five Nonna's Gnocchis, two boxes of diet Cokes, and a six-pack of Asahi she'd shoved onto the belt.

"Having a party?" he asked.

Akira grinned. "No time for parties. Besides, this one would be boring."

"Yeah, you're missing Fritos, tequila, real beer, and some sweet Mary Jane."

"What's wrong with my beer? I love my beer."

"It's made in Italy, girl! Don't you read the labels?"

"Yes, you knucklehead, but it's the other way around. It's a Japanese company operating a brewery in Italy. It's smooth and silky, just like me."

"Smooth and silky? Sounds boring."

"I'm boring, Chad. What can I say?"

"Whatever floats your boat, baby. It's Miller time for me!"

He nodded toward the pasta boxes. "Or maybe you married into a large Italian family. Rad!"

She laughed and picked up a tabloid from the magazine rack.

The door chimed and swung open. Sunlight reflected off the glass, blinding Akira momentarily. Then she got a look at him. *Surfboard guy*.

He waltzed over to Chad, and they high fived.

Akira peeked above the magazine, then looked down and flipped a page. "Look here. A woman in Brazil gave birth to a thirteen-pound bat baby with a three-foot wingspan. God, I hope she had a C-section," Akira said, and continued scanning the page. "Ugly as hell, too."

"I guess you don't have kids then."

It was the guy who'd answered, not Chad. He'd taken over the station and now held up the scanner.

"Do you?" she asked.

The guy ignored her question and said, "Did you find everything you were looking for, miss?"

"How about you? Did you have a good look?"

"One has to look in the right place at the right time."

Akira smiled. "Some people get distracted by the littlest things."

"You mean the littlest dresses."

"Maybe you should keep your eyes on the road next time."

"You made it pretty hard to do that. Are you buying that?" he said, nodding at the magazine.

"Sure," she said, and handed it to him.

"See? I like an honest woman."

"And how do you know I'm honest?"

The guy picked up a box of Nonna's Gnocchi, "maybe you could persuade me over a g-nuschi dinner," the guy said.

Akira cracked up, "oh, we're having dinner now?"

"Don't I deserve a little something for all the trouble that little dress put me through?"

"Yes, probably a ticket for reckless driving."

He pulled out a citation from his back pocket, "Got that!"

Akira shook her head.

———

Two weeks later, a full moon lit up the living room of the huge oceanfront modernistic villa Akira had rented. Not bought. That would have cost her three million-plus. Kyle—*that guy*—stood naked by a large open window overlooking the beach.

On a glass coffee table sat two half-empty champagne flutes and two untouched plates of gnocchi in a creamy white sauce. From a silver ice bucket peeked the neck of a Dom Pérignon bottle.

Akira inched toward Kyle, her bare feet caressing the cool slate floor. She was naked too, except for the white feather boa draped around her neck and dragging on the floor behind her.

"Hey, you," Akira said.

Kyle turned around and gazed at her. "You're stunning."

They met in the middle of the room.

"Are you okay?" she asked.

"What do you mean?"

"Well, it's a big house. Men can sometimes get—how should I say this—overwhelmed. You know … mine's bigger than yours?"

"It's you who's doing the overwhelming, not this house."

Akira traced her fingers over his face, then moved them to his neck, digging them in just ever so slightly.

"I can't quite feel my heartbeat. I think I may be dead," Kyle said.

"Maybe you are, and this is all a dream."

He placed a hand over hers. "It's been seven hours and fifteen days, and I know everything I want to know about you."

"You don't know who I am … What I do. You should probably stay clear of me," she whispered.

"You don't know me either," Kyle said, and they kissed. "But I have a feeling we have more in common than Van Halen."

CHAPTER 13

Ambulance

Sir Charles paced across the room, looking ready to murder. "Do you understand the words that are coming out of my mouth?"

Bobby sat on the sofa and bobbed his head agreeably. The man's question had been rhetorical. Best not to answer. His stomach felt icy cold, like he was developing an ulcer. The reason wasn't medical. The reason was Stan and Jo, who'd conned him out of a password. His hand went to his belly.

"Have you spoken to anyone about what we're doing here, Bobby?" Sir Charles asked.

"What? No. I don't know what we're doing here, boss."

"Don't be a cunt. What do you mean, you

don't know? What is there to know?"

Bobby searched Sir Charles's face for a clue.

Oh, shit. Had Stan and Jo gone ambulance on this? That's not what they did, though. It was too risky, they'd said. He fought the panic rising from his gut and gripping his throat. He needed to stay calm to stay alive. If he didn't get out of the suite before Jimmy got back, he'd end up like Lily. And although he was angry, that anger had to take a backseat.

"So what, I wonder, what were you doing in Beverly Hills last night?" Sir Charles asked.

"Nothing."

"Nothing?" Sir Charles spat. "Even if one is breathing into a fucking pillow, one is still doing something. Were you breathing? Because that's doing something, you pig fuck."

"I'm sorry. I told you guys, I was just drinking with a friend, that's all."

"See? You were doing something. You were drinking. That wasn't too hard, was it?"

"Sorry, boss."

"Shut the fuck up, you imbecile." Sir Charles pulled the Macallan off the shelf, then opened the fridge.

Bobby stood, grabbed the empty ice bucket from the side table, and said, "Boss, can I get you some ice?"

Sir Charles nodded, tapped his mobile phone

and spoke into it. "Yes, I'll hold."

Bobby headed for the door. It swung open. Jimmy stepped in, running his wet hands through his short hair. He was stripped down to white Adidas pants and a wife beater, and carrying a gym bag.

"Hey, Bobby." Jimmy reached into the bag and produced a shoulder holster packing his SIG-Sauer. He placed it on the coffee table. "Where are you going?"

Bobby tried to swallow but any remaining saliva seemed to have dried up on his way to the door. "I'm–I'm getting ice for the boss."

"No, you're not, mate. You'll do that later. I need you here now. Sit the fuck down."

Jimmy unholstered the SIG and checked the chamber, then pulled the magazine out and checked that too. It was fully loaded.

"What's wrong, Jimmy?"

Jimmy reached back into the bag and pulled out a suppressor.

"Nothing you need to concern yourself with."

Bobby sat down, cradling the ice bucket as Jimmy twisted the silencer into the barrel and gave Bobby a look.

"Are you going to keep hugging that bucket?"

"Yes. I mean no." Bobby placed it back on the side table.

"You, okay?" Jimmy asked.

"Yeah, I'm cool, bro," Bobby said, feeling beads of sweat popping on his brow.

Jimmy's eyes narrowed as he holstered the gun. "I didn't ask you if you're cool, bruv. I asked you if you're okay. Because if you're not, it's cool."

"Yeah, yeah, I'm okay. Back off, bro."

"Okay, if you say so." Jimmy said.

———————

Sir Charles glanced at the laptop. The battery was at five percent. He slapped it shut. "Jimmy, fetch me the charger."

"Charles," Helger barked into the cell phone. "What is it? I told you not to call."

"What the hell's going on?" Sir Charles said. "It's not working."

"Yes, we can see that. We're looking into it."

"Looking into what?"

"Looks like you got hacked."

"What? How?"

"We tracked the hack to the parking lot at your location. It's a mobile unit. Someone was waiting for you to log in to your laptop. They had your password, Charles. And they've taken all your funds."

"Jesus fucking Christ. You promised me my bloody money was safe!"

"It's too late. It's gone," Helger said. "All

twenty-two million. The signal's still bouncing around. We may be able to track it but I can't make promises. I'll call you back. Stay put."

The line went dead.

Jimmy came back and plugged the charger into the laptop, then joined Bobby on the sofa.

Sir Charles watched the screen as it refreshed. The account page was still there, staring at him like an incoming train.

And the balance was zero.

"The money's gone, Jimmy. The laptop got hacked. Someone in this hotel."

Jimmy looked puzzled. "Here, in the hotel? But who else knows about this?"

Something flickered in Jimmy's face. And then the bodyguard turned and stared at Bobby. Bobby's eyes widened, showing too much of the white part.

———————

Jimmy leaned over him. "Bobby, where did you say you were last night?"

"I said ... I-I was in ... Beverly Hills, having drinks."

Jimmy straightened himself, then stretched his neck, twisting it from side to side. It cracked loudly, and Bobby flinched.

"You sold us out?" Jimmy asked.

"No. No fucking way. I … I …"

"Pull yourself together, you cunt!" Sir Charles said. "The bank said I'm completely wiped out. Clean. Someone has accessed the account and taken everything."

"Bobby, where's the money?" Jimmy hissed.

Sir Charles walked over to the sofa, veins bulging from his temples.

Fuck. "Okay, okay," Bobby said, the words tumbling from his mouth. "I don't know. They drugged me. Last thing I know, I woke up on a bench in Beverly Hills. But it's not possible. They can't do the ambulance in the US. But they got me drunk. I didn't know what I was saying."

Jimmy pushed his face right up to Bobby's. "What are you fucking saying? Ambulance? What the fuck is that?"

"You monumental goat fuck," Sir Charles screamed, foaming at the mouth. "Were you drunk or drugged? Which one is it?"

"I don't know. Wait, listen—"

Jimmy pulled the gym bag toward him and the next thing Bobby knew he'd flicked open a nine-inch switchblade. Bobby recoiled against the back of the sofa.

"Who, Bobby, who?" Sir Charles said. "You're telling me you met some strangers, and they drugged you to get the password for my account? How did you even have it in the first place?"

"Tell us where the money is, you cunt," Jimmy hissed.

"I-I don't know them. Never seen them before, I swear. Th-they tricked me. I took nothing!"

Sir Charles slammed his fist down on the counter. "Nonsense, I want their names."

"It's not what you—"

Jimmy stretched his neck, and once more it cracked. Bobby swallowed, his throat dry as sandpaper, and imagined drinking the sweat prickling on his forehead and running down his back.

"This imbecile has blown our plan to bits," Sir Charles said.

"No, boss, I didn't steal your money," Bobby said.

Sir Charles picked up his cell phone and redialed. "There must be something Helger can do."

"If it wasn't you," Jimmy said in his ear, "then who took the money?" The tone was now calm, almost friendly, which somehow unnerved Bobby even more.

"Don't know. I shouldn't have … but they made me."

"Bobby, I'll take care of you, but how did you know the password?"

"I just found it. And it was … it was easy to remember."

Jimmy chuckled. "Yeah, I know."

He grabbed Bobby's index finger, and it snapped like a breadstick.

Bobby shrieked.

"You should have told us. We would have changed it, you stupid fuck," Jimmy said. He pinned Bobby to the chair, shoved the SIG against his mouth and pulled the hammer back. "Continue."

Jesus Christ. Bobby wondered if he was about to piss himself.

"Hang on! Calm down. I'll tell you everything. After I left the suite, I went to meet with this girl—"

"Who?"

"Jo. And he was there too, this guy, the pilot, Stanley. He wasn't supposed to be there. Then she said—"

Jimmy pressed the gun into Bobby's face. "Who the fuck is Stanley? Are you a fag, Bobby?" His hand whipped around Bobby's middle finger and broke it.

"Fuck you!" Bobby screamed, the pain making him dizzy for a moment.

"Hush, hush, Bobby." Jimmy pressed the SIG's barrel into his cheek.

"I told you, I don't know a fucking thing."

Jimmy looked over at Sir Charles, whose face was like thunder, and waited. His expression said it all—he was seeking approval to kill Bobby.

Sir Charles put his hand up. "He didn't take the money. He got played. Right, Bobby?"

Jimmy climbed off Bobby and got up.

"Yes! That's what I've been saying," Bobby said.

"Okay then. Tell us everything," Sir Charles said.

Bobby's mind whirred, grasping at the seconds he'd been granted. Question was, how could he turn that commodity into minutes, into an escape?

Sir Charles stared into Bobby's eyes. "The clock is ticking, Bobby, you hear me?"

CHAPTER 14

Hassan

Jimmy moved the cursor over a satellite view of Los Angeles and zoomed in on the airport until a dozen red hotel markers appeared. One was The Concourse Hotel on Century Boulevard. Close by was a small bright-green X. Jimmy clicked on it and read the data in the drop-down menu: Robert Banks, AT&T Customer ID 213-LAC-5656 Acct.# 213-5656. Another label tagged the number with *Signal Origin Relay*. He clicked on the point of origin.

Sir Charles hung over his shoulder, sipping Macallan from a tumbler. "What the hell? Is that—"

Jimmy clicked on another label marked Connect. A red line appeared, connecting the signal origin to another spot on the map—the hotel's parking lot. He zoomed in again, until another X popped up over a fuzzy image of a parked vehicle.

"It's a van," he said, "but the picture's too degraded so we've got no model."

He clicked on the tag next to the image. Another drop-down menu appeared: Receiver, AT&T Customer ID 213-LAC-5656 Acct.# 213-5656. Another tag read *Signal Clone. Not Identifiable*.

"What the fuck's happening?" Sir Charles said.

"Looks like the hackers were in that vehicle."

"Are they still there?"

"I wouldn't be, would you, sir?"

"Yes, that would be stupid, and they don't seem to be the stupid types. We're the lucky ones who ended up with the idiot." Sir Charles glared over at Bobby, who was still on the sofa, nursing his broken fingers. He'd improvised a splint with toothpicks and duct tape.

Jimmy shrugged. "That's it, sir. That's as far as we go without proper equipment. I think they conned our idiot. He wasn't the one doing this—definitely not."

———

Bobby looked down at his injured hand and winced. *Fuck me*. At least he was alive, for now at least. But these psychos were going to kill him as soon as they no longer needed him. Making them think he could help them was the only way out.

Then a light bulb went on in his head.

"I have an idea," he blurted.

The game was a dangerous one, but it wasn't as if he had a lot of choice.

Sir Charles and Jimmy looked at him.

"Do you now?" Sir Charles said.

"Spill it," Jimmy said, his forehead creasing.

"Two years ago, a company—Axis I think they were called—made these cameras, closed circuit but connected to the internet. It's a new thing."

"Go on," Sir Charles said.

"Well, they can be hacked, but in many hotels like the Bonaventure in Downtown, they don't even need to be. They're public access—used as a publicity thing."

"What are you thinking, Bobby?" Jimmy said.

"I'm thinking we find out where the video files are stored, and scan through the footage. See who was in that parking lot."

"Look at you," Jimmy said. "You're not as stupid as we thought. Just a massive pig fuck."

"Very well, Einstein. How are we supposed to get that footage?" Sir Charles asked.

"I could go down to reception and try to bribe one of the bellboys for it. If we can get the plate on their vehicle, I have connections at the DMV.

We can find these fuckers. Trust me," Bobby said, "I know what they look like and I want a piece of them too."

Jimmy patted Bobby on the shoulders, but it was hard, threatening rather than friendly.

"Just so we're clear," Jimmy said, "you're not going anywhere. Go to the guest bedroom and call the bellboy with your cell. You better find something we can use to get these pricks."

So that was it. Bobby was out of ideas. He needed to get out of the suite, but it wasn't happening.

"Get on with it, then," Sir Charles snapped.

Bobby jumped up from the sofa and headed for the guest room.

Sir Charles's cell phone rang. It was the bank. And the news wasn't good. Helger had left for the day. A woman spoke. "He asked me to call you and tell you we had to close the account. I'm—"

Sir Charles killed the line. "We're fucked, Jimmy. And right there in that guest room is the cunt who fucked us."

"How much cash do we have with us, sir?" Jimmy whispered.

"About 400K. US dollars." Sir Charles stared at the map on the laptop screen. "Is there a way to find out where these fuckers are? To trace that IP address?"

"If the idiot is correct and there's an IP camera somewhere outside the hotel, I say it's a probability."

"I have a deep desire to choke this cunt with my bare hands when this is over," Sir Charles said.

"It relaxes me just to know that you feel the same as I do, sir."

"You think Hassan could help?"

"I do. He's a communication specialist, a high-paid hacker himself. And I worked with him back in Somalia. He's loyal and he's the best."

Bobby had learned three things: The Concourse didn't have IP cameras, the CCTV was out of service, and the bellboy was who the fuck knew where.

None of that was information he needed to share with Sir Charles and Jimmy. As long as he could bluff it out.

He emerged from the guest room with a smirk on his face, as if he had something to contribute. Just enough to look smug, but without pushing it.

"There are cameras in the hotel as part of some promotion thing, boss. Bellboy's looking into it. As soon as he has the IP addresses, he'll call. Said he'll sneak into security on their break in about twenty minutes. I promised him five hundred dollars."

"Then I hope you have that kind of money, Bobby, because you're sure as fuck going to need it," Jimmy said.

Bobby nodded. All good. He was going to pay the non-existent bellboy for non-existent information.

And now, the clock was ticking.

Sir Charles turned to Jimmy. "I'm glad we paid Hassan in advance. What's his ETA?"

"Should be here soon, just before our Asian pizza with extra cheese arrives," Jimmy said.

Bobby sat back down on the sofa and wound more tape around his splint. "That's a great idea. Asian pizza."

"Yeah, Bobby, hope you like cheddar on top," Jimmy said.

He and Sir Charles began to laugh, and for a second Bobby was relieved. Then he realized it wasn't a fun laugh; it was full of spite and sarcasm.

Jimmy grabbed both his shoulders and stared him down. "Come on, mate, don't worry. It's all good. We're going to find these fuckers."

Sir Charles lit up a cigarette, Jimmy went back to the laptop, and Bobby took himself to the bathroom. He relieved himself, then looked in the mirror over the sink. He was a mess, his face pale and puffy, eyes bloodshot. His hands trembled as he washed them. He'd not yet processed Lily's death—couldn't allow himself to go there.

Then he heard a beeping sound. *What the heck?* Of course. It was the Motorola pager tucked in one of his boots. Why hadn't he thought of that? Raffi had given it to him a few days earlier but Bobby wasn't used to it and had completely forgotten about it. There was a message from Raffi on the small screen: *wh4t up? u dig ur pgr?*

For a moment, he couldn't remember what to do, but then it came back to him and he turned the tiny selector switch to SMS mode. Ignoring Raffi's message, he scrolled through his contacts, selected a number and punched in some pager-speak. *911 h31p n33d u h3r3 4s4p 911. c0m3 4rm3d 70 kill. c0nc0ur8 h073L rm1405 82.*

The Motorola beeped, indicating that the SMS had been delivered. Bobby turned it off and hid it back in his boot, then flushed the toilet and looked in the mirror again. Beads of sweat had collected on his forehead. He opened the faucet and splashed his face with cold water, then dried up with a hand towel. *Stay cool.*

Even the towel felt amazing and smelled fresh. He wasn't used to the perks of a high-end hotel. At least he wouldn't die in a dump, if dying's what it came to.

Back in the living room, he grabbed a Michelob and took a long cold pull.

Sir Charles was slamming back yet another shot. Jimmy was still on the G3. The bodyguard's cell phone rang, and he turned to Bobby. "It's Hassan. Let him in."

Bobby walked into the foyer and opened the door. Hassan stared him down. The man was a giant—six-eight, pushing three hundred pounds, as solid as a tree. He pulled a large military-grade roller, and held a duffle bag over his shoulder. At first glance, his attire seemed black casual, but it wasn't. It was low-key military-grade clothing. Bobby moved aside and nodded. Hassan flicked his chin up and ducked a bit as he walked through the door and into the foyer. Bobby eyed a bulge at the man's side. Hassan's jacket flapped open a little revealing the handle of a large knife and a pistol concealed under his armpit.

———————

"Hassan, mate, how did you like first class?" Jimmy asked in Arabic.

They shook hands.

"It was good, my friend. I thank you for that," Hassan replied.

"Welcome to the team, Hassan," Sir Charles said, also in Arabic.

"Thank you, sir." Hassan bowed slightly. "It is

my great honor to serve you. The blood of Sudan is in my veins, as it is in yours. I know who you are, sir. When Jimmy called, I couldn't say no."

Sir Charles gestured toward the driver and switched to English. "This is Bobby, our connection in LA."

Hassan barely acknowledged him, and Bobby returned the favor.

"Yes, Jimmy filled me in. I know what happened. Let's get right to it, sir," Hassan said.

He opened the roller and pulled out a large soft black case. It housed a beige laptop that dwarfed the G3.

"This," Hassan said, "is the Hewlett Packard Internet Advisor 486. And with it, my friends, we can find these fuckers and get your money back. Every single cent."

A tiny smile grew on the side of Sir Charles's mouth.

"That's the attitude," Jimmy said.

Hassan plugged in the 486, connected it to the G3 and the phone socket, and powered it up. A series of dial tones settled into a hum, and the screen came alive with applications and browser icons. Hassan double-clicked on Freenet.

"Okay. Everybody go eat. This will take a while."

"Where's that Asian pizza?" Bobby asked.

Sir Charles and Jimmy laughed. Bobby

shrugged, sat back down on the sofa, and took another pull from his Michelob.

———————

An hour later, the table in the suite was littered with beer bottles and fast-food cartons.

"So, what about this Y2K bullshit I keep hearing about?" Jimmy said.

"What do you mean?" Hassan answered without taking his eyes off the screen.

Jimmy chuckled. "You know, computers will freeze up and the world will end kind of bullshit."

"Bullshit? Y2K is as real as the Qur'an. Got my family ready to head for our bunker in the mountains not too far from Juba. We stockpiled arms and supplies up there. We can survive ten years." He turned to Jimmy. "Nah, my friend, this is not some bullshit conspiracy. Computers were not designed to reach another digit pass 1999. Everything will stop working, and I'm ready for it. You better be too."

"No shit."

"You've got nothing to worry about. You'll be in Riyadh by then. I have friends there. I'll connect you. I got your back, Jimmy."

"Sounds like a pig fuck. How about the government? What are they doing?"

"They've tried to stop it, but nobody has a

solution. They're lying, telling us everything will be okay. But I have connections and they tell me the politicians all have classified locations where they'll be protected. No one cares about us."

"That's bonkers."

"Yeah. See this hotel? In two years it won't exist. Everything will come to a standstill; people will start looting and then there'll be a civil war."

"Like Sudan."

"Yes, my brother, like Sudan—the old days. And we've seeing it way too many times to let it sneak up on us like this." Hassan's eyes pierced Jimmy's. He grabbed his hand. "You have nothing to worry, my brother. I got your six."

Jimmy patted Hassan's shoulder. "Thank you, brother."

Hassan turned back to the monitor and punched the return key.

Sir Charles wandered into the living room, still wearing the same suit but without his jacket and tie. He picked up a large slice of garlic bread and stuffed it in his mouth.

"Would you like a drink, boss?" Bobby asked.

"There it is," Hassan said. "I found them. I found your thieves."

"Where are they?" Sir Charles said, nearly choking on his garlic bread.

"Thank God. Can we get the money back?" Bobby asked.

They all turned toward him, like starving hyenas eyeing up a big fat steak. Dead eyes all around. Bobby right in the middle.

CHAPTER 15
Extra Cheese

Akira stepped out of the elevator and eyed the sign. *There you are: 1405. And there I am: 1411.* She scanned the hallway. Blocking the path was a sawhorse with a sign that read *Remodel in Progress. Keep Out. Authorized Personnel Only.*

She inserted her keycard in the lock. It beeped. She pushed the door open and stepped inside. A manila envelope lay on a console. She opened it and dumped four letter-size sheets on a dining table.

The photos were of the mark, Sir Charles Barton, and the two adjuncts, James Craw and Robert Banks. Another picture showed the room's layout. She examined the faces and the floor plan, forming a mental picture of it all, then emptied the fruit bowl, placed the photos in it, and torched the lot with a cigar lighter from her clutch.

———————

A few minutes later Akira stepped into the hallway, still wearing the dress, but not her jacket. Parked in front of the suite next to hers was a cleaning cart. She peeked inside the room. A maid with her back to Akira was leaning over a small cleaning bucket and ringing a mop. Akira continued and stopped at 1405. She knocked on the door.

A few seconds went by, then the door opened. Towering over her was Craw, his eyes filled with malice. Beyond, Barton was at the bar, filling a tumbler with ice. Craw looked her up and down and gestured for her to pass, but left so little space that she had to squeeze past him. He grabbed her arm, pulled her close, and sniffed the top of her head. Then he cracked a devious smile. "What's your name, luv?"

She looked straight into his eyes and smiled. "I'm Winter," she said, and ran her hands through her platinum-blond hair.

"Fuckin' hell, and my name's summer's eve. Well, chop chop, Extra Cheese. Get in there and make yourself comfortable."

———————

Sir Charles grabbed his cane and walked over to the girl. "Let me look at you," he said, and smirked.

Bobby felt sick to his stomach. So they'd ordered another prostitute? Another Asian girl? What the fuck was going on? Who were these two—straight-up serial killers?

He'd believed what his referral had told him, that Sir Charles was a British ex-pat on the run who needed a few days to hide before leaving for an undisclosed location. And that was it. Nobody had told him they were killing Asian girls. Fucking unbelievable.

"Winter?" Sir Charles said. "Ha! Now is the winter of our discontent, made glorious, made glorious. God, you've got to love old Bill."

Winter lowered her chin and walked to the center of the room.

"Look at him," Jimmy said.

The girl looked up at Sir Charles as he circled her.

"That's why I love Los Angeles. Here, no matter what, you can always say 'Have a nice day.' What do you think, Winter? Are you going to have a nice day?"

"I'm not here to have a nice day. I'm here to please you," she said.

"We're told that you're an expert, a real pro with pain," Sir Charles said, "yet you seem so frail, so slender, so smooth." The back of his hand traced her bare arm. "Good grief, you're an icicle. Are you cold? Or are you afraid?"

"Is that what you'd like me to be?"

"Oh no, no. Nonsense. Not yet. I take my time. I like to inspire fear. You know, there's nothing like the real thing, don't you agree?"

The girl pulled a Vertu from her boot and waved it at Sir Charles. "Should we negotiate extra service?"

Jimmy slapped her across the face. The blow sent her careening into a shelving unit. She fell to her knees, barely holding on to the cell phone.

Bobby winced, taken aback, but remained seated.

Jimmy stepped closer and cracked his neck.

Bobby's muscles twitched; he was a ball of nerves, ready to explode, but knew he needed to restrain himself. Hassan was armed, and in the next room. Now was not the time.

Jimmy grabbed Winter by the hair and lifted her. The girl was punchy and looked up, though Bobby could see the pain in her eyes.

"Look at me, cunt. Look into my eyes. Focus!" Sir Charles barked.

Her left eye was bloodshot.

"Get up," Sir Charles said.

Jimmy wrapped his muscular arms around her like a vise, and Winter gasped for air, her feet scraping the floor as he lifted her. Surely her ribs were close to the breaking point.

Sir Charles moved in closer, looking at her as if he was about to flick an insect off his lapel.

"I will tell you when you can so much as flex a muscle. You understand?"

The girl nodded meekly.

Sir Charles twisted the silver handle of the cane, unlocking a razor-sharp twelve-inch blade, the steel ringing as he pulled it free.

The girl squirmed and tried to pull away, but Jimmy's grip was unwavering.

She caught her breath. "I thought pain had to be negotiated."

Sir Charles pointed the blade at her throat, carefully, deliberately, without piercing her skin. Jimmy cracked a sadistic smile.

"You're wondering what I want," Sir Charles said, and moved his face close to hers. "I want your dignity, your humanity, your sacred self. Translation: I want to wrap you up with barbed wire and desecrate you. Can you handle that, Ms. Winter?"

Bobby fought his instinct to get up, and gripped both armrests. They creaked under the pressure.

"You're determined," Sir Charles said. "You appear so cool, but deep inside, your bladder's about to let go of all its confidence. But that's what I've paid you for, after all, isn't it? So, get on with it."

Sir Charles pulled the blade away and inserted it back into the cane. Jimmy released the girl and dumped the contents of her clutch on the side table next to the sofa.

"Speak," Sir Charles said.

"Yes," Winter said, "that's fine, but I have to get approval."

Sir Charles leaned into her ear. "You tell them I'll give you an extra 10K, and I'll try very hard not to hurt your pretty little breasts."

Jimmy cracked his neck and sat down on the sofa right across from Bobby.

The girl nodded, keeping her head low.

"Very well," Sir Charles said, "make your call, but keep it short."

———————

A huge man walked back into the living room. Akira locked eyes with him, trying not to reveal how startled she was. Who the fuck was this? Why hadn't she been told about a fourth?

He looked back at her, his stare impassive, the eyes dead. There was a large tactical knife in his belt holster, but no guns. He headed to the bar and leaned back against the counter.

An extra body in the picture would be difficult to handle; Akira needed to speed things up. She went toward the sofa, where Craw was now sitting next to Robert Banks, and put a foot on the coffee table in front of him. She hit the speed dial on the Vertu as Craw stared at her legs. He grinned, aroused, wanting to see more. The Vertu rang.

"What's the deal?" a male voice said.

"I'm with the client; I need approval for the extra service. Bondage but with barbed wire," Akira said, smiling at Jimmy.

His eyes followed her hand as it crept up her inner thigh and under her dress.

"How's the view, Jimmy boy?" Sir Charles asked.

"A rather delightful sight from here, sir. Spread them a bit more, darling."

"Hassan, would you mind fetching the wire?" Sir Charles asked.

So that was the big guy's name.

Hassan opened the cabinet next to the bar and grabbed a roll of barb the size of a bowling ball.

Jimmy looked back at Akira's crotch.

And his expression turned to shock.

Instead of the cell phone, she was aiming a .38 Walther PPK at his face. It had been hidden in a crotch holster under her dress.

He went for her wrist but Akira popped him twice in the chest. Jimmy's wife's beater blossomed red. He looked down at his torso, then up at her, an expression of fury on his face, then took one last breath and stopped moving.

Robert Banks was next on her list, but he'd jumped behind the sofa. Instead, Akira spun around and aimed at Barton. Both shots missed and hit the wall. Barton limped into the hallway and ducked into the bathroom. A wide-eyed Hassan charged Akira like a bull, but she shot him twice in less than a second. He kept on coming, protected by a Kevlar vest no doubt, and was on her before she could aim at his head. He barreled into her, and the next shot hit the ceiling as she crashed into the drywall behind her and got stuck halfway. Hassan gripped her neck with both hands. She tried to catch a breath and reached for his eyes, nails at the ready, but he head-butted her and pulled out his Bowie knife.

Red sprayed her face, and the smell of gunpowder assaulted her nostrils. Hassan released her throat, his face now blooming like a rose.

And then he fell.

Revealing Banks behind him.

Pointing Jimmy's pistol in Akira's face, its suppressor smoking.

A second passed, and Akira winced as she took a deep breath. Her last breath. She closed her eyes and waited for the shot.

But the shot never came.

She opened her eyes. Banks had lowered the weapon, and now extended his arm toward her. Akira grabbed it, perplexed, and he yanked her out of the wall. The sound from the suppressed gunshot and Hassan's head popping still echoed strangely in Akira's ear. She straightened and patted herself, checking if anything was broken.

"You okay?"

"Yeah, I think so," Akira said in a hoarse tone, then brushed a chunk of drywall from her shoulder. "Fuck."

"You sure you're okay?"

"Why didn't you kill me?" she said to Banks.

"My best friend is in the bedroom. These psychos, they killed her. You take care of the old geezer. I think he's hiding in the bathroom. Be careful. He's got a shotgun in there," Banks said in perfect Japanese.

The language switch took Akira aback. Who was this guy? Was he with Wilshire? Nah, they'd never do that.

"And if he's in the other room?" she asked in Korean.

He responded in the same. "If he's in the other room, you're fucked. He's got an MP5."

"No shit," she said.

"No shit."

Akira wiped brain matter off her face with the back of her forearm. Banks handed her a bunch of paper napkins.

"Thank you, Robert."

"It's Bobby. Who are you?"

"I'm Akira."

He nodded. "Okay, my friend Lily, her body, I need it for a proper burial. I'll be back for it."

"Of course."

He locked eyes with her for a moment, then handed her the SIG and walked out of the suite.

CHAPTER 16

Eye

Sir Charles sat squeezed between the tub and the toilet. He gripped his cane.

So they'd found him, just like he'd known they would. Fuck.

He glanced left. Near the glass wall of the walk-in shower was a pack of Marlboro. Now more now than ever he needed those vials of PCP. And propped against the opposite wall was Hassan's shotgun.

He used his cane to drag the Marlboro toward him, bit the cap off a vial and snorted half the contents. The skin on his forehead started to itch, and a sensation that was both pain and pleasure crawled like an army of fire ants to the back of his head. As the angel dust took control of his mind, he imagined his pupils oscillating laterally, his face flushing red as his brain vacuumed the blood from the rest of his body. His heartbeat sounded like a high-pitched jackhammer—

And then he was falling from a skyscraper. The traffic below hurtled toward him as he flew past windows at a velocity he couldn't comprehend. Surrounding him were walls containing his mortal enemies. A voice that sounded like a department-store PA system urged him to kill everyone in isle five.

He threw a punch, connected with ceramic tiles, then withdrew his fist. It was bloody, but he felt nothing. His mouth leaked, and he wiped away saliva and foam, then he stood up and spun around, now wielding the shotgun he had no memory of picking up. His forehead felt hot and dry as sandpaper.

Then the bathroom door spoke to him.

"Come out, Charlie. Make it easy on yourself," the woman said.

Winter. Fucking Winter. If that was even her real name. "Fuck off," he screamed, his voice echoing in his own mind.

"You can make all the noise you want, Charlie. We've secured the entire floor of this hotel just for you."

"I'll kill you, you fucking cunt!"

"What did you do, Charlie? Anything you want

to share?"

"I'll give you the disk. They'll give you anything to get what's on it. And if you're here for the money, you can have it," Sir Charles said.

"You're pathetic. Wilshire got all of your money, Charlie. That's not what I'm here for. You're the period at the end of my assignment. Come on, open up, show me that old-fashioned dignity."

Sir Charles looked straight at the door, his eyes narrowing to slits. "Whoever this Wilshire is, it's the disk he wants, not me. They're petrified of it! If you have the disk, you hold all the cards. You can be anybody, do anything you want."

Sniper shots were easier. You didn't have to engage the mark face to face, listen to them coming up with reasons why they needed to live. But Akira was used to it. *Rule number one: don't listen to a word they're saying.*

But something else had crept into her mind, and for all the wrong reasons. And that was to tell Wilshire to go fuck themselves. This clusterfuck had almost gotten her killed. It was still debatable whether she'd even survive the job, let alone finish it. And then she'd probably be held responsible, which meant she was pretty fucking sure she'd be dead by the end of the week.

"You can write your ticket," Barton continued. "It's right there on the shelf next to the CD player. In the small wall safe. The code is 0-8-5-0-1-2-5-8. The Vivaldi CD is lovely, but it's the Wagner you want. You hear me?"

Akira went to the living room and punched in the code. Underneath *The Four Seasons* was a Richard Wagner *Siegfried Idyll* CD. She placed it on the counter, then inserted the Vivaldi disk into the player.

The Spring concerto filled the room. Akira took a deep breath and turned the volume up. The Walther was relatively quiet, but she didn't want people dialing 911 if Barton ended up firing his shotgun.

Akira caught her reflection in the mirror by the wet bar. A bruise ringed her entire neck and her face was speckled with blood. And, fuck, she looked tired. Her eyes filled with tears and she vomited into the sink, the Walther still in her hand.

She'd been lucky this time. That fourth man—why hadn't she been told about him? Wilshire's oversight had almost gotten her killed.

Memories of years of abuse began to surface. She pushed them and the tears away, not wanting to think about the past right now. Did she have a death wish? Was that what Kyle had been trying to tell her?

Akira ducked into the hallway and snuck back to the bathroom door.

"Are you out there?" Barton called out. "Did you take the disk?"

———————

Senses sharpened by the drugs, Sir Charles focused on trying to pinpoint her position. He edged toward the door, gripping the shotgun, his hand shaking with hatred and fear.

Aimed the barrel forward, and squeezed the trigger.

The blast was loud. The breach created a hole the size of a coffee mug in the thick oak.

Sir Charles backed away and waited, then inched forward, pointing the shotgun ahead, ears straining to catch any sound, even a breath.

He reached the hole, peeked through—

And found himself at the edge of a volcanic crater a mile wide. He looked down. Millions of eels had formed a whirlpool in the lava. In the middle was the woman—Winter or whatever her name was. She was naked, wearing a crown of barbwire. Blood trickled down her face.

"You are astonishing," Sir Charles said. "I love you to death."

———————

With her back against the wall, Akira angled the compact. Then she saw him. His eye.

She snapped it closed, spun around, and fired through the hole.

One shot—her final bullet.

One minute the eye was bloodshot, its pupil dilated. The next it bloomed red as it swallowed the bullet.

There was a thud.

She peeked through the hole. Sir Charles Barton lay in a pool of his own juice. Akira walked back into the living room and turned the music off, then called Wilshire.

"I hope you have good news," the male voice said.

"I do. All clear. Send her in."

And the line went dead.

CHAPTER 17
Siegfried

Five minutes later, the door lock beeped. Akira's mind whirred, imagining the various outcomes of a path already set in motion. She looked down at the Wagner CD in her hand, the disk her boss wanted. The disk with the embedded data. The data everyone in that room had gotten killed for.

Thought usually happens faster than physical movement, but not today. Before Akira's brain could reason with her body and stop her doing anything incredibly stupid, it was too late. She'd pocketed the CD.

She then ejected the Vivaldi and placed it in its jewel case. It was this she'd turn over to Wilshire.

The front door opened, and a uniformed cleaning lady pushed a cart into the foyer. The forty-something had a wide frame and thick ankles, and her hair was pulled back under a headband.

Vera.

The door swung close behind her.

No turning back now.

Akira sat on a stool by the counter, her right leg shaking, fingers tapping nervously on the Vivaldi CD.

Vera locked eyes with her. "Talk to me," she said in a clipped tone.

"The one on the sofa, two shots to the heart. The one by the entry, one shot to the back of the head. The principal's in the bathroom—single shot to the head also."

"Only one shot for the principal? Why?"

"Ran out of .38s."

"You could have tapped him with that SIG," Vera said, nodding at the gun hugged against Akira's side. "Got quite a large suppressor there. Muy bonito, uh?" She smiled. Not a human smile; more like a Badger baring its teeth.

"Fuck you, Vera."

Vera ignored her remark. "I see. There's a master bedroom and two guest rooms off there, correct?" She glanced toward the hallway.

"The master bedroom's down there. I'm using it. You can have it when I'm gone."

"You got something for me?" Vera asked.

"Yeah, this." Akira waved the Vivaldi CD case and placed it on the counter.

"Está bien, guapa. Go make yourself even prettier. I'll be busy chopping up this big boy." She grabbed a roll of polyethylene from the cart and laid it across the floor, then pulled up her sleeves and rolled Hassan's body onto the plastic.

"How did you shoot this man in the back of his head? That's a mystery I'd love to understand," she said, and cackled.

"Same answer as before. Fuck you," Akira said.

"What's going on with you? Usually you're a bitch, but today you're just unfriendly."

Akira stilled her trembling leg.

Vera, though strong, struggled to drag Hassan's dead weight along the hallway and into the small bathroom where Sir Charles lay. Akira followed behind, watching the cleaner sweat, listening to her huff and puff as she hauled him into the shower. Vera took a series of slow breaths and headed back to the foyer. Picked up a large duffle bag from the underside of the cleaning cart. Then returned to the bathroom and shut the door behind her. For which Akira was grateful.

———

Akira went into the master, pulled Lily from under the bed and lifted her over her shoulder. She'd expected the body to weigh more but the poor girl was light as a feather. As she made her way back to the foyer, a high-pitched motor switched on and off, then back on again.

Vera was testing her tools.

Akira scrolled through the contacts the agency had programmed into the Vertu. And there he was. Bobby. Her angel from nowhere. She hit speed dial.

The line rang a few times, then Bobby picked up. "Who's this?"

"It's me, Akira," she said in Japanese.

"I was about to call you. We're here. Just got out of the elevator."

"Who's we?"

"I brought some friends."

"I have Lily with me. I'm bringing her out. But whatever you do, don't come in. Got a cleaner in here. You understand? Just collect your friend and go."

"I hear you," Bobby said. "I still have the key card. Don't shoot."

The line went dead.

The door lock beeped.

Akira looked back down the hallway. If Vera had heard, it was all over. The cleaner would have come with an ex-SWAT backup team, stationed a block away in two unmarked Suburbans. They'd kill Bobby and his crew in minutes.

The door swung open. Akira stepped outside the suite and leaned over, letting Lily slide off her shoulders. Then looked down the hallway.

It was lined with over twenty men—Bobby's friends, all dressed casually, irezumi tattoos visible on their bare skin. Yakuza gangsters who would help get Lily a proper burial at any cost.

She stared, and they stared back as Bobby walked through the line-up, Lily in his arms. They were all armed. Knives, hammers, axes—anything that could kill a person quietly.

Bobby stopped at the elevators. A chime announced the opening doors. Bobby stepped in. The men turned to Akira, muscles tense, ready to pounce and destroy everything in their path. But it was as if a switch had been turned off. In unison, they nodded subtly, then turned and walked away.

Some followed Bobby, others took a service elevator further down, and yet others dispersed into the stairwell. Their departure was perfectly choreographed, and took only seconds.

Akira ducked back into the room, put the items spilled out over the table back into her clutch, and exited the suite.

———

Akira headed across the busy lobby toward the exit.

A police officer was conversing with the reception-ist. Two more were outside, talking into their radi-os, patrol cars blocking the driveway.

Someone had called the cops. But Bobby and friends seemed to have made it out, and for the first time in years, Akira felt like she was com-ing out of a tunnel and into the light, rather than running toward an oncoming train. This was what Kyle had been tried to tell her the whole time. He wasn't trying to control her future, as she'd thought. He wanted her to be free from the past.

A large man bumped into her, and her clutch fell onto the floor, spilling its contents. The jew-el case split apart, and the CD rolled over the marble and toward the reception desk.

The man who'd bumped seemed oblivious and kept on walking.

Akira scrabbled around on the floor, repacked her clutch, then hurried over to the reception desk.

The police officer stopped the CD with his shoe, picked it up and smiled. "Wagner?"

Akira shot him a glare. He could fuck off. It was none of his fucking business what she lis-tened to. She waved the jewel case, and the offi-cer handed the disk back to her.

A smirk grew under his large mustache. "You Asians like classical?"

"Thank you, Officer."

"I didn't think so."

Fuck you, bigot.

Lisa glowered at him, then turned to Akira. "I'm so sorry, Ms. Winter. Let us know if there's anything we can do for you. We want you to be absolutely satisfied with your stay." She smiled, then gave the officer another critical look.

"Thank you, Lisa," Akira said, and pocketed the CD.

Minutes later she was in her car. The engine roared and Akira drove the Porsche away from the hotel.

———

Vera—now donned in a hooded rain suit, gloves, goggles, and a breathing mask—leaned over Hassan's body.

Engelbert Humperdinck's "Spanish Eyes" played through the headset connected to a Rio MP3 player, the very latest in digital-music devices, as she lifted the Sawzall and closed her eyes.

It went to work, its motor whirring as it chewed through muscle and bone. Vera smiled as the long carbide blade went through Hassan's arm like a knife through butter, spattering blood over the shower wall.

By the time she was done, Hassan had been distributed into several heavy-duty trash bags, any resemblance of a human being long gone. She'd been careful not to put too many pieces in a single bag. Too much weight could mean a sharp edge of jagged bone piercing the plastic and spilling the contents.

Vera switched off the heavy Sawzall and laid it on the floor, then wiped blood from her goggles with a hand towel. She cranked up the volume on the MP3 player and sang along to the haunting lyrics. Just like Engelbert said, it was just adios, not goodbye.

CHAPTER 18

Uncle William

The Porsche's headlights illuminated the road, dancing over the treetops, flashing over the rocky mountainside, and lighting up the night sky beyond the cliffs. Akira turned onto Mulholland Highway, came to a turn and shifted down to second, revved the engine, tires smoking, went up to third, hit the gas and furiously gained momentum on a short straight, then repeated the process all over again.

Sir Charles. She didn't want to think about him right now. Especially because he'd reminded her of Uncle William and the abuse her mother had endured. Steering on the winding road was a distraction, but the tears still welled, blurring her vision for a moment.

The coyote came out of nowhere. It froze in

the middle of the road, blinded by the headlights.

Akira stood on the brakes. The wheels screeched, the car slid, and smoke hissed from the rubber trail on the road.

She stopped ten feet away from the animal and locked eyes with it. Then it was gone.

Akira took deep breaths, unable to fight off the memory ...

1982

KOREATOWN, LOS ANGELES, CALIFORNIA

It was a beautiful sunny spring day on a residential street lined with trees in the middle of K-Town. A Caprice station wagon pulled up to the curb in front of a modest two-bedroom home. Ms. Lee was behind the wheel. Her daughter, Jane, sat in the backseat with twelve-year-old, Akira.

Akira grabbed her Star Wars backpack, got out and ran up the driveway. She and Jane waved at each other as Ms. Lee drove away. Akira walked up the dozen steps to the front door and looked up at the perfectly blue sky. She could hear birds chirping and the sound of a lawn mower in the distance. A gentle breeze played with her long black hair. The oak trees rustled, and a leaf fell from a branch, spinning, dancing with the wind.

That's when time ceased.

Akira heard a scream inside. It was the sound of suffering, of pain. And it was coming from her mother.

She opened the door and bumped straight into Uncle William, holding on a Budweiser can, his thin hair pulled back in a short dirty-blond ponytail.

He blocked the doorway. "Hey, Akira, what's the hurry, uh?"

Akira peered around him and into the living room, searching.

And saw her.

Sung-soo was huddled on the couch, sobbing. Her clothes were in disarray, her lips bloody, one eye black. On seeing Akira, she shielded her face with one hand and pulled her dress down over the bruises on her legs with the other, her face etched with shame.

"Mom!"

Sung-soo staggered to her feet and retreated to the kitchen.

Akira hated this man her mother made her call Uncle. Wished for him to be gone, to disappear, just like her father had.

Uncle William stroked her hair but wouldn't let her pass him. "You should come to the house later. What do you say? Remember, you wouldn't want to break a promise, right?"

He laughed, revealing two silver crowns at the side of his mouth. Akira held back tears and squeezed by him, running into the kitchen.

"Momma, are you okay?"

But Sung-soo kept her face hidden with both hands and turned away. "Go to your room. This doesn't concern you."

Akira stormed out of the kitchen and up to her bedroom. The promise she'd made to Uncle William meant nothing. The deal was off. He'd broken his side of the bargain, and now she knew he would never leave them alone, no matter what she agreed to do for him.

―――――――

Drones of irregular hexagons invaded a black void, exploding as they were hit by tiny white dots fired by a triangle in the blackness of space. Electronic machine guns chirped and electric whiplash explosions increased a sequence of numbers at the top of the screen.

Akira played Asteroids to escape the horror surrounding her. Shooting saucers as they hurled toward her ship made her feel in control. They were the villains, and she was killing them all. These battles went on for hours. If only it could be this easy to defeat the monster in her life, she thought as she maneuvered the Atari's joystick like a pro.

Someone downstairs started yelling. Her mom was crying, pleading. Again.

Uncle William was back. Akira ran down the stairs and into the living room. Her mom was on the floor, pinned underneath him, both his hands wrapped around her throat.

"You slut! I know how it is with you bitches. I see you! I know what has to be done."

Akira pulled at his arm, trying to hold him back, but he swung his hand around and hit her square in the face, knocking her out. Her mother tried to fight back, but he was stronger. Sung-soo's mouth was full of blood, her lips swollen. A bruise circled her throat. But for him it wasn't enough; she was still conscious.

"Shut up!" Uncle William yelled, and swung his arm.

The powerful blow knocked Sung-soo out. He tore off her nightgown, pulled down his pants and forced himself inside her. A few minutes later, he was done. He gulped from a beer can, stood, pulled his pants up and left.

———

The television woke Akira up, static from the screen showering her face with a flurry of pixels. She bolted out of bed, gasping for air, disoriented.

"Mommy!"

No answer.

She looked at the small digital clock. She'd overslept and her mom hadn't woken her. It was now past ten, the school bus long gone.

Then the power went out.

Akira peered into the hallway. No sign of Uncle William. She headed downstairs and peeked into the living room. No sign of her mother either.

She edged along the short hallway toward the kitchen. As her angle of vision changed she spotted the coffee maker floating in the sink, submerged in dishwater. Still plugged in.

She entered the kitchen, and something to the side of her moved, startling her.

She turned toward the island. Feet brushed her face.

Delicate feet.

Her mother's feet.

Akira looked up and screamed.

Sung-soo hung from a heavy-duty extension cord tied to a ceiling fan.

Akira hurtled out of the house and onto the street. She ran and ran, and then she stopped and looked up at the sky and realized she'd returned home but didn't know how she'd gotten there.

A horn blared. Tires screeched. Akira nearly jumped out of her skin as a van shuddered to a stop a few inches away from her.

"Watch where you're going, kid!" a man yelled, then took off.

An older woman crossed the street and went into Akira's house. A few seconds later, the neighbor began screaming.

For years, Akira had been terrified, but in that moment, something snapped and she began to walk toward Uncle William's house with only a single thought in her mind—the man responsible for her mother's death was alive. And that was unacceptable.

The garage door was a third of the way up. She ducked and slipped in, then crept around the rear end of the 1969 Chevy Nova. The front of the car sat on one hydraulic jack, the hood propped open. One wheel was off its hub, leaving the brake drum exposed. Uncle William lay underneath, his back on a creeper, legs sticking out.

"Hey!" she yelled.

He slid out from under the car and stared at her. Then he grinned, showing off his silver crowns, and stood up.

"What's going on, stupid? Don't you see I'm busy?"

He slapped her on the back of her head, but she didn't flinch, just wiped tears from her cheeks. Uncle William looked down at her, a cigarette smoldering from the corner of his lips, then grabbed her chin. Akira recoiled.

"Did your mother send you? I don't have time for your nothing bullshit right now. I'm busy."

He placed the cigarette on a toolbox next to the car, then picked up a gasoline can from a workbench, poured a bit of fuel in the carburetor, and propped the can by the brake booster and the engine.

He winked at Akira, grinned again, showing his gleaming silver. "Wanna hear this bitch roar?" He reached across the engine bay, pulled on the carburetor throttle and revved the engine.

Akira eyed a screwdriver in his back pocket.

The car vibrated and the engine choked. He reached behind him and grabbed the screwdriver, and adjusted a screw on the throttle body. The car sputtered, but he kept on turning the screw until the engine purred—the perfect mixture of gasoline and air.

He handed her the screwdriver. "Hold this, stupid."

Akira grabbed it and looked at the tip. It was long and sharp, a flathead.

Then she looked at Uncle William's neck.

Uncle William lay back down on the creeper and rolled himself under the car.

Akira's eyes filled with tears. If only she had the courage to … the screwdriver fell from her hand and she looked down, steadying herself on the front fender as she searched for it. The fender bumped up and down and little, shaking the gasoline can perched in the engine bay.

"Hey watch out, stupid! I'm under here," Uncle William barked.

Akira's heart began to thump like a trip hammer as she took in the hydraulic jack, then its release lever, and then his body under the Nova.

Suddenly everything became clear.

She stepped on the lever, and the car dropped.

"Fuck!" Uncle William screamed as the wheel hub crushed his pelvis.

The gasoline can toppled over, and fuel poured down into the engine bay, splashing on his face, neck, and chest.

Akira's self-doubt vanished. Her sweat had dried up and she felt suddenly cold. She picked up the smoldering cigarette, looked at Uncle William—pinned, drenched in fuel—and took a long pull from the butt.

Her lungs were used to the smoke; it was the first thing she'd learned for him. It made her a woman, he'd said.

He looked up at her, and his eyes widened as understanding dawned.

"Fuck. You little bitch. Fuck! Don't you dare."

Akira took another long drag, then tossed the cigarette through the open hood.

"I'll fucking kill you!" He screamed.

Embers sparked as it bounced off the intake manifold. The car lit up, and Akira jumped back, intending to run. But something was holding her dress. She glanced down. Uncle William's hand clutched at the hemline, and he began to scream and flail as the flames seared the flesh of his forearm.

Then there was a surge of heat and the bottom of the car caught on fire. His hand fell, and Akira was running out of the garage, free.

CHAPTER 19

Vera

Vera was the daughter of a butcher in Sinaloa, Mexico. She'd lost her mother at an early age—a life-changing moment that had shaped her very being. Vera had been eight years old when she'd watched her mother kill the Policía Federal officer who'd raped her, then chop him up and store him in their shop's freezer. Her mother had been given a life sentence. Years later, in an act of revenge, the Sinaloa chief of police had arranged for her mother's murder.

As Vera had grown up, the anguish and horror of that time had replayed over and over in her head. And so she'd shut off those memories and put all her attention into learning the art of true nose-to-tail butchering from her father.

Years had passed, and the best restaurants in Mexico City would send their chefs to her father's shop. Many customers connected to the Federales would gossip about her mother's killers, some even mocking her, but Vera was patient and careful, until she'd discovered who'd been responsible for her mother's death.

When Vera was nineteen her father had wrapped his truck around a tree—a death born of too much grief and way too much drinking. She'd taken over the business and begun looking for the people who'd killed her mother.

Eventually, she'd killed them all, displaying their body parts in a public square, on an altar constructed with human remains.

The news had made it to Mexico City, the papers speculating that the assassin was a woman. *La Prensa* had coined the name La Cortadora de Sinaloa—and Vera, codenamed The Butcher, was born.

Her professional career had begun in Puerto Vallarta, but she'd soon realized that moving to Juarez where the demand was much higher was her only option. She'd served the drug cartel for years, until one day she traveled across the border for a vacation in Las Vegas. And it was there she'd found the love of her life.

In one man's voice: Engelbert Humperdinck.

Vera knew she was a sociopath, that she would

never feel empathy, yet somehow this man had given her something that could fill the black void in her soul. His songs spoke to her, and so Vera had made Las Vegas her home.

——————

THE CONCOURSE HOTEL
LOS ANGELES, CALIFORNIA

Engelbert continued to grace her ears as she tossed a bag filled with bits of Hassan into the cleaning cart. One body bagged, two to go.

Sometimes even professionals worked with idiots, but it was the pro's responsibility to get the best out of everyone, no matter their limitations. Vera's idiot was her son, Rigo, a FedEx courier who freelanced for his mom anytime she needed.

Vera removed her gloves and called him on her cell. The line rang for more seconds than she liked.

"Mom?"

"Are you where you're supposed to be, hijo?"

"Well, yeah, of course, Mama. I'm in the elevator. Be up in a few."

"Good."

Vera placed the CD Akira had given her inside a FedEx envelope and walked over to the sofa. Jimmy lay in a pool of blood. What a mess that bitch had made.

There was a knock at the door, and she opened it. Rigo's hair was unkempt, his standard issue uniform rumpled. Vera shook her head and tutted.

"Hi, Mama," he said, and recoiled for a moment. It wasn't the first cleaning job he'd come to, but her boy had never gotten used to the smell.

"You're late," she said. Rigo gagged. "Are you going to pass out again?"

That's what he'd done six years earlier at one of her jobs, and Vera would never let him forget it; she brought it up every single time.

"Like I said, son, you're late."

"But you didn't give a time. How can I be late?"

"How can you be late? You work at FedEx. How you've managed to keep your job is a mystery to me. Are you all set?"

Rigo nodded. "I got the label made this morning. We are absolutely all set. Yeah, no, I'm sure of it."

"Great, I'm glad you're sure. Now, can you fucking do this thing you've got to do, ASAP?" She handed him the envelope.

"No tip?" Rigo chuckled, then walked out into the hallway. Vera stepped in front of the door, stopping it from closing.

"Tip? Can you tell I'm busy? I don't have time for comedy, idiot. Get the hell out of here before

I put you back where you came from."

A grim look washed over her son's face.

"Yeah, okay. That's just ... weird. Why would you say that?"

Vera shut the door in his face.

"Nice seeing you too, Mom," Rigo called out.

Vera put her gloves back on and turned to Jimmy's body. Air hissed out from the two bullet holes in his chest. Then he gasped as droplets of blood sprayed out of his mouth.

Look at you. We have a squirter. The brain was still going, but the ticker had stopped pumping. Looked like he was going to need another pop. What a fucked-up job. Vera looked around for the SIG-Sauer Akira had placed on the bar counter, but it wasn't there anymore.

"Triple fucking bitch. Puta madre de mierda," Vera hissed, throwing up her arms in frustration.

She headed for the hallway, and was about to walk into the bathroom to get the shotgun, but stopped. No, too loud. She went into Hassan's room instead, and in a duffle bag found a 9mm H&K with a suppressor already attached.

Then it was back to the living room.

Only there was no Jimmy.

The squirter had gone.

Vera didn't startle easily, but this was like one of those supernatural movies, and she never watched those because she found them spooky.

And spooked she was. The hair on her arms stood up as she took a quick step back into the hallway, gun up close to her chest, senses sharpened.

Where the fuck was he?

She scanned around, then glanced to her right at a picture frame. And there, reflected in the glass, was Jimmy. Standing behind her. Wielding a nine-inch switchblade.

He lunged but missed and knifed her respirator instead. She ripped off her goggles and mask, and spun around. Jimmy swung the knife again, skewering her hand, and then grabbed her throat.

They both fell backward. Vera dropped the gun but ended up on top. A dazed Jimmy reached for her face and grabbed her hair. Vera pulled her hand out of the blade, then punched him square in the face, breaking his nose. Blood sprayed everywhere. She hit him again, blood from her hand mixing with blood from his face. She punched him one final time.

Jimmy dropped the knife, twitched, and stopped moving.

Dead. Finally.

Vera shot him twice in the head. Then six more times. Then another seven, until there was no head left to speak of. Now out of rounds, she locked the slide open and examined the wall behind him.

This was not cleanable.

And her hand was bleeding and needed stitches.

"Puta madre." That fucking bitch had ruined her day.

She headed for the master bedroom, ripped her rain suit off, and threw it on the floor.

CHAPTER 20

The Sweep

Leaving her DNA behind was no longer Vera's primary concern; the cleaning job had gone way beyond that. First, she'd need to tend to her wound. Second, she'd need a very different kind of support. Now that the job had gone south, the two Suburbans with eight men, weapons ready, on standby in case things got dicey, no longer passed muster. What she needed instead was the sweep.

Big Mac's two-man team offered three tiers of deep cleaning. Tier-1 comprised a non-destructive method of cleaning such that affected areas were returned to their original state. Forensic decontamination and DNA swab collection were included as proof that the mark had been eliminated.

Tier-2 was more aggressive, and included all of the above plus gas treatment, even the use of UV radiation for deeper decontamination. It reminded Vera of when houses were treated for termites.

Tier-3 was destructive. It included all the services in Tiers 1 and 2. The site was then sprayed with industrial bleach and torched. Tier 3 was rarely used but absolutely necessary when a cleaner had lost control.

And Vera had lost control.

Twenty-four stitches later, Vera secured the bandage on her wound with medical tape, and flexed her fingers. She could still make a fist, meaning she'd been lucky; the tendons hadn't been damaged. And thank God for local anesthetics, cocaine and tequila.

Her cell phone rang. She pulled it out of her bra and said, "Things have changed."

"Really?" a male voice said.

"It's out of control, stand by. I'm calling Mac."

———

Sir Charles groaned, pulled himself to his feet grabbed the side of the tub. He scanned the room, and caught his reflection in the mirror. His left eye was missing, and blood trickled from the empty socket and down his cheek. Christ, he could see inside his own head. A wail echoed around the room, like the sound of a dying cat. And Sir Charles realized it was coming from his own throat.

And yet ... he was alive!

He rolled sheets of toilet paper into a ball and stuffed them into the gaping hole in his face, groaning as white-hot pain lanced through his head, then pulled a vial of PCP from the cigarette packet and snorted it all. His head tilted back, then forward, connecting with the mirror, shattering his reflection. The pupil in his remaining eye dilated as a bolt of energy shot through his nervous system. He clenched his teeth, muffling a scream as he began to convulse violently.

He fell to his knees. Seconds went by, and the drug stabilized. The pain was gone, leaving him with a blissful sense of absolute invincibility.

He got back up on his feet and looked into the broken mirror. *What the ...?* Two shiny black horns had sprouted from his temples. Enthralled by the transformation, he traced his fingers over the newly acquired appendages, then exited the bathroom.

Instead of a hallway, the Greenwich foot tunnel stretched ahead of him for a quarter mile. At the end of it was a table on which lay the Lincoln's keys. He reached forward into the space, arms bending impossibly, like they were rubber. And then he was holding the fob.

He saw the door, opened it, and walked out of the suite.

CHAPTER 21

Big Mac

A large shirtless African American man in his fifties sat in an office in the back of a tanning salon. A gold chain hung around his neck and he wore an LA Rams cap. The sounds of the neighborhood and the smell of traffic flowed in through an open patio slider. World Wrestling Federation and Hulkamania posters covered the walls. Paint peeled off the ceiling, and the stained nylon shag carpet, uncleaned for years, had become a flakey beige crust of DNA.

Across from his desk was a coffee table and a sofa. One end was occupied by a blue-haired White girl. She was topless and smoking a joint. Next to her, two Black twins wearing identical shorts and crop tops shared a slice of pizza. The table was littered with crumpled Budweiser cans, empty Fritos bags, and three opened Pizza Hut boxes.

Wheel of Fortune played on a large television set on a commode at the far end of the room. The three women watched intently.

Big Mac's cell phone rang in a drawer, the sound further muffled by the din of the TV.

"Hey, turn that shit down," he yelled as on the screen Vanna White gestured toward the wall of squares and the chyron read: *Fictional Character.*

"Am I chewing too loud?" one of the twins asked.

The White girl picked up the remote and muted the TV.

Big Mac rummaged in a drawer, put a Desert Eagle. 357 Magnum in a gold finish on the desk, then dug around for his Motorola. He pulled the antenna out with his teeth and flipped it open.

"Mama bella! Been waiting for your call. All going well today?"

"Why so fucking long to answer? You keep that phone I gave you inside your ass?" Vera said.

Jesus, the woman bit like a viper.

"Sorry, Mama, what can I do?"

"Change of plans. My day is fucked, and you know what that means. Burn it down."

"Tier-3? Fuck, sorry about that. That's another twenty kays."

"Bueno, I knew this much. I sent the money five minutes ago."

Big Mac punched a few keys on his computer and checked his bank account. "Yeah, Mama, I see you did."

"Listen up. You're going to need one more cleaning carts to remove all three. One's already bagged. That'll be an easy one. I didn't chop the rest. Everything went to shit, comprende?"

"I gotcha, Mama. We'll take care of it, as usual."

"Great, make it melt."

"Smores in a cracker; it'll melt like smores in a cracker."

The line went dead.

Big Mac wiped his sweaty forehead with his forearm, then brought up a live feed on another monitor. The black-and-white image of Benito appeared, a skinny El Salvadorian wearing a cap with the logo reading *Die Hard Pest Control*. He was in the back of a van, sitting at a small makeshift desk. A shelf next to him was full of cleaning supplies and other tools of the trade.

"Hey, boss," Benito said, looking straight into the screen.

"Yo, Benito, where are you?"

"Exactly where we're supposed to be—in the parking garage under the hotel, not too far from the elevator."

"Good man. Where's Bruno?"

"On his headset, in the driver's seat."

Benito lobbed a pack of cigarettes to the side, and Big Mac heard Bruno say, "What's up? Are we doing this?"

"Yeah. It's time, bro," Benito said.

Bruno appeared next to Benito and looked into the screen. "So what's the deal?"

"Forget taking out the trash. This is a Tier-3," Big Mac said.

"Right now? Shit, I thought we had another hour. I'm gonna miss *V.I.P.*," Bruno said.

"Can you tape it? Benito asked.

"The VCR's broken," Bruno said.

"I'll do it," Big Mac said. "Don't be worried about missing Pam in action. Focus on the job. Now listen up. I need you two to focus."

Benito and Bruno leaned closer to the screen.

"You have three bodies," Big Mac said, "and you need two more carts. One's already in the suite, and one of the bodies is bagged and—"

"I don't remember packing the torch," Bruno said.

Benito slapped his shoulder. "I always pack the torch, baby."

"Okay people," Big Mac said, "I don't give a fuck who packs what. Just do what you gotta do and get back here. Finish this fucking thing."

"Okay, motherfuckers, Bruno's coming to

play," Bruno said, and loaded a pesticide sprayer with bleach.

Benito grabbed a small Benz-o-Matic torch kit and a fire extinguisher.

Big Mac disconnected the call. *V.I.P.?* He'd record their fucking asses first.

They opened the suite's windows, duct-taped the fire alarms, and covered the sprinklers with heat-absorbing cups. Benito set up two large fans to vacuum the fumes toward the ducting in the ceiling. Bruno tossed a respirator over to Benito, who fired up the torch and began to burn anything that looked like blood. Each scorching session was followed by a short burst from a small extinguisher, ensuring the wall, carpet, and furniture didn't go up in flames. Then Bruno sprayed sodium hypochlorite over the burn marks, dampening the smoke and dissolving any DNA residue.

They worked methodically, eliminating any forensic traces in less than two hours, and leaving behind what seemed to be a puzzling act of vandalism. Wilshire's lawyers would reimburse the hotel for the damage, and pay triple the actual expenses. That way, nobody would be reporting any damage to the authorities.

CHAPTER 22

Ski Mask

WILSHIRE LOGISTICS, INC
LOS ANGELES, CALIFORNIA.

Rigo arrived at 5900 Wilshire, holding a pad and pen and a small FedEx parcel. He ran up the white sandstone steps next to a large fountain in the center of a small lake—a Los Angeles billionaire's announcement to everyone that money could buy anything. It was the weekend so this should be an easy delivery.

He entered a cavernous lobby. Two men in sharp black suits stood guard in the middle. Behind an impressive desk, surrounded by white marble, glass, and steel, an attractive and impeccably dressed blond woman smiled as he approached. Above her, a sign read *Wilshire Logistics, Inc.*, though there was no explanation of what exactly the company was or offered. The logo featured a red and black target with a gold lightning bolt in the middle that screamed private military.

Rigo explained why he'd come. The woman's long-manicured fingers tapped a Motorola two-way radio. There was a moment of silence. The radio beeped twice and Rigo was cleared for the penthouse. She handed him a lanyard with *Wilshire* stamped on the pass.

"Wear it at all times, please. Take the one marked P"—she gestured toward a bank of elevators—"right there by those two gentlemen."

The two men wore tactical gear and held H&K MP5s.

Rigo slipped the lanyard around his neck and headed for the elevators. As he passed the sharp dressers, one whispered something into his wrist, but Rigo couldn't make out what it was.

One of the elevator guards examined Rigo's badge and pressed a button. The door opened and Rigo was whisked at terminal velocity to the thirty-first floor.

Another large lobby, another impressive desk, more glass and steel, the same white marble. And a stunning 180-degree view of Los Angeles.

He stepped out and walked past two more armed guards in tactical gear. Another impeccably dressed receptionist pointed to a man wearing khaki pants, black Skechers, and a black shirt.

Rico extended the FedEx pad and pen. "I need

a signature here."

The man raised his hand, then turned and headed for a hallway. "Follow me."

Rigo rolled his eyes and followed the man into a large glass-walled office. At the end of an imposing desk sat a figure wearing mirrored Ray-Bans over a black ski mask, and black suit and tie. Next to him, an Asian man in his thirties wearing jeans and a baseball cap sat in front of a laptop.

"I'm Adriano. You must be Rigo. Have a seat."

"What the fuck is this? No, I'm good. This will be quick. I just need a signature." Rigo extended the pad and pen.

"Sit," Adriano snapped.

A pistol was holstered under the masked man's blazer. *Shit*. Rigo took a deep breath and sat down.

Adriano came over to him and extended his hand, and for an instant, Rigo thought he wanted to shake hands, then realized he was asking for the parcel.

"Oh, yes! Here."

Adriano opened it and produced a Vivaldi compact disc, "Ha! *Le Quattro Stagioni*. One of my favorite." He looks at Rigo, "You have great taste in music, Rigo."

"I-it's not mine."

Adriano pasted a smile on his face and handed the CD to the man on the laptop.

The computer hummed, and Rigo fidgeted. He had lots of deliveries scheduled. No way did he want this one jeopardizing his good standing at FedEx. He eyed the door, but one of Ski Mask's escorts had blocked it. Rigo could see a pistol tucked in his waistband.

He began to sweat.

The man on the laptop looked up at him, then at Adriano. He shook his head and ejected the disk.

"What?" Rigo asked.

"Vera's kid, right?" Adriano said.

"Yes, what's going on? I need to go. I have deliveries."

"Oh, don't worry, we'll be done soon. What deliveries? I don't have you scheduled for others."

"That's because I don't work for you. I'm a freelancer."

"Yet your jacket says FedEx," Adriano said, and chuckled. He turned to the Asian man. "You see that, too, right?"

The man nodded, his expression blank.

"I mean I freelance for my mom."

"Mamma Vera! I see. So what's with the bullshit uniform, Rigo?"

"It's not ... it's not bullshit. I'm employed at FedEx too."

Rigo stood up. Adriano pushed him right back down. It was a hard push, more strength from a man that size than he'd expected. Rigo winced. And that fucking ski mask was unnerving the shit out of him.

"Did you make any stops, Rigo? Maybe you lost the CD and replaced it with this shit."

"What? Look, I'm Vera's son. You can ask my mom. I came straight here. Trust me, I'm no fuck-up. I do this all the time."

"You steal all the time?"

"That's not what I said. I didn't say that."

"I need you to shut up, son."

Adriano pulled a cell phone out as the Asian man closed the laptop and exited the room.

Vera sat behind the wheel of a white Cadillac Escalade parked in front of the iconic Dresden Room, a restaurant and lounge few miles north of K-Town.

"Why are you calling me?" Vera asked.

"A sweet boy you got here, Vera," Adriano said.

"You don't have to get sarcastic with me. Get to the point. Where's my son?"

"He seems to have delivered the wrong disk. The package—we don't have it."

"I don't give a shit about your disk. I delivered what I got from your bitch. Now, because of her sloppy work, my goddamn DNA is all over that suite, and that's going to cost me, which means it's going to cost you. Now let my son go."

"No."

"Mom, help," she heard Rigo squeak down the line. "He's got a gun on me."

"I said let my son go. I will not repeat that, capisce?" Vera said.

"Okay, mama bear, I can respect that. But don't worry about your son. I promise he'll be okay. But we need that disk. And we need you to find it."

"Fuck you. The job's done, and I'm done looking. I guess your sloppy bitch has it. Do you want me to fix that? Are you asking me for something?"

"Yes, we are. Wilshire has approved you for a change of order. That disk is our top priority. This is your new task. What do you say, mama bear?"

"Don't get parental with me. I already had a father, and he taught me to cut meat in ways you'll never understand, capisci, Italiano?"

"Por supuesto, Vera. Te entiendo perfectamente," Adriano said.

"You know what I like about the Olive Garden?" Vera asked.

"Nothing?"

"Everything. Theirs is the best Italian menu out there."

"I don't think so, Vera."

"It has the most important ingredient of all.

I'm surprised you didn't notice, being Italian and all."

"What's that, Vera?"

"Consistency."

"I agree—consistently shitty."

"Oh, come on, let's be fair. You know that even though it's not the best, it's got to be a four. See, I've been to Italy. I've traveled the entire country."

"Yes, Vera, I'm aware of that. They're still looking for you. What's your point?"

"My point is, dear Italiano, that I like consistency. Back in Italy, everywhere I went they cooked pasta, but the sauces were always different. I had the best pasta at one restaurant, but I could never have the same dish somewhere else. The chefs are so busy trying to outdo each other with their narcissistic fuckery that they forget the original recipe. But at the Olive Garden, it's always the same. I know what to expect. Yes, it may be less than average, but it is *always* that."

"Why do I feel you're going to ask me a question, Vera?"

"So, my point is, Italiano, are you going to be consistent?"

"I see, like il giardino degli olivi?" Adriano asked.

"Yes, like the Olive Garden. Is my son going to be safe?"

There was silence. Had he lowered the gun?

"Yes, Vera, your son is safe. In the end, I'm a businessman working for businessmen that want the outcome to be good for everyone. So, yes, I'm going to tell you what I'm going to do, and I will do what I said I was going to do. No surprises. You have the word of Wilshire, and that's a contract," Adriano said.

"You understand if I'm a little skeptical."

"I do. Just send an address as soon as you have her location."

"You're dreaming. I'm doing this alone, using my men, end of the story."

"Okay, you call the shots on this one."

"Good. I need two-hundred-fifty kays in the first account. Then wire the two million for the change of order to the other account. You have one hour. Meanwhile, if you don't mind, I'm going to enjoy some live music. And you, be nice to my son."

Vera killed the line.

Adriano turned to Rigo. "Sorry, my friend, but I can't let you leave yet. You hungry?"

"Yeah, I can eat."

"You like those things with the tomato sauce in them? Like a calzone—you take them out of the plastic, put them in this pouch thing, and in the microwave. You Americans love microwave!"

"You mean Hot Pockets?" Rigo asked.

"Sure, but no. These are not pockets, it's closed all around like a burrito with marinara sauce."

"I don't know those."

"Anyway, we have a fully stocked kitchen with all the pockets you want. Go ahead, it's back there. Make a right, then first door to the right before you get to the conference room."

Rigo stood, relieved he didn't have to be in a room with a masked psychopath holding a gun to his face.

"You know how to make coffee?" Adriano asked.

"Yeah?"

"Great. Make a fresh pot."

"You want me to make coffee?"

"Yes, and bring me some pronto or I'll fucking shoot you," Adriano said with a smirk.

CHAPTER 23

Kyle

Akira sped northbound along Pacific Coast Highway toward Kyle and the safe house. They needed to leave, and that was okay. There were options in place; they'd prepared for this exact moment.

She eased off the accelerator and pulled into a vista-point parking lot.

Waves crashed onto the jagged rocks below, spraying foam into the air. Akira ripped the door open, got out of the Porsche and vomited in the dark.

Her Vertu vibrated. "Kyle?"

"Hang on, baby," Kyle said.

She heard footsteps. Was he heading upstairs?

"Talk to me," he said.

"Kyle, get out! They know you're there. I'm on

my way to Gaviota. I'll wait for you."

"What?"

"You're burned. Leave. I fucked up. I led them to you. I took—"

"Calm down. It's going to be okay."

There was a click—an incoming call.

"It's Wilshire," Akira said.

She put Kyle on hold.

"What's going on?" A male voice asked.

"I'm done."

"You left quite a mess back there."

"I'm out. *We* are out."

"Hang on. First things first, right? You have something for us that we need to send to our client. We must fulfill our obligations, and you must fulfill yours. Agreed?"

"Too late. I want to be done. I *am* done."

"I hear you. That can be arranged. First, I want to make it easier for you. Take your time. Give us a location and we'll pick it up."

"Fuck no, I'm keeping it until I know we're safe."

"Okay, forget it. I'm not angry with you. But you need to keep an open mind. I'm in a tricky spot—help me out here. How about one more assignment? One for the road. You with me?"

"You've bought five more seconds."

"Find Vera. Kill her. And burn everything she has on her. Then call us. Once we have the disk, you're free, both of you. Copy that?"

"Bullshit. Fuck you."

Akira switched over to Kyle. "We're fucked. They are coming for us. Watch your six. It's Vera."

"It's okay. I'll deal with it. I need you to pull it together, though."

"Are you still in the house? You've got to get out! They're going to sweep it."

"I'm leaving right now. We'll finish this. We'll wrap this bitch up like Van Halen's guitar."

PASADENA, CALIFORNIA

Kyle opened a large hidden panel at the back of the closet and took out two pistols, a shotgun, ammo, and two detonation devices. Then he grabbed a few stacks of currency, four passports and a black velvet pouch from the wall safe. The whole lot went into a sports bag. Four minutes later, he peeled the Mercedes E500 out into the street, eyes on the rearview mirror.

Two blocks from the residence, he spotted a blue Ford Taurus pulling away from the curb. He pulled a Colt M4A1 assault rifle from the sports bag, lowered the passenger window and slowed down, baiting the car to come closer.

As it approached, he made a sudden stop, reversed, and hurtled backward, stopping along-side the Ford. The driver had little time to react. Kyle raised the Colt and sprayed his face and the interior of the Ford. A red-haired woman in the passenger seat fired off four shots but missed. Kyle riddled her with bullets, ejected the spent clip, and slapped in a fresh one.

As he pulled away, leaving the two assassins slumped dead in their seats, his phone rang.

"You okay?" Akira asked.

Kyle let the silence hang for a moment.

"Kyle?"

"Yeah, I'm good. Just sent two to the morgue. Got out just in time."

"What the fuck? That's Vera's team, right?"

"I don't think so. I think it's Wilshire. Looked like a clearance to me."

"You sure?"

"Baby, they wanted us dead as soon as they gave you this fucking gig."

"Fuck."

"Yeah. Some chick tried to kill me. Looked like someone I've seen before. You remember that analyst sitting in the corner at the end of the hall, like three years ago? Looked like her."

Fuck. He'd just dropped a stick of dynamite on a campfire. He could see Akira now—her fore-head crumpling, her eyelids forming two lines under her dark, arched eyebrows. It scared him, but it was so damn hot too.

"Was she pretty?"

Jesus. Only Akira could feel jealous in a life-and-death situation.

"Who?"

"The redhead—Amber?"

"I had a feeling you'd remember her."

"Well," Akira said, "that bitch was hitting on you the whole fucking time, and we were in LA for just a week."

Kyle rolled his eyes.

"I was going to kill the bitch, remember?"

"Yeah, I do."

"You talked me out of it. You remember that?" Akira snapped.

"Yeah, I do. I didn't think it would be conducive to our relationship with Wilshire if you killed one of their employees."

"Forget it. Fuck that bitch. You sure she's dead?"

"Positive."

"Shit, why I didn't see it? Wilshire I mean."

"Probably coz you've been busy, you know, surviving? Where are you?"

"I had to park. I'm on PCH a few miles away from Hueneme Bay. At the vista point just before the rock."

"Okay, so, what did you do, baby?" Kyle asked.

"Well, a couple of things. First, I've been

throwing up all week, and I missed my period."

"What? Are we … pregnant?"

"No, Kyle, *I'm* pregnant. It was supposed to be a surprise."

"I am. I'm also super fucking happy."

"But you're also mad at me, right?"

"Yeah, I'm so mad at you I could kiss you right now. Holy fuck, this is awesome. Wait, I'm going to be a dad?"

Kyle merged on to the 134 West Freeway.

"Well, yes, but there's the other thing."

"Do you need to tell me? I'm happy with the first thing."

"It's the reason everyone's trying to kill us. I quit."

"Okay, but this is good, right? I mean, you could have—"

"There's something else …"

She told him about an encrypted disk she was supposed to turn over to Vera, and how she'd swapped it with a Vivaldi CD.

"That dumb ass didn't even check it," Akira said.

"That's pretty funny."

"Whatever, Daddy, I'll meet you at home."

"Nothing can't stop me, babe," Kyle said. "I'd kill everyone in the world if I had to, just to get to you—just to get to you both."

"I love you to death," she said, and disconnected.

———————

Forty-minutes later Kyle made a left on Sunset Boulevard and drove for about a mile before making a right on Pacific Coast Highway.

Two SUVs appeared behind him. One, a black Suburban, blew past him and swerved, pulling up in front. An Escalade raced up behind him, slammed its oversized brush guard into the rear of the Mercedes. Kyle's neck snapped back. The rear brake lights shattered, sending red plastic fragments flying up as the trunk buckled.

"Fuck you," Kyle screamed, and tried to wiggle the E500 around the Suburban, but it swerved and blocked him every time.

Its tinted rear window lowered, revealing a large man, mercenary type, dressed in black tactical gear, holding an M-16. He sprayed the Mercedes, cracking the glass of the bulletproof windshield, then reloaded. Kyle crushed the gas pedal and steered right. Still in full control as the wheels skimmed the asphalt. The man pointed the M-16 at Kyle. The Suburban slowed down as the Mercedes veered left, then right, performing a vicious pit maneuver. It hit the Suburban's rear panel, sending it fishtailing out of control. The shooter lost his balance as he fired, showering parked cars, street signs, and a few lamp posts.

The Suburban crossed in front of Kyle as the Escalade crashed again into his rear, ramming him toward the Suburban. Kyle hit the brakes and swerved again, barely avoiding the SUV but heading for a fire hydrant. The Escalade turned, hit a curb, then ran over a sidewalk and crashed into a bus stop, leveling it.

The Mercedes snapped the fire hydrant out of the water main like a toothpick, then toppled end over end and cartwheeled among a cloud of debris. It landed upside down as water spewed from the pipe, obscuring the Mercedes.

The Suburban careened into a phone booth and hurtled toward a gas station. The shooter was thrown out the back window like a rag doll onto a concrete column as the car collided with a fuel pump. The driver was thrown from the vehicle into a parked dump truck.

The Suburban's gas tank ignited. Then the pump caught fire. Like dominos, one pump after another exploded. The vehicle was launched a hundred feet into the air. The ground rumbled, and the corner of the gas station collapsed into a flaming sinkhole.

Across the street, pedestrians ran for cover behind parked cars. Kyle crawled from the wreckage of his Mercedes, holding the sports bag and a Beretta. Two men emerged from the Escalade, both wearing khaki pants and black shirts. One stared toward the Mercedes, obscured by the gushing water main, and scanned the perimeter with a Glock outfitted with a laser sight.

The other, a large man wielding an AR-15 sprayed the area behind the fire hydrant.

Kyle fired two perfect headshots, and the man holding the Glock collapsed. Then, like a ghost, he inched forward until the barrel of the Beretta was a few inches away from the back of the large man's head. Kyle depressed the trigger without blinking. The spray from the hydrant turned red as the man fell dead on his knees.

A biker on a yellow Ducati SS arrived at the intersection and stopped next to Kyle.

"Hey, bro, you okay?" the biker said as he lifted his visor.

Kyle raised the Beretta and pointed it at his face. "The helmet and the bike."

The biker complied, and Kyle slung the sports bag over his shoulder and sped away.

MALIBU, CALIFORNIA

Paco, a cholo in his late twenties sporting a tattoo of a gun and the number 13—a reference to the Mexican cartel he ran for—rubbed the sweat off his neck and hit the speed dial.

"I got news from one of my boys," he said into his cell. "That man you looking for—Kyle right? He started a war a few miles back. Gas station on Sunset just blew up. Then he popped a tag. My boy tells me he's heading my way on PCH."

"Keep an eye on that shit," Big Mac said. "Don't lose him, brah."

"You got it, boss."

Paco walked out of 7-Eleven holding a six-pack of Modelo, put the cell phone back in his Dickies and tossed the six-pack on the floorboard of a purple 1964 Chevy Impala low rider.

A minute later, the Ducati raced past him. Paco floored the Impala. No way could he catch up with the bike—it was doing over a hundred. Instead he put his foot down and followed as best he could. A few miles later, he passed the rider filling up at a gas station. Paco drove by and parked by a side street.

A few minutes later, the rider drove past him again. This time, the Ducati was keeping to the speed limit, meaning no one would call the cops on a speeder ... and Paco could follow at a safe distance.

CHAPTER 24

Spanish Eyes

Vera sat at a booth in the corner of the busy lounge and sipped from a glass of lime water. With her bandaged hand, she sliced into a T-Bone steak and looked over at a stage area near the stone fireplace.

A couple in their sixties, dressed in matching sequined ensembles, were about to perform for the patrons. The man sporting his trademark blond pompadour, put a microphone on a stand and leaned into it. The mic squealed.

"Sorry about that, folks. I'm Jesse and this is my one and only Marlene. We are so glad you could join us on this special Sunday afternoon."

He fumbled his way behind the drum set. Marlene smiled and took a seat behind her mic and an electric organ.

"Anything you want to hear?" Marlene asked.

"Please let our lovely waitress know, and we'll take care of you," Jesse added with a wink.

The server made her rounds, collecting dollar bills, then stopped next to Vera. "Still working on that?" she said, and nodded at the steak.

"Yes, leave it. Until that bone is white as a Bernini, I won't let go of it," Vera said, and smiled.

"Got it. Anything else, hon?"

Vera handed her a hundred-dollar bill. "Give this to Jesse."

"Off course."

"And more of the same water. I love that lime."

"Gotcha."

Vera picked up her cell and dialed.

Rigo answered. "Mom? What the hell." His voice trembled.

"You okay, hijo?"

"Yeah, it's all good. They put me in the kitchen."

"Got a guard there?"

"Yup."

"They won't hurt you, I got this. Hang on tight, son."

She killed the line.

Jesse and Marlene performed Michael Jackson's *Beat It*. Vera hated pop music, but this couple were legendary for their renditions and had even had a cameo in a feature film just two years

earlier. The movie had been a hit, and their per-
formance had shot them into pop-culture star-
dom.

You couldn't judge Jesse and Marlene's musi-
cal talents by their covers, but there would always
be a few confused patrons who didn't understand
why people loved them so much.

Vera had to find Akira—her son's life depend-
ed on it. And until she was given the woman's
location, she was on idle. Which was stressful.
And when stressed, Vera's only cure was a dose
of Humperdinck. This was the closest she could
get to it.

Jesse and Marlene marched through the song
like a stoner eating a bag of Fritos, and everyone
in the lounge applauded.

Vera crushed her lips together, wrinkled her
nose, and closed her eyes, then applauded using
the back of her hands, appreciating at least the
connection and love they had for one another.

It put a big smile on her face, albeit a short-
lived one.

A wannabe punk rocker sat on the other side of
the lounge. The guy was thirty-something, with
dirty long black hair, dark glasses, a thrift-store
faux leather jacket, mesh top, and torn jeans. He
was flanked by two girls who looked like underage runways. They gawked at him like he was the
smartest human being on the face of the planet.

He looked at the singing duo with disgust and whispered to the girls, who giggled.

Vera was enraged. Nothing worse than a heckler who didn't have the balls to heckle.

Jesse stood up, sipped water from a glass perched on a bar table next to his drum set and went up to the mic. The crowd cheered him on.

"Thank you, thank you, you're so kind. We're Jesse and Marlene. This next song's a request from a generous member of the audience."

Marlene caressed the keyboard as Jesse sang "Spanish Eyes."

Vera smirked. The song reminded her of more than just her idol, Humperdinck. As she looked over at the young punk, she recalled another singer, a blue-eyed punk rocker named Woolsey, a young man she'd met long ago in Vegas, but very much like the one sitting across from her.

And just like the young punk, Woolsey had been in Vera's path.

1977

LAS VEGAS, NEVADA

Before Vera had retired from killing and gone on to clean stages for Wilshire, she'd redefined the word "gruesome." Las Vegas in the mid-seventies had been her second busiest killing ground in North America—the first being Juarez, Mexico—although occasionally she'd flown out of her comfort zone to South America, Caracas specifically. There she'd settled for targets in the banking industry. However, she'd found Venezuela's politics volatile and law enforcement too unpredictable, so she'd stopped taking jobs there.

Vegas was different, not just for the obvious contrast between the Mexican cartel and the Italian American mafia's vindictive styles, but also because killing in Sin City, wherever possible, was done on the down-low. Most of the cleaners Vera had known in Vegas back in 1975 had worked construction sites and knew that the best way to hide a body was to put it thirty feet underground, mixed in concrete and rebars.

In Vegas, a mark would just vanish, whereas in Mexico she'd been notorious for making a splash. That way, the cartel who'd hired her could spread fear among their enemies.

The cleaners were called decorators. They'd use the body parts Vera had so meticulously butchered to decorate streetlights and hang under bridges. They'd prop up heads and limbs on the roofs of city buses—brazen, macabre shows of brute force and power.

Vegas had been at a crossroads. There was chatter about the state authorities working with the government to revoke some of the casino's licenses. They preferred licensing corporations without ties to the Mob, and Vera had known that leaving Vegas would become a reality soon enough.

She'd decided there and then to give Vegas a going-away present, and became obsessed with that idea. No more hiding bodies. She wanted to make a big splash on her way out, but it couldn't look like a hit.

She'd met her mark at an afterparty given by her friend, Marcus Greene, an executive at the Stardust. Woolsey wore dark glasses, skinny black jeans and a gold lion's head buckle on his studded black leather belt. He'd immediately eyed Vera, who'd brought five-year-old Rigo.

The young punk had looked at her son in a devious way, then squatted so he was down at Rigo's eye level and caressed his face just a little longer than felt right. A pedophile punk rocker? Was that even a thing?

Vera had chatted with Marcus, her gaze darting back and forth from him to Rigo and Woolsey, who was now showing his belt buckle to Rigo. Vera had struggled to keep her composure, still engaging Marcus but keeping Woolsey in her peripheral vision as he placed her child's hand playfully on the lion head.

As Rigo touched the buckle, his hand now in

close proximity with the punk's crotch, Woolsey became aroused.

Fucking jackpot.

This was the man who'd be her going-away present to Vegas.

Over the next twenty-four hours, Vera learned that Woolsey had moved from LA, where he'd already inflicted damage on a few dozen boys. His sudden move to Vegas had been prompted by allegations of child molestation.

Vera had a container parked on a remote property outside Las Vegas, right off Route 95—a five-acre lot with a small building she used to store weapons. Inside she'd set up an autopsy table complete with instruments and other tools of the trade.

Three weeks passed, and Vera learned Woolsey's routine. She gained access to his apartment at the Hilton, injected him with M99 in his sleep, then transported him to her remote building.

There, she chopped off his right pinky finger, the one least used when playing the guitar, then cauterized the blood vessels and grafted skin over the injury site. Then she transported him back, undetected, to his apartment.

Woolsey was a quick healer. Two weeks passed. He was feeling himself again, he told friends, after the shocking discovery of his missing finger. But no one believed his story; he was a drunk and an addict after all.

A week went by, and Woolsey was back on Vera's autopsy table. Chop. The ring finger went.

Recovery was harder this time, but he got through it. She gave him two weeks' grace then returned. Once a week, she'd pick him up, chop off another finger, and drop him home.

This continued until there were no fingers left.

Woolsey recovered one last time and went into hiding.

As for Vera, no, she would not hang him from a bridge or display his body in some other way as to shock law enforcement. Rather, this goodbye would be on the down-low. Sort of.

She would leave that to Woolsey himself. He would be the one to make a splash of his own death—Vera's perfect postcard to Vegas.

Over the next two months, Vera bombarded him with mock letters from his molested children. These were supplemented with phone calls, emails, threats and blackmail. The relentless psychological attack made Woolsey's life unbearable—he just couldn't switch it off.

And then Vera sent him a gift.

All his fingers in a little box.

The police found them lined up next to a mound of cocaine on the coffee table. It was the last thing he'd done before leaping off the Hilton's roof.

Some witnesses were quoted as saying that Woolsey's body had exploded on impact, forming a bloody snow angel on the marble sidewalk.

It made for one of the most infamous photographs on the front page of every single newspaper in Nevada that year.

———————

Jesse and Marlene packed up their instruments and left. The punk rocker went to the bathroom, leaving his giggling girls no doubt wondering what magical time awaited them in Hollywood.

Vera stared at the girls, smirked, then picked up the steak knife and got up.

CHAPTER 25

Hot Dog

One of the twins was bent over on the sofa, her skirt pushed up to her waist. Big Mac knelt behind her and ran his hands heavily from her ass to her breasts. She moaned, and he grabbed her hips and thrust hard into her. He groaned, she moaned again, louder this time, then she sank her face into a pillow.

"I'm gonna come!" she screamed.

His cell phone vibrated in an empty pizza box on the table.

"Shit, hang on."

Big Mac pulled out of her and shoved her to the side.

"What the fuck!" she said. "What are you doing, Papi?"

"I've got to take this," he said, and pulled his pants up.

He flipped open the phone. There was a text from Paco waiting. He squinted, straining to read the message. The twin continued to pleasure herself while Big Mac walked over to his desk and put on his reading glasses.

1958 Seagull Road, Mussel Shoals, Ventura. Yellow Bike.

Holy shit. Big Mac scrolled through his contacts and stopped at Vera's number.

THE PENINSULA
BEVERLY HILLS, CALIFORNIA

Vera always stayed at the Peninsula when she was in Los Angeles. Loved the classy atmosphere, the service was of the highest standard, and the location was central—she could be anywhere in about thirty minutes. There was a spa too. She could eat the best food in LA. And downstairs was her favorite hairstylist, Danilo.

Except this time, her stay was a clusterfuck. She'd slept only briefly in the past forty-eight hours, and the job was getting messier and more tedious with every day.

She was watching a repeat of the previous

day's *The Tonight Show* when her cell phone vibrated. A text from Mac. With Akira's location—an artsy-fartsy community for millionaires past Oxnard.

She picked up a note from her nightstand written to herself earlier in the day. *Rita Gonzalez, 1050 Grissom Way, Oxnard.*

Vera had leased her white Escalade and paid the valet to keep it in front of the Peninsula's driveway, where they kept a handful of other VIP cars. He gave her the key, and she handed him a one-hundred-dollar bill.

Traffic was light. She drove down Santa Monica Boulevard and connected with the 405, then went onto the Ventura Freeway. Her mobile rang.

"Mac. Tell your boy to stay put until I arrive. I'll be in a white Escalade. Hard to miss."

"I don't want no boy of mine ending up as a loose end on my conscience."

"Just tell him not to look at me," Vera said. "If I see him, it means he saw me, and I'll kill him."

———

Big Mac's phone rang. *For fuck's sake*. He looked wistfully at the twin on the sofa, then answered.

"He's here," Paco said. "And she's here too, bro."

"Be cool. Do nothing. Wait for the cleaner.

And make sure you get outta there as soon as you see Vera's vehicle—a white Escalade. Don't cross her. If she sees you, I'll end up missing you, bro. You feel me?"

"Gotcha. Can I go get some food? I crave a sandwich."

"No, Paco, you can't go get some food."

"But I'm starving, bro. There's a Wiener-schnitzel down the street. I'll be like a minute."

"That's not a sandwich, it's a hot dog."

"What? No, it's bread, with meat in it. It's a sandwich with a sausage inside. It's a hot dog sandwich."

"So, if you fold a slice of pizza, you got bread on the outside and pepperoni on the inside, right? No, pizza is pizza, not a fucking sandwich. Are you the kind that chops spaghetti up too?" Big Mac asked, rolling his eyes.

"Fuck, yeah, I chop it so small I can eat it with a spoon. I heard that's how the pope does it."

"The pope is a decrepit fuck. I don't use him as a measuring stick for how to feed myself."

"May God forgive you for what you just said, bro. That's the pope you're talking about."

"Oh, fuck me. Really?"

"Whatever, I'm starving bro."

"Okay, well, you know how you're not feel-ing hungry?" Big Mac said. "If you're dead, that's how."

"What? I mean—"

"If you fuck this up because you need food, you're going to be dead before you digest that shit. Feel me, amigo?"

"Yeah, okay, okay. Pump the brakes, bro. Was just asking. You know what I'm saying? We just talking here."

"I don't care what the fuck you're saying, you dumb fuck. If you're not there and something happens, I'm certain of only one thing. You be dead. You getting' this through your taco-light motherfuckin' skull?"

"You don't have to insult my heritage, bro. I'm staying here. No food for me today."

"Better hungry than muerto, right?" Big Mac said.

He killed the line and turned to the twin. "Hey baby, I'm starving. Want some hot dogs?"

CHAPTER 26

Lincoln

The pimple-riddled valet in the elevator looked terrified as he and Sir Charles made their descent. Sir Charles didn't blame him. His face was ruined, and sporting a bloody paper tissue packed into his eye socket wasn't exactly haute couture.

"S-sir, this is t-the s-service elevator. You—"

Sir Charles growled. The valet began to tremble and his voice became a high-pitched squeal that sounded something like a question.

Sir Charles gripped the bloody wolf's head on the top of his cane. It clicked and a steel blade emerged.

The valet yelped as Sir Charles whipped the cane forward, severing his carotid artery and jugular, and spraying the elevator walls with blood.

The valet crumpled onto the floor. Sir Charles searched the valet's pockets and found a master key. The elevator stopped and the doors opened.

He was in an underground corridor beneath the hotel. A few minutes later, he stumbled upon a door with a sign that read *Janitor Room*. He tried the master key. It opened. Sir Charles switched on the light and closed the door behind him. The room smelled like acetone and sweat.

To one side stood a cot, a shelf unit with tools, a wall cabinet, paint cans, rolls of old carpet, and a large trash bin. None of this shit was of any use if he was going to get to the Lincoln without blood pouring out of his face.

Sir Charles searched the cabinet and found a first-aid kit. On the shelf was a piece of leather and a pair of scissors. He trimmed the hide into an oval, then attached the patch over his eye with a carpenter's stapler, puncturing skin and bone. It held fast and he'd barely felt a thing. Fuck, these drugs were good.

Sir Charles's cell phone vibrated. It was an unknown number.

"Who the fuck are you?" he growled.

"We're friends of Helger's. The girl who has your disk—we know where she is. We'll text you the address. Watch your back. An armed man is in that hotel looking for you."

The line went dead. A few seconds passed, and

a text popped up on the phone screen.

1958 Seagull Lane, Mussel Shoals, Ventura. 1hr drive.

Sir Charles's eyes widened. He needed that disk. With it, he'd be on the space shuttle, fighting Moby Dick with a golden harpoon. Which meant nobody was going to stop him getting to the Lincoln.

Then he heard someone coming down the metallic staircase, one foot after the other. More footsteps. Closer now. Just outside the door. There was a burst of gunfire. Then the door opened.

A man stepped in, wielding an H&K MP5 submachine gun that could fire up to 1,200 rounds per minute.

Sir Charles speared him with his cane blade, cutting up from under his chin, through his mouth, and into his brain, killing him instantly.

He made his way to the parking lot. The sun was sinking behind the horizon, giving the night sky a slight orange glow.

And there she was—the Lincoln.

He fumbled with the keys. Having only one eye was a bitch. And floating in deep space surrounded by jellyfish didn't help. He grasped at something in the air, but his hand came away empty. Finally, he managed to slip behind the wheel. It turned into an octopus, its tentacles reaching for his face. Sir Charles chuckled, hit the gas and swerved into the Century Boulevard traffic.

"This is so embarrassing, Helger. I'm a man of my word!" he said, and ran a red light.

Car horns honked and tires screeched. A large pickup truck barely missed him and swerved badly, causing some of its cargo to fly off the bed and into the street.

After a few blocks, Sir Charles arrived at another red light. This time he stopped. The pickup driver stopped beside him. He was late twenties, African American, built like a refrigerator, and wearing a hoodie with a Gold's Gym logo on it. And he was furious.

He banged on the Lincoln's driver-side window and pulled on the door. "Get out, you piece of shit."

Sir Charles stared at him. The man's muscles flexed, and tendons bulged from his neck.

"Get out of the fucking car!" the man screamed, hammering his fist against the glass. "I'll teach you a lesson, motherfucker!"

Sir Charles lowered the window. The man's hand shot in and grabbed the lock, then wrenched the door open. He reached for Sir Charles's throat.

And stopped.

Sir Charles raised the MP5 and fired two dozen rounds into the man's neck and mouth. Blood sprayed everywhere, and the man dropped to the ground, half his face gone.

Sir Charles placed the submachine gun on the passenger seat and crushed the gas pedal, propelling the Lincoln through the red light. The door slammed shut and the tires squealed. He drove off, clipping a pedestrian, swerved into the left lane, crossed oncoming traffic as he sped onto a freeway ramp, and merged with the 405 freeway north.

He pushed the accelerator—eighty-five, ninety, a hundred miles per hour.

Blood pooled at the bottom of his eye patch as the road in front became a collage of melting tar and ships chasing the whale of all whales, Moby Dick. He rode the Lincoln hard, surfing on thick black waves, sailing north to Mussel Shoals.

CHAPTER 27

Gaviota

Gaviota was the nickname Akira and Kyle had given their three-thousand-square-foot sanctuary. The modernistic beach house was in Mussel Shoals, Ventura, about an hour north of LA. Much of the rear had been constructed from large glass panes, providing stunning ocean views.

Rita came twice a month to clean, sort any mail, and ensure the home didn't look vacant.

Akira headed for the kitchen and tossed her black clutch on the counter. Opened the fridge, twisted the cap off a bottle of water and took a long pull.

There were fresh apples in a fruit basket. She grabbed one and took a big bite from it, then ripped open a bag of Lays and stuffed her face with a handful of chips.

Yeah, she was supposed to be eating for two, but no one could call this eating, and she wasn't consuming enough even for one. She ducked into the living room, crumpled into a lounger, and fell asleep.

———————

Kyle arrived around four. Akira bolted into his arms. Then she pulled away and looked down at the bags by his feet.

"Are we going to war?"

"Just a precaution. I love you, baby. I'm just glad you're okay."

"I love you too, but I fucked us royally."

"And yet here we are."

They headed for the kitchen. Akira took the CD case out of her clutch and slid it over the counter.

Kyle picked it up. "Wagner? What's this?"

"It's encrypted. That's what I took."

"All right. We'll figure it out."

"Yeah, but are we safe here?"

"There's no way anyone knows where we are. And we weren't followed."

"Then why all the artillery?"

Kyle shrugged. "Just in case we *were* followed."

"I think something's wrong," Akira said. "You

know Wilshire. They'll never stop looking. I'm not sure I can bring a child into that."

"That baby is the best part of both of us. We'll work it out. You take a shower and get some rest while I work on that disk."

She left him alone and he went into the study. He'd installed the latest software and two top-of-the-range CRT monitors, one connected to a Mac G3, the other to an IBM Aptiva.

Kyle sat down and popped the CD into the disk tray.

———

Akira bolted out of bed, hyperventilating, and sat on the floor, breathing in and out, trying to calm herself down. Once the sweating had subsided, she went to the bathroom and vomited into the sink.

She changed into a workout outfit, headed downstairs and peeked into the study. Kyle was fixated on one of the monitors. They exchanged gentle pleasantries, and then Kyle leant back in his chair.

"I'm having a hard time with this. You're sure you grabbed the right one? I can't find shit in it."

"Want to come for a walk? It'll refresh you."

"No, babe, I want to give it another shot." He placed his hand on her belly. "How's that baby coming along?"

"You idiot," she said, and ruffled his hair. "It's the same as a few hours ago."

Akira left and Kyle set the encryption program to run again. He glanced outside just in time to see Akira being swallowed by the thick marine layer.

The screen displayed what the program had harvested—metadata, track titles and duration, sound levels, inputs, outputs, file types. There was a beep and the progress bar moved across the screen to Analysis Complete. Kyle punched a few more keys, then moved the cursor to Scan Again.

A message came up: *Error 218M. Audio file 1 Damaged.* The computer beeped. Kyle ejected the disk, examined it for a few seconds, then tossed it on the desk. It slid under the printer next to the hard drive.

Fuck.

Kyle debated retrieving it, but he was exhausted. It could wait.

CHAPTER 28

The Cleaner

Paco jolted awake and fumbled with the Nokia, its Grand Valse assaulting his ears like a grenade. "What's up?" he said, and rubbed his eyes.

"I knew you'd fall asleep, you dumb fuck. She's there. You've got to bolt, bro," Big Mac said.

Paco dropped the phone and fired up the Chevy just as the white Escalade appeared in the rearview mirror a few hundred yards behind him.

———

Vera cruised the Escalade past the exclusive beach homes and pulled up in front of the modernistic house. A magnetic decal on the side of the SUV read: *Rita's Cleaning—We are the Best!*

She climbed out of the vehicle, wearing Rita's branded uniform, opened the liftgate, and fumbled with a cardboard box with six half-gallon jugs of Simple Green liquid cleaner.

There was a CCTV camera atop one of the columns by the entry gate. A plate above an intercom read *The Johnsons*. She rang and looked straight up into the camera, adjusting her cap so her face would be obscured.

———————

Kyle stepped out of the shower, slung a towel around his waist, and headed for the foyer. He checked the monitor next to the intercom panel and pressed the TALK button.

A woman wearing a Rita's Cleaning cap stood by the gate, but she wasn't Rita.

"You have the wrong house," Kyle said.

The cleaner cracked a big smile, her cap still covering most of her face.

"It's Maria. I'm here for Rita. Don't mean to be intrusive, but I don't know how long
I can hold this box."

"Thank you but Rita does our house. I'm busy. Would you mind?"

"I do the Wilsons' house, Mr. Johnson. Your neighbours down the street? And I saw Rita
yesterday, and she asked me to drop off some

Simple Green for her. I guess she ran out. She swears by it. I like 409, but, you know, Rita gets what she wants. She's the boss."

Kyle opened the drawer of the console table by the entryway and took out a .357 Taurus.

He checked the chamber. Loaded. Pulled the hammer back and placed the revolver behind a fruit bowl. Then he looked back at the monitor; the cleaner turned to her left and waved to someone beyond the camera view.

"I'll be right over, Mrs. Wilson!" she yelled. "No, no worry, I don't need help." Then she turned to the monitor again. "Sorry, sir, I need to go work. You know, the early bird gets the worm. She's a sweet person, Mrs. Wilson, but such an early riser. I'll leave these by the front door if that makes you feel more comfortable, but I don't want to leave them outside the gate."

She started to yell over at the neighbour again.

Something about that smile that felt familiar, but sure, why not drop off that shit?

"Come in. I'll leave the front door unlocked." Kyle buzzed the gate open.

Clothes. He needed to get dressed. Now.

He grabbed the gun, ran to the bathroom, and yanked on his sweatpants. That smile, that face under the cap. Fuck. *Vera*.

He peeked back into the hallway. Thirty feet away, the door opened.

Think, Kyle, think. Couldn't shoot—didn't know for sure who else was outside. And Akira was on the beach, meaning he couldn't protect her.

"Hello?" Vera called.

She'd know she was dealing with a trained special op. But he'd been out of the game for a while. Maybe she was hoping he was little rusty. And perhaps he could turn that to his advantage.

"Okay, okay," he said. "Just come on in. You can leave them by the door."

Vera entered, her head down, carrying a box awkwardly with both arms. Then she bumped into the console table, knocking the fruit bowl over and spilling the contents all over the floor.

This was bullshit. What the fuck was she up too?

"Oh, my goodness. So sorry about that! I'm such an idiot!"

"It's okay, just leave it there," Kyle's voice cracked. "I'll take care of it." His cell phone rang. *Fuck.* He took two steps back to grab it. The screen was flashing *HER*.

By the time he'd turned back toward the foyer, the cheery smile had gone. The hair on his arms stood up. Vera sneered and offered him a scornful smile.

"Hey, big boy, remember me?"

————————

1989
VILLAVICENCIO, COLOMBIA

It was a typical tropical summer—humid as hell—
and Kyle had landed at Vanguardia Airport, a five-
hour drive from San José Del Guaviare, a small
town on the fringe of the Amazon basin. The CIA
had been surveilling cultivation of new coca fields
that had been springing up fast in the region.

Kyle wasn't alone. There were three other
agents and one civilian—a woman, Vera Maria
Delacruz, who was with them in an unofficial ca-
pacity.

The mark was liberal presidential front run-
ner Raúl César Vargas, a cartel-fighting general
protected by eighteen armed bodyguards. Vera
had taken over the operation after the team had
secured Vargas's campaign building.

Her task was to convince the general not to
give his inspiring speech, but to replace it with
one prepared by the CIA that undermined his effort to stop the Colombian drug cartel and win
the support of the people.

Ordinarily, Kyle didn't see left or right when
it came to political parties; he had a job to do for
his country, and he would do it no matter what.
But what came next was something he'd nev-

er forget. She was the kind of psychopath he'd thought only existed in horror films. She started with his wife, her tool a butcher knife sharpened to within an inch of its life. And made Vargas and his children watch.

Outside Vargas's headquarters, a crowd of ten thousand chanted his name, which inspired the general to reject the speech prepared by the CIA. At that point, the team was instructed to kill Vargas before he could make it to the podium. Vera took everyone by surprise, and butchered him and his whole family.

She sliced through each one like it was a chunk of beef hanging in a butcher shop. And throughout, there was madness in her eyes.

After the fact, the team were so upset that they requested a private jet just for Vera. That way, they wouldn't have to share a flight with a monster.

———————

So, yes, Kyle remembered her. She was heavier, with shorter, darker hair, but the essence of her was still there—the madness still in her eyes. The skin on the back of his neck tingled. This motherfucker was the only person with the power to give him the creeps.

Kyle nodded and clenched his jaw.

Then green fluid exploded from the box as two shots rang out. They caught Kyle in his side. He dropped the cell phone as two more shots hit his thigh and one blew off his index finger. Blood sprayed everywhere.

He sank to the ground, Taurus aimed ahead, and landed two slugs square in her chest. She was thrown backward against the door and dropped the box.

Kyle tried to get up, but slid and fell again, hitting his head on the wall behind him.

Vera lay unmoving on the floor, still gripping her gun.

Kyle looked over at his cell phone a few feet away from him, it had stopped ringing. The battery had detached. He sat in a pool of his own blood, his lungs calling for breath. Blood gushed from his leg.

But he was alive. For now at least.

The smell of black powder smoke filled the hallway, and green liquid from the cleaning product had spilled all over the marble floor.

Vera coughed, stood up, and steadied herself against the door frame. She clutched her chest and ripped her uniform open, exposing a bullet-proof vest, the bullets from the Taurus embedded in it.

"Whew! You've got me, motherfucker! Damn! This fucking hurts!" Vera shot him a glare. "Lost your touch?"

"Fuck you, I shot you right in the chest, you bitch."

Kyle eyed his Taurus, but it was out of reach.

"Yeah, you got me, and actually, you're the first person ever to shoot me. Motherfucker." She walked over to him and assessed his wounds. "Look at you, I ruptured your femoral artery. Didn't mean to, just worked out that way. A lucky shot, I guess."

"Fuck you, Vera."

"You can't stop the bleeding. You'll die slowly, but at least it won't be painful. Unless ..." She looked at her watch. "Probably about an hour and a half tops. Yeah, you'll be dead soon enough. And I'll make sure it's painful." She took a deep breath.

Kyle laughed, spitting up blood. "I shot you square in the chest."

Vera pointed a Ruger at him and stepped closer. "Where's your messy bitch? They told me she was here. Tell me where the disk is and I promise I'll make it quick."

"Those are two questions I won't answer," he hissed.

Vera chuckled and inched a little further toward him.

That's it, bitch. Nice and close.

Kyle pulled a small knife from the band of his

sweatpants and stabbed her calf. Vera screamed and collapsed onto the floor. The Ruger slid away from her.

"Puta madre!"

Kyle swung the knife again, but she'd crawled just out of his reach.

"Fuck you, bitch."

Kyle stood up and lunged at her. Vera's lips formed a tight line, and she delivered a sidekick to his wounded thigh. Kyle fell backward, heard a crack as the back of his head connected with the marble floor, then everything began to go black.

———

Vera got back to her feet. "Dios mio, motherfucker, maybe I'm the one losing the edge."

She checked her leg. She could walk at least. She picked up the Ruger and limped up the stairs. No Akira. She checked the ground floor. No sign of her there either. She found a door that led to the garage. A silver Porsche and a black Mercedes-Benz were parked in tandem. Where was Akira? Had she taken a taxi to Camarillo? She could chart a private plane from there and vanish for good.

Vera's phone rang. It was Big Mac. She rolled her eyes.

"Why are you calling? I'm busy," she hissed.

"My guys are telling me they were a body short at the suite."

"Oh, for fuck's sake, Mac, that's not possible. You've got to contain that bullshit. I'm too busy to listen to this. Tell those fucking clowns to be done with it."

"They are done, but—"

Vera killed the line.

CHAPTER 29

Katana

Akira had walked for almost an hour to Rincon Point before she thought of calling Kyle. His cell went straight to voice mail. Jesus, maybe for once he could take his head out of his own ass and answer the damn thing.

She stood on top of a rock overlooking the ocean. Ion-rich air filled her lungs with every breath. She felt serene and thought of the child who'd be born into such a violent world. The waves crashed on the rocks below.

Akira doubled over and vomited.

Morning sickness. Like an alarm clock in her stomach. She put her hand on her tummy, smiled, then glanced over her shoulder back at the road.

A car came up the freeway ramp—a purple low

rider, hard not to notice. A Chevy Impala with sparkly gold pinstriping was merging onto Pacific Coast Highway. The driver was a cholo in his late twenties. He drove the car up the ramp while eating a hot dog. And even though he was about forty feet away, the neck tattoo and his face were visible for just a second.

Akira's eidetic memory rarely failed her. It was like scrolling through microfiche— images, words, faces. And bingo!

Francisco Morales. His friends called him Paco. He worked for Big Mac, a drug dealer in South Central.

Fuck, they were here.

Her hand shook as she speed-dialed Kyle again, and still got no answer. Shit.

She had three miles to cover, and it would take at least twenty-five minutes.

Akira began to run.

———————

No Akira. And no CD. Vera had gone through the entire house and come up with sweet fuck all. She returned to the hallway and stood over Kyle.

"I'm impressed. You're still awake, though you look a little dizzy, motherfucker."

"F-fuck you."

"Hey, amigo, you understand my situation

here? I could have been done with this job back at the hotel, but I'm here, wasting my precious time killing you and looking for shit I can't find."

"Fuck you."

Vera opened her purse and pulled out a CD. Kyle looked puzzled for a moment.

"I know what you're thinking, but nope, this is not the disk I'm looking for. Sometimes it can take a while before I get what I want, so I bring music to cheer me up. Vera spun the case around, revealing the label: *Engelbert Humperdinck's Greatest Hits.*

"Saved by the Dinck, amigo! I hope you have an excellent stereo system in this crib. Are you two audiophiles? You've got three minutes and twenty-nine seconds—the length of this song—while I relax. Then you're going to tell me what I need to know," Vera said, still gripping the Ruger.

She stepped into the living room. The furniture was modern. A white sectional faced a large glass window overlooking the ocean. And next to a large media console was the entertainment system.

One wall was decorated with masks, swords, and hilt weapons displayed like they would be in a modern-art museum—white shelves, teak and walnut detail, glass cases. The works.

To the side, two free-standing pedestals held two sixteenth-century samurai suits of armor. Accent spotlights illuminated the collection beautifully. Above a walnut credenza was a glass enclosure containing two ancient samurai swords—a nodachi and a katana—and below them, an exquisite tanto dagger. The case was shallow, about four feet wide and six feet tall. The swords hung in an X, the nodachi pointing downward, the katana up. Vera was beside herself.

"Is this what I think it is? Boy, you two are raking it in if you can afford these marvels."

She placed the Humperdinck CD and the Ruger on the credenza and looked around the room. There was a small teak side table by a chair. She dragged it in front of the credenza, then climbed on it and opened the latch on the glass door. The aroma was heavenly and she inhaled deeply—centuries of carbon-steel-forging legacy, and cherry wood in the handles. If these blades could have spoken, they'd have terrorized a mind for eternity.

Just the katana alone was worth over a million dollars. Vera examined the incredible craftsmanship that had gone in to the making of the weapon.

"Some collection you've got here," she yelled. "Too bad you didn't get the chance to show me your skills, amigo!"

Vera took down the katana and stared at it. This weapon was sacred ground. A venerable instrument of honor, of war, of death.

Kyle pressed on his wound and blood rushed through his fingers. He inched across the floor toward his cell phone, fading in and out of consciousness, seeing at first no one, then Vera, then a man with an eye patch and a harpoon. Was he a pirate? The man leant over him, cocked his head, examined him.

Kyle lost time again, and Vera was back, holding the Ruger a few inches away from his face and yelling at him.

Kyle reached his cell phone and grabbed it, wanting to dial. All will, no strength. And the battery lay a few feet away.

Again, he must have blacked out because Vera was back at the end of the hallway, this time holding the katana.

Time skipped again, and the sharp tip of a blade tapped him, piercing his chest.

Kyle screamed and unconsciousness beckoned.

"Don't you leave me now," Vera yelled as she raised the sword. "There's still more fun to come!"

Dazed, Kyle looked at the cell phone in his hand.

"Trying to call your sweetie? You can't do it

without that." She pointed to the battery, then poked him again with the razor-sharp katana. "Why is she not here? Where's the disk?"

"Fuck you," Kyle mumbled.

She raised the blade and laid it reverently on her palm. A drop of blood splashed on the marble tile—just the weight of the blade on her hand had been enough to cut her.

"Euuuweee, that's sharp! I know exactly what this sword is. You must be quite the connoisseur. Fascinating. Did you know these swords were tested on prisoners?" She examined the blade, then the handle. "Mid-1600s Japan, they'd hang the poor bastards from their wrists, then a renowned sword tester would be given the honor of testing this weaponry miracle. This actual sword was tested by Yamano Ka'emon. I recognize the marking on the blade. He was sixteen years old when he sliced through his first body as an official sword tester. He cut a man in half with one supreme stroke. This here is not a sword, it's a divine object. You should feel honored to perish by this blade. So, where's the disk?"

Kyle chuckled.

"What did you say? Speak up, boy. Can't hear you when you mumble." Vera raised the blade again.

Kyle stared right into her eyes and raised his arm instinctively, a futile attempt to shield himself.

———————

Kyle was in a slim black Gucci suit and tie. Akira wore a yellow sequined dress and black Valentino ankle-strap sandals. Together, they watched the crowded lobby at the Standard on Sunset.

As they headed toward the exit, Kyle glanced down at his own legs and realized he was walking backward. They passed white bubble chairs hanging from the ceiling in a crowded lounge, its patrons conversing, listening to music, regurgitating their drinks into glasses. A man at the bar received money from the bartender.

In a smaller lounge they took money from the bartender as he took his check back and pushed it into the cash register. Then they took turns regurgitating their drinks until their tumblers were full. The bartender picked up their glasses and smiled as the liquid rose from their glasses into a vodka bottle he was holding. Then he stored it back on a shelf behind him and placed the dry tumblers on a rack.

Kyle and Akira turned and walked backward toward the exit.

At the entryway, Akira gave a ticket to the valet and received the keys to a red Ferrari 355 GTS parked in front. Kyle bumped into someone in his peripheral vision. It was Vera.

The valet opened the car door for Akira and she slipped behind the wheel. Kyle tried to get her attention, but no sound came out of his mouth. The Ferrari engine rumbled, and Kyle watched in horror as Akira reversed down the driveway and out into the backward flow of Sunset Boulevard traffic.

Someone tapped him on the shoulder. "You with me, amigo?"

Kyle opened his eyes. He was back in the hallway. Vera stood in the middle, still wielding the katana.

The darkness descended again.

Kyle and Akira were having sex on the floor next to an open window overlooking the ocean. White silk drapes billowed in the breeze. Akira was on top, moaning, grinding. Kyle pulled her face close to his and watched her pupils dilating. Her lips parted and she licked her upper lip. His fingers traced her nipples. She moaned again.

Something next to him moved. He turned. A white boa constrictor was crawling toward them.

The serpent coiled around her waist, then moved up to her shoulders as it blended with her irezumi. She arched her back and pulled on the drapes, grinding against Kyle. The boa coiled around her neck, then wrapped itself around his right arm. The pain was crushing, and Kyle recoiled.

Confused and fear-stricken, he looked back at Akira, but she was oblivious. As she reached her climax, the boa ripped Kyle's arm off.

He screamed, the pain excruciating, and then Akira was gone. Instead, Vera loomed over him. The katana's blade had sliced through his left shoulder and his collarbone and lodged right below it.

Vera stepped on his chest and pulled the blade out. "Fuck, you moved your ass. That was no good. We'll have to try again." She lifted the katana, her arms stretched, the blade pointing up at the high ceiling. "I read once that a Shogun cut down a fleeing enemy horseman with such vigor that the blade went clean through the enemy's saddle, not mentioning the obvious."

The blade came down.

Kyle's arm was severed. Blood sprayed everywhere. His vision blurred.

"Now that's vigor!" Vera said. Her face speckled with blood "I always wondered what happened to the horse. Did you?" Maybe not. You didn't like what I did to that family back in Colombia, did you? Wow, sending me home by myself. That was mean."

The carbon steel flashed as it came down once more.

Akira drove the Ferrari along Sunset Boulevard. Her dress fluttered like a yellow sparkly butterfly wing, revealing her stunning legs. Kyle placed his hand on hers. She shifted gears through the twisty canyon road, and they glanced at each other at every turn.

Sunset Boulevard's oncoming traffic moved backward away from them in a milky neon streak. As dusk became dawn, the Ferrari parked into an overlook and a cloud of dust was vacuumed back under the car. Akira and Kyle came together in a kiss. As their lips parted, Akira disappeared into the crimson-red sky.

He tried to reach for her, but she was gone.

CHAPTER 30

Moby Dick

Vera placed the katana on the living-room table and went into the dining room, Ruger at the ready. Again, the decor caught her attention. On one wall was an impressive collection of fishermen's tools: a cross-staff, an astrolabe, fishhooks, knives, and three rare whaling harpoons dating back to eighteenth-century America. These beauties had been used to hunt creatures larger than any dinosaurs that had ever walked the earth. Sperm whales, maybe even blue whales.

One had a sharp barbed tip at the end of its iron shaft, designed to embed deep in the whale's flesh, making escape difficult. Vera examined the shaft; it was inscribed with two words: *Moby Dick*. She smiled.

———————

Akira snuck up the path next to the neighbor's house—currently vacant—and jumped over a short fence. She opened the door, padded across the kitchen and peeked into the hallway.

And there she was—Vera. She wore a bullet-proof vest and was holding a Ruger. And on the floor was Kyle, lying in a pool of blood, his arm severed.

An involuntary whimper burst deep from Akira's throat. She clapped her hand over her mouth but it was too late.

Vera turned and fired two shots at her. The slugs took a chunk of wood out of the door frame. "You're too late, you sloppy bitch."

———————

Vera went after her. "It's no use, darling. I killed him."

Vera peeked into the dining room. Clear—no sign of Akira. But the Moby Dick harpoon was missing.

"Are you serious?" she called out. "You want to use a harpoon? Come on, princess. Moby Dick? That's so over the top." Vera edged forward, leading with the Ruger. Where the hell was she?

"Don't be calling me names now, just because I'm not a skinny bitch like you."

Vera went into the living room. The katana was no longer on the table. A warm draft came from behind her. She spun around as a concealed wall panel opened six feet away from her.

Akira emerged and took a migi-jodan stance, arms up, the katana pointing up toward the ceiling, its blade streaked with blood.

The Ruger was pointing down, and Vera knew that if she lifted the gun, she'd lose her arm before she'd even had a chance to take a shot.

Akira inched closer, gliding almost. Vera stepped back through the doorway.

"You killed him," Akira yelled.

Vera took one more step back and nodded at the katana. "Yes. With that."

"Now, an eye for an eye," Akira said, changing her stance to waki-gamae—blade toward the side and the floor. Ready to strike.

Vera began to shake.

———

Sir Charles climbed out of the Lincoln, flipped the cap off a vial of PCP and snorted the whole lot.

The drugs kicked in faster than usual, sharpening his mind, enhancing his vision. He could have spotted a fly a mile away.

He stood atop the mast of a whaling ship, watching the vast waters of the Bering Sea as Moby Dick breached the crimson waves and rose toward the sky.

Sir Charles gripped the harpoon. "Die, you monster!"

Then he barreled toward the whale and speared its back.

———————

Vera dropped the Ruger. One eye twitched, and a puzzled expression formed on her face. She looked down at her chest as a bulge formed in her bulletproof vest, pushing outward. Akira remained completely still.

A metal tip poked through the Kevlar, and she stumbled forward.

Akira understood what she was looking at now. A harpoon. And the wielder? Sir Charles Fucking Barton.

Vera clutched the iron shaft as she sank to her knees.

"Sink all coffins and all hearses to one common pool!" Barton bellowed maniacally. "And since neither can be mine, let me then tow to pieces, while still chasing thee, though tied to thee, thou damned whale! Thus, I give up the spear!"

Akira brought down the katana, cutting the

shaft behind Vera, disconnecting her from Barton's grip. Then, without breaking stride, she stroked the blade sideways and severed Barton's head.

Blood sprayed everywhere as he collapsed behind Vera.

Akira ran into the hallway and kneeled next to Kyle. He was still alive, but fading fast. She cradled his head, and Kyle opened his eyes.

"Protect her," he whispered.

CHAPTER 31

Agony

Akira sat at Kyle's desk, tears streaming down her face, the Ruger pointed toward her own mouth. She trembled violently, her finger caressing the trigger. Kyle was gone. Without him, there was no reason to live.

And then her stomach cramped so hard that she had to put the gun down. She grabbed a small wastebasket and threw up into it.

Her child was calling. That there was her reason. That was why she had to survive.

She took a deep breath and slumped back in the chair. Something was just visible under the printer. She pushed it back, revealing the Wagner CD. The edge was damaged and it was splitting apart.

Akira pushed the tip of a fingernail into it and peeled away an inch-sized section. What the hell was under there? She dug in again until she'd removed the whole top layer, then inserted the CD back into the drive.

There was a beep, a message about a protocol initializing, and a progress bar appeared on the screen. A list of folders popped up, labeled A–Z. Eighty percent were highlighted in red; the rest were grayed out. She double-clicked on "A." There were three dozen files inside— A1.mov., A2.mov., and so on. An inquiry window popped up, and a list of selected programs opened.

She selected the icon DivX Player and clicked PLAY. A slate labeled "Alfieri, Paolo" appeared. A video recording with no sound started to roll, taking over the screen. An underage girl tied to a bed was being raped by a fifty-something priest in a black robe. He reached for something out of frame while the terrorized young girl sobbed. His hand came back into frame, holding a small metal case. He locked eyes with the girl, opened the box, pulled out a syringe and injected her.

Boiling with rage, Akira clicked on the pause button. The scene froze.

She took a deep breath and fast-forwarded, then stopped and pressed PLAY again. The clergyman was lashing the girl with a whip. At first she screamed, but then a state of euphoria seemed to take over, perhaps induced by whatever she'd been injected with.

Akira fast-forwarded again. Now, the girl was convulsing. Her body went limp. Her mouth hung open and her eyes stared lifelessly into nothing. The priest walked up to the camera and the screen went black.

She clicked on more folders. Most contained snuff movies featuring different clergymen. Many of them digitized from Super 8 to video. The date stamps went back thirty years.

A familiar face appeared in several—that of Sir Charles Barton, the mark she'd been hired to take down. In one, the man was strangling a young girl. Then he beat her with his cane until she stopped moving. When it was over, he looked straight into the camera, grinning like a hyena.

The sick fuck.

Akira headed back into the living room. Barton's headless body was sprawled where he'd died, but Vera had crawled toward the patio door and now lay in a pool of her own blood. Akira searched her pockets. Bingo—cell phone. She texted Wilshire, assuring them that the job was done and that she was on her way back to Los Angeles with the disk. Then she tossed the phone on the floor.

"You're a dead woman," Vera hissed.

Akira grabbed the tip of the harpoon and

pulled. Vera passed out.

Now it was time to clean up. Sort of.

Akira spent the next twenty-minutes cleaning Vera's wound and packing it with gauze. Once she was sure the woman wouldn't bleed to death, she collected a rope and two pulleys from the garage.

Then she made a call.

"I need a favor," Akira said.

"Ask away, my friend," Bobby replied. "Anything for you."

———————

Finally she was ready to disappear. The neighbor's Landcruiser had been loaded with everything she needed. There was just one more thing that needed to be done.

She took a wooden box from the credenza and opened a small black jar with a gold kanji on the label. There was a small mirror on the inside of the box lid, and Akira checked her reflection as she painted a large red dot on her forehead and streaked her cheeks with two lines that went down to her jaw.

This was not war paint; this was Akira's design. And it signified the invocation of agony upon her enemy.

She walked outside and onto the sand, the katana in her right hand, then looked over at the horizon. The sun had risen, cruelly and beautifully, unveiling a new day. As if nothing had happened. How could the earth show so much disrespect? Nothing would ever be the same without Kyle.

Light glittered on the dark waters, creating a kaleidoscope of color—reds, yellows, blues. It was just a molecular trick of the eye, of course. Yet the eye could perceive what wasn't really there. Kind of like Kyle, who was gone, but somehow she could feel him in the very air she was breathing.

Akira turned and looked back at the house. Vera hung from the porch, trussed up in the rope-and-pulley system she'd improvised. Gagged and blindfolded. Wrists and ankles zip-tied. Bare feet barely raking the sand beneath her.

She was conscious and still in her clothes.

Akira approached her and stopped a few feet away. Then, using the katana's tip, she removed the blindfold without putting as much as a scratch on the woman's face. Vera's eyes widened and trailed the movement of the blade.

"Just so you know," Akira said, "I'm very good at this. That's why I have this sword. I used to dream of being an expert as a child. Truth is, like my female ancestors, who immortalized themselves as Onna-Bugeisha, I am a martial arts master." Akira looked at the blade. "This katana has a name. My ancestors named it Itami. It means 'agony.' And that is what you will experience."

She looked back at Vera.

"Because if you think this is going to end quickly, you've got it all wrong. It will be a quick cut, yes, but a slow death. Long enough for you to see and feel what agony is. And yes, Vera, I'm sublime at this sword-swinging shit, you cunt."

Light bounced off the blade, and in it Akira saw the reflection of her own face, the rising sun, and the color of the ocean.

Vera squirmed and mumbled behind her gag. The words were muffled, but Akira could make them out well enough: "Save him. Save my son."

Then Akira swung the katana with the fury of a typhoon. A masterful stroke, as magnificent as it was deadly. And it was done.

Vera was forced to witness her lower body detaching from her hips and her organs spilling onto the sand beneath her feet.

If her eyes could have made a sound, it would have been deafening.

CHAPTER 32

Adriano

The Prophet Elias monastery stood above a rocky landscape overlooking the Aegean. For three hundred years, the building had sat in judgment of all in its sight. Fifteen hundred feet below, the crystal-clear turquoise water reflected the afternoon sun, shimmering like razor blades scattered over a sheet of glass.

Adriano was at the wheel of a rented red Lamborghini Miura P400 SV, one of the most beautiful cars that had come out of Italy since World War Two. The car was old but mechanically sound, and drove like a dream.

He drove it fast, windows down, wind in his hair, a pair of mirrored Ray-Bans shading his eyes. The shifter fought him with every gear change, but Adriano paid it no heed and raced the V12 engine uphill and onto a stretch of a road with twelve razor-sharp turns, like something drawn by a five-year-old having a tantrum.

At the top, he parked up at a vista point with a 360-degree view of the island, and climbed out, smoothing the fabric of his signature black suit. He took off his Ray-Bans and checked his reflection. Dark-red tie, perfectly ironed black shirt. Excellent.

He checked the map and walked to the cliff edge. The view was spectacular, impossible to tell where the turquoise waters ended and the sky began. He stared at the vanishing horizon for a minute, then looked back at the car. Like a Monica Bellucci with wheels. Fucking sexy as hell.

Not that he was here for a drive in a hot Italian exotic. He was there to scope a target.

He studied the map for a few minutes, comparing it with the landscape below, particularly interested in a Cycladic villa a half mile away. The summer rental had been built right by the water.

Adriano pocketed the map and used a small Swarovski hunting scope to home in on the villa. Aleppo pines and cypress trees surrounded the property, providing privacy. A sliver of a gap in the treeline revealed large glass windows, a step-down pool near a private rocky beach, and a single lounge chair.

He put the scope away, fired up the Miura's massive engine, and drove back down to Mesaria, a village not too far from the airport.

———————

The morning after, Adriano loaded a van with a small ice chest and a large case containing a Barrett M82A1—a powerful military-grade sniper rifle. He'd picked a slow day—no tourists, no groups, and no special holidays. This would give him the advantage he needed: solitude.

The roads were clear, but the climb up the road in the van was slow-going.

At the vista point he'd scouted the day before, he backed up to the edge of the cliff, climbed into the back of the van and opened the rear doors. The view was breathtaking—just the sky and the island below.

He opened the case and got to work. In two minutes flat, he'd assembled one of the most lethal rifles in the world, a weapon capable of striking a target two miles away. Plus, the subsonic bullets ensured he could take a second shot at the target without having alerted them.

Adriano had gone through this process many times. During the war in Iraq in the early eighties, he'd been a sniper for the Italian Secret Service (SISMI), assigned to covert work with the CIA,

and had unofficially joined the American-led co-
alition during Operation Desert Shield, during
which he'd delivered fifty-eight kills.

Next, he connected an iPod to his earpiece,
moved the click wheel and selected Tomaso Albi-
noni's *Adagio in G Minor*.

He closed his eyes and took a series of controlled breaths for eight minutes. When the song
was over, he was ready.

In the scope, he sighted the villa, then Akira in a black two-piece swimsuit. She lay on the
lounge chair, her child in her arms.

This was not an easy shot. He was using a .50
BMG round that weighed three quarters of a
pound. The night before, Adriano had calculat-
ed the impact of the weight on the bullet's trajectory. Because of the drop, he'd have to shoot
way up above the mark if he wanted to achieve his
goal of a headshot. The digital readout marked
the distance as 821 yards. With the ten-foot gap
in the treeline, it would be like shooting through
the eye of a needle.

Akira stood up and took the child inside the
house, then returned a few minutes later with just
a book and sat back down in the chair. The title on the front was written in Korean. Adriano
didn't speak Korean but liked to imagine she was
reading a romance novel.

He chambered the round, took a deep breath,

then let the air out of his lungs as his trigger finger depressed.

Then the bullet was gone—he felt it more than saw it, a sharp recoil and the familiar punch of physics set loose. Supersonic, silent, merciless. It cut through the air like a whispered execution, unbothered by weather or altitude. Gravity could fight it, but not stop it. The shot was clean. Cold. Like he'd planned it.

The white wall behind Akira was painted violently with human debris and blood as her head exploded. It was a perfect headshot. Not only that, the bullet had destroyed one of her shoulders. Blood drained into the pool, turning the crystal-clear water into an expanding cloud of dark crimson.

Over the next sixty seconds, all the tension he'd felt dissipated. The muscles in his face relaxed. The painstaking task had taken three years to plan. Now it was complete.

This trip to Greece had been out of Akira's comfort zone, but hiding in remote locations had taken its toll, and cabin fever had set in. She'd gone to Indonesia six months earlier, but after only a brief time there had realized her days in Jakarta were numbered. She'd spotted a US intelligence officer. And if she could spot one of them, it wouldn't be too long before someone spotted her. Wilshire was still actively searching for her, and the Vatican couldn't allow anyone in possession of such explosive and damaging secrets to remain alive.

She'd befriended a Korean student on a backpacking trip. Sara was young and needy, an expat like herself, and they looked a lot alike. The women had immediately hit it off, and Akira had hired Sara as a nanny. Sara had been thrilled. Instead of backpacking, she could stay in expensive villas and see the world from a different perspective. Plus, she adored babies and was in absolute awe of Mina.

Sara brought Mina inside for a nap, then grabbed a book and headed back to the pool where she sat down to read.

Akira put Mina in her cot, then filled a tray with food and drinks. As she headed out the door, she allowed herself a smile, enjoying the view of the turquoise water bleeding into the horizon as millions of swallows, on their way to South Africa, formed a spectacular murmuration.

As she wondered how such a miracle might come to be, Sara's head exploded.

Fuck. Akira froze.

There'd be another bullet, this one with her name on it.

Only it didn't come.

And then she realized—whoever had taken the shot couldn't see her. The treeline was blocking their view. The shooter might not even realize they'd shot the wrong person. Might not even know there were two women in the house. Which meant they didn't know Akira was still alive.

She had to move fast. The sniper's next move would be to come and clean up. And judging from the trajectory, the road on the other side of the hill was a fifteen-minute drive to where she was.

She'd need to avoid the roads and Santorini Airport, but the house had a dock with a small boat. She could sail to Rhodes, then to the shores of Turkey, and on to Istanbul. A long way but doable.

Akira ran inside, put Mina in a car seat and set her down in the master bedroom. Then she loaded the boat and went back inside. She caught her reflection in the glass—still wearing her swimsuit, her body covered in blood spatter.

Mina was crying. Akira gave her a bottle and ducked into the shower.

Adriano stopped at the side of the road. pulled the antenna up on the sat-phone, and called Thomas Wilshire.

"It's done."

"And the child?" Thomas said with a slight German accent.

"The child's in the house."

"We don't need the child."

"I know," Adriano said. "I'm getting the CD and I'm done."

"No one is to be left behind."

"What do you mean?"

"It cannot remain alive," Thomas said.

"I don't do back-to-back. That wasn't the plan, capisci? I didn't bring a pistol, and I'm not killing a baby with a rifle or a knife."

"Of course you are," the German hissed. "We need it done."

"I don't like to veer off a plan."

"We need it done."

"You keep saying that. Do I sound like a Golden Retriever?"

"Check your phone," Thomas said.

Adriano looked at the phone screen and read the text. He swallowed, furious and astonished at the same time. "That's a lot of zeros."

"Are we on?" Thomas asked.

"Consider it done. Pezzo di merda."

The line went dead.

The van made it to the villa in seven minutes flat. Adriano picked the gate lock and pushed it open, then unzipped his bag and took out a knife that had once been the weapon of choice for hand-to-hand combat during the First World War. A 1918 Knuckle Duster Trench Knife. The six-inch blade came with brass knuckles, sharp spikes, and a pointed pommel at the top of the handle that allowed soldiers to stab and bludgeon their enemies. It had well and truly earned its nickname—the skull crusher.

He gripped the hilt, walked up the driveway, and ducked into the living room.

There, ten feet away, was the woman he thought he'd killed.

"Akira? Motherfucker." Adriano blurted out.

Her hair was wet. Dark and shoulder-length; not the short platinum-blond style she'd sported in LA three years earlier.

She was naked too. And while fighting a naked woman would be weird, Wilshire had paid Adriano too much money to feel odd about anything. All he knew was that he must not underestimate her, not on any account. The stats the agency had recorded for Akira were off the charts, and he knew it.

CHAPTER 33

Titanium

Akira eyed the trench knife, grabbed an ashtray to her right, and threw it at her assailant. He ducked.

"Fuck you, Adriano," Akira muttered.

She scanned the room. What else did she have that might level the playing field? The damn Beretta was in the duffle bag at the end of the hallway.

"You need something? You find what you were looking for?" Adriano asked.

Akira had trained for this exact scenario. Sort of. It had never included fighting naked. Which would have been useful right about now.

She'd made plans to move to Seoul, it would have been the perfect place to hide as a South Korean ex-pat. Making a stop in Greece instead, was a mistake. And now this.

And why the knife? Why didn't he have a gun? It made no sense.

Adriano's knuckles turned white and he bolted forward and swung the knife toward her belly. Akira stepped back just in time. He punched her in the face, then landed a perfect one-two. She parried one punch, but not the other. The brass knuckles of the trench knife barely touched her jaw but knocked a tooth from her mouth. It bounced off the ceiling.

Adriano smirked. "Was it a molar?"

Akira blinked, alert to the adrenaline rush, then straightened herself and took the praying-mantis stance.

Adriano charged her again. She ducked and shoved him toward the window. His blade caught Akira's shoulder but the glass shattered, slicing his hand and forearm, and he dropped the weapon.

Akira grabbed a table lamp and smashed it against the side of his head. Adriano dropped to the floor, stayed down for a whole two seconds, then stood up as if nothing had happened.

"Seriously? What the fuck," Akira said.

She inhaled deeply and took two steps back. Adriano's chin came up, and the stare of his intense blue eyes drilled into her soul. She changed her stance—a jiu-jitsu pose—exhaled, hardening her core, and pushed a loose strand of hair behind her left ear.

Then she bolted forward.

Too slow. Adriano delivered a sidekick to her liver that sucked the air out of her, and she fell to her knees. He kicked her again, this time on the side of her face, sending her down onto her back. He stood right over her. Akira stared at the ceiling, helpless. Oh fuck, this was it. She was going to die.

Adriano eyed the trench knife a few feet away. Mina's cry came from the bedroom. He looked at the door, then leaned over and picked up Akira as if she were weightless.

He charged through the bedroom door and threw her against the wall. She smashed into a lamp and a picture frame, and slid down onto the bedside table. Akira stood up. Dazed, she glanced at Mina, secured in the car seat next to the king-size bed, startled by the commotion, still sucking on a pink pacifier tethered to her wrist.

Adriano stared at Mina.

"Don't you fucking dare," Akira hissed.

Mina began to sob. Adriano cracked an unnatural smile, revealing gold-capped teeth. His eyes glistened.

"No, you motherfucker. Don't even—"

Adriano spun around, hit her with a roundhouse kick to her head that sent her slamming into the bedpost. She dropped to the floor. He leaned over and grabbed her hair. Blood dripped from her forehead and into her eyes. She tried to wipe it away.

"This is the good part," he said, and spun her around like a marionette. "This is where I ask you to give me what you took. Then I won't kill you. Yet." He looked over at Mina. "Give it to me now or I'll kill that thing first, just to shut it up. Capisci?"

"It's in the hallway closet, under the carpet," Akira whispered.

"What? Come again?"

Akira tried to point but her body wouldn't comply. "Closet. Under ... carpet."

"Good."

Adriano lifted her over his shoulders and launched her over the bed like a rag doll. Her body crashed into a tall dressing mirror, and it shattered above her. Time seemed to slow down as she locked eyes with Mina. Her daughter stared at her, silent now, eyes full of fear.

"You know that's seven years of bad luck," Adriano shouted, then adjusted his tie and walked out into the hallway.

Akira listened as he rummaged in the closet. For a moment, she blacked out, then came to, wincing as she flexed her hand. A shard of glass was implanted in her left palm, and she used her teeth to pull it out. Mina was sucking on her pacifier.

So beautiful, so perfect. She'd gotten the name from Bram Stoker's *Dracula*, hoping her daughter would one day be with someone who would love her, do anything for her, even if it meant coming back from the dead. It was Mina who'd changed Akira. Before, she'd always been on the other side of this scenario, killing people who deserved it, and many who didn't. Following protocol, no emotions, just the job and nothing more. When Wilshire hired you to kill someone, you didn't expect them not to hire someone to kill you too. That was always implied. But even so, assassins tended to forget. She had. And now Adriano, formerly a colleague, was now the enemy.

Akira unbuckled Mina from the car seat and carried her to the doorway.

A square of carpet and a plank landed with a *thunk* on the floor in front of them.

Akira crawled toward her sports bag and pulled the zipper open. Grabbed a Beretta 92.

Adriano stood in the doorway holding a small pouch, opened it, and cracked a smile.

So he'd found the CD case.

"I hope this is what I think it is," he said.

Akira raised the Beretta. Mina right behind her.

"Ha! Una pistola Italiana! What a bella cosa!"

Akira fired, once, twice, three times. Adriano's knee buckled and he dropped the pouch and screamed.

She took another shot. It hit the television set. Adriano limped over to her, wincing, and slapped the Beretta out of her hand. She punched his shattered knee.

He screamed again, his voice an octave higher.

Akira staggered to her feet and pushed him, putting all her weight behind it. He fell backward and landed next to the trench knife. Akira rummaged blindly in the sports bag and grabbed whatever came to hand.

Oh, shit. A grenade.

Adriano looked at her. "No fucking way."

Akira pulled the pin with her teeth and tossed it toward him, then scooped up Mina, charged into the bathroom and slammed the door. She dove into the tub, cradling her daughter, anticipating the blast.

Two seconds went by. Three. Four.

There was a bright flash, a deafening bang, and the unmistakable smell of magnesium-based pyrotechnic chemicals.

Shit. Not a grenade then. A flash-bang.

Akira eyed the window across from the tub. She imagined jumping through it with her daughter, but her body wouldn't respond.

Then the bathroom door swung open, and

Adriano limped over to her.

"Look at my suit," he said, his face twitching. He pointed at where one of his pant legs had caught fire. "Jesus Christ! That was close. I thought it was a bomb."

Akira helplessly pulled at his jacket. But her brain wouldn't let her do more.

Adriano plunged the knife into the side of her head. But the blade jammed halfway into her skull.

A shard of glass matted into her hair sliced Adriano's hand.

"Fuck," he screamed, and recoiled as blood sprayed the tub and wall.

He looked down at his hand—his pinky was bent backward. Instinctively he grabbed it and cracked it back into its place.

"Fuck me," he screamed again.

Akira was lifeless, still shielding her daughter. Adriano looked around, picked up the Beretta, and aimed it at Mina.

———

Minutes later, Adriano slipped behind the wheel of the van and hit the speed dial on the sat-phone.

"Do you have good news?" a male voice said in Italian.

"Of course I do."

"Bravo. We have wired the money."

"On my way."

The line went dead.

Adriano tossed the phone onto the passenger seat, started the car, and drove away. Behind him, fire engulfed the villa.

———————

Akira staggered to her feet, the trench knife still stuck in her head, and barely made it out.

Outside, she turned and watched the house go up in flames. A column of putrid smoke plumed up into the sunset sky. She ached for little Mina, but it was too late. She looked down at her hand; she was clutching something. Mina's pacifier fell out of her palm. She stared at it.

Instinctively, her hand went to her head and she pulled the knife out. The pain was white hot, and she collapsed to the ground.

The blade was bent at an odd angle.

And then she remembered. And understood why she was still alive.

During a mission exfil a decade earlier, Akira had been shot in the head. Her ballistic helmet had caused the bullet to deviate, but the impact had shattered part of her skull. Against the odds, Akira had survived, a testament to the power of sheer determination and the best that modern neurosurgery offered. A few months after the cranioplasty, she'd returned to training and put her harrowing experience behind her.

Except for excruciating headaches when the weather changed, she forgot she even had the plate.

Now, for the second time in her life, the titanium had saved her.

CHAPTER 34

Phoenix

Doctor Alexander Athanasiou stood at the foot of the hospital bed and flicked off a piece of lint off the Metropolitan Hospital logo on the pocket of his white coat. The thick eyebrows and streak of gray in his hair made him look older than his thirty-six years.

He looked at the unconscious woman on the bed, a proud smile frozen on his round face.

"With an anxiety that almost amounted to agony, I collected the instruments of life around me, that I might infuse a spark of being into the lifeless thing that lay at my feet."

Then he laughed. The line from Mary Shelley's *The Modern Prometheus* was one of his favorites.

"That would make you Frankenstein, you know," Nurse Liosis said.

He smiled. "Yes, but still a doctor."

She looked at him. "Touché, Doctor."

The nurse rolled her eyes. His joviality was infectious, his talent unmatched, and everyone thought he was godsent. Which is why they tried not to mind when he quoted Shelley every time a patient opened their eyes after surgery.

Over the past three weeks, their patient had undergone multiple surgeries and been in and out of the ICU. Nurse Liosis brushed a strand of the woman's black hair off her face. The left side of her scalp had been shaved during pre-op—a style a punk rocker could have pulled off except for the two dozen staples holding together a ten-inch C-shaped scar that would have horrified Jack Skellington.

———————

Akira came to, unsure who the laughing man was but glad she could at least breathe without the aid of a ventilator. Her brain tried to assemble the puzzle unfolding before her, but couldn't. There just weren't enough pieces.

A child. A fire. A helicopter ride. The laughing man.

"Ms. Winter, I'm Doctor Athanasiou, your

surgeon. And this is Nurse Liosis, our floor supervisor."

"Who are you?" Akira said, slurring her words.

"You're still under the effect of the meds, but you're okay. The firemen found your suitcases, and the police turned everything over to the Japanese consulate. Right, Ms. Liosis?"

He turned to the nurse. They both smiled.

"Yes," the nurse said. "Someone from the consulate brought your documents and suitcases here a couple of days ago. They're in the closet."

"The police?"

Akira looked down at her left arm, where an IV had been inserted.

"You'll stay here a while longer," the doctor said. "Then we'll move you to rehabilitation therapy at the end of the hall."

Akira looked at his face, then turned to the nurse.

"Where's Mina?"

———

No sooner had their patient asked the question than she fell asleep.

The doctor shrugged. "Do we know who this Mina is?"

"No idea who Mina is, but she asks every time."

Akira Winter was a mystery. After the fire,

she'd been airlifted by the Hellenic Coast Guard to Metropolitan Hospital in Pireas, a brand-new medical center on the Athens Riviera where Dr. Athanasiou was head of neurosurgery. He'd been in the Greek Corps during the peacekeeping operations in Serbia and had the experience of treating wounds of war. Akira's story interested him.

"She's not strong enough yet," Nurse Liosis said. "She suffered so many injuries."

"Yes, the cranioplasty's the least of my worries. Whoever stabbed her brutally attacked her in ways I've never seen before."

"You think it was a robbery?"

"No. I served in two wars, and this wasn't a beating or a burglary gone wrong. Someone tried to kill her. But she just wouldn't die."

He picked up a clipboard at the foot of the bed and examined the patient's chart.

"Four broken ribs, a punctured lung, a missing tooth, glass debris cuts, knife wounds ... the obvious one, the cranioplasty. Bruises all over. A few defensive wounds. Reminds me of when we treated that underground mixed martial arts fighter last month. Remember?"

"Like she was the attacker too," the nurse said. "What about those bullet fragments in her shoulder?"

Dr. Athanasiou flipped a page. "They're old,

like the cranioplasty. There's a dent in the titanium but it's still intact. It saved her."

"And the scars on her side."

"And the elephant in the room."

"The tattoo?"

"The yakuza-style tattoo, and the old scars," the doctor corrected.

"She's a puzzle, this one."

He chuckled. "I love puzzles."

"Really?"

"Yes, sorry. Not funny."

"Don't be, Doctor. I was thinking more like Humpty Dumpty." She laughed.

"I love it when you're evil, Ms. Liosis."

"I skipped my lunch hour. I need food. That's what you're hearing."

Then he flipped through more pages. "By the way, did the police come back?"

"Haven't seen that prick today. Why?"

"With the house fire and all these wounds, this didn't even make the last page of any papers. An expensive Santorini villa goes up in flames and no one talks about it? God forbid something happens on the island and we lose a couple of tourists this year." He looked at Nurse Liosis. "You think the mayor covered it up?"

"I've learned one thing, Doctor. When dealing with the police, I don't even ask questions in my own head just in case they're listening."

"They covered it up," the doctor said. And placed the chart back into the cubby.

"Hear this—we saved a life, and that's all the hospital is here for. I'm famished, I haven't slept in thirty-six hours, I have a break coming up in ten minutes, and I need to see Mrs. Demogerontas before she shits her bed. I'll see you in the cafeteria." Nurse Liosis patted the doctor on the back and left the room.

———————

A week went by and Akira remained in the ICU, where she could be monitored constantly. The police had either lost interest or were too busy reeling from the shock of Vladimir Putin's visit following Prime Minister Konstantinos Simitis's interest in befriending the Russian dictator.

A story that was all over the news, twenty-four-seven. And the only thing Akira could watch.

Still, she'd kept herself busy—stolen a patient's cell phone, money, clothes, a couple of small tools, drugs, and an EMS response kit. She'd stashed her loot behind a plumbing service panel in the closet wall.

The plan, of course, was to leave the hospital, because even though her ordeal hadn't made the news, it was still in the police reports, and she needed to be dead if she wanted to survive out-side Greece.

A plan had formed in her head, but she needed more time.

———————

More weeks passed, and she managed to connect her Swiss bank account to a few in Japan and a doz-en more in the US where she could transfer large sums of money without triggering any government red flags. She'd also wired money to the hospital, paying for a transfer to a private room, away from Dr. Athanasiou and his nurses, from where she could execute the plan for her vanishing act.

Then one morning, wearing a big smile and holding a boombox, he stopped by.

"I thought you'd like this," he said, and pulled a CD jewel case from his white coat pocket.

It was the Richard Wagner CD case.

Shit.

"I completely forgot to give it to you," the doctor said. "It's been in my desk drawer, and then this morning I saw it and ... well, here it is. You were gripping it so tight when they brought you in that it took two nurses to get it out of your hands." He chuckled as he held the CD in front of her face. "You must love this classical stuff! I'm a Country boy myself."

"W-where d-did you ..."

Akira coughed and tried to draw air into her lungs. She told herself to relax but the panic wouldn't subside ... images of Adriano, then Mina, flooded her mind. She'd gotten stabbed trying to protect her. And yet neither the doctors nor the police had mentioned a baby being found in the fire. Was Mina dead? Or had she been taken?

Akira grabbed a paper bag from the nightstand and blew into it.

"That's it. Breathe in ... through your nose ... That's it. Exhale even slower. Count to four. And again," the doctor said.

A few minutes went by, and Akira finally calmed down.

The doctor took her hand. "This is what happens when you don't take anti-anxiety meds."

"I-I prefer not using drugs."

"Well, let me know if you change your mind. I have plenty," he said, and chuckled. He placed the CD in her hand. "Take it easy, okay?"

The doctor left and an avalanche of memories assaulted her. She remembered. In the seconds before Adriano had stabbed her, she'd grabbed his jacket and picked his pocket. That's how she'd taken the CD from him.

Adriano would have figured that out, but it would have been too late for him to go back. By then the house would have been crawling with firefighters and police officers.

Akira began to sob. If Mina's body hadn't been found, Adriano must have taken her. But why? And where was she?

The days passed, and with each one Akira got stronger, driven by the need to find Adriano and Mina. A plan began to forge in her mind, as sharp as the katana forged in the hands of her ancestors. She would bring death to the doorsteps of Wilshire and the clergymen in those videos. But how?

Getting on the bad side of the Vatican wouldn't be a smart move. It was the largest organization in the world, with over 1.3 billion members, and had the money and resources to control mercenary groups and assassins everywhere. That was why she was in this damn hospital in the first place.

Finally, she was ready. It was a big and busy hospital with mostly outpatients—a chaotic environment perfect for slipping out unnoticed.

She'd used the night wisely, and located her first mark—a man admitted for psychiatric evaluation. The process would take a few days, and by the time he missed his car she'd be long gone. Akira would pack the stolen Fiat with her belongings, then park up several blocks away from the hospital.

She'd studied the hospital routines closely too, particularly when a patient died. She'd clean out her room, just like the nurses did for the deceased, then fill out the necessary forms and switch charts and ID with her second mark—a woman who'd just died. It would be at least a day or two before someone discovered something wasn't right. By then, she'd be out of Greece.

CHAPTER 35

Lady Kage

Akira sipped on a glass of Cristal. First class had never felt so good. There was nothing like champagne to forget her fucking headache. And codeine mixed with the alcohol felt even better. Her fractured clavicle wasn't healing as fast as the rest of her body and hurt like hell from time to time. And the tinnitus she'd been experiencing since her departure from Athens was like a new friend.

She'd driven from Athens to Turkey, a fourteen-hour trip with only a few quick stops here and there for fuel or to pee. Once she'd had to hide from Kalashnikov-wielding soldiers in a pickup truck. After a two-hour power nap in the car, she'd crossed the border—mercifully without having to show her passport—and ditched the

Fiat, selling it to a garage owner who was happy to take it off her hands, no matter the missing paperwork.

Then she'd checked into a motel in Gebze, thirty minutes east of Istanbul. It had cost her a little extra to procure a false passport from the man across the way, but had been worth the lira. Since Wilshire thought she was dead, her passage home to the US should be safe.

The new passport had worked just fine through customs. That guy had been right when he said his documents weren't fake—just not legal.

Akira smiled as she looked at the prefecture of Osaka below. This was the first she'd been to Izumisano in twelve years. Her last visit to Japan had involved killing an investment banker traveling on the Shinkansen. *Oh boy, that was so stupid.* She'd been so eager. She'd killed that man before they'd even reached the second stop, but had been so fascinated by the speed of the bullet train that she'd hidden the body and stayed on board for the whole two-hour trip to the end of the line. She could have jeopardized the entire operation, could have gotten killed for it. It was true what they said—youth was wasted on the young. Still, the ekiben they'd served on that train was the best.

———

As the airplane approached the artificial island, Kansai, the new Osaka International Airport shone like an enormous flag floating outside the bay. A bridge shaped like a flagpole linked the airport to the shores of Izumisano and as they began their descent, the Rinku Gate Tower, the fifty-six-story skyscraper owned by Hong Kong conglomerate XiS Technologies, reared into view. There, Akira's first boss and mentor, a woman who went by the name of Lady Kage, was expecting her visit.

The Boeing 747 yelped as it touched down, the sound of the reverse engine's thrust oddly soothing to Akira. But even that couldn't stifle the dread deep in her core, like a blade piercing her heart. Mina. Where was she? What had happened to her?

Kansai's terminal was the longest structure in the world and one of the busiest pieces of real estate she'd seen in years. It was nothing short of breathtaking. Hordes of people spewed out of the gates like spiderlings bursting out of their nests. Except, the spiders were escaping the egg sac to begin a new life. Akira couldn't help wondering what reason people had? What were we running toward ... or from?

She collected her baggage and walked over to a porter holding up a cardboard sign that read *Ms. A.*

He bowed, then bobbed his head meekly. "Follow me, Ms. Akagi."

Outside the terminal, a parade of flight attendants wearing colorful silk scarves passed by them. The porter walked up to a tall man with short black hair and a square jaw, who wore a tailored black suit and tie. Akira joined them.

"My name is Ken. I'm your driver," he said in Japanese, and bowed. "I'm driving you for the duration of your stay."

Akira thanked him. Ken popped the limo's trunk. The porter loaded the luggage and left. Ken opened the door for Akira then navigated them through the immediate traffic jam and headed for the Sky Gate Bridge—the flagpole shape she'd seen from the air. This was the longest double-decked truss bridge in the world, with six lanes. And it was the only road connecting the airport to the mainland, a three-mile ride into Rinku Town.

They exited the bridge and drove across the primary avenue, leaving the hustle and bustle of the airport behind. A short while later, Ken pulled the limo into the driveway of the Rinku Tower and lowered the tinted glass partition between them.

"Ms. Akagi, let me know if you need anything else. I will take care of it. I'll be parked in front, waiting for you." Ken smiled and the partition went back up.

A valet opened her door and bowed as Akira stepped out. She took a few steps up to a turnstile and went into the modern Japanese-styled lobby. Dark-green stone floors cut in between red-carpeted meeting areas decorated with tategoshi latticed walls and a reception desk accented by gold laminated ukiyo-e paintings.

Akira joined the line, but a young woman approached her, bowed in saikeirei style, and said, "It is a great honor to meet you, Ms. Akagi. I'm Suki. No need to go to reception. Please follow me. I'm Lady Kage's assistant. She is waiting for you."

Akira nodded, returned her smile, and followed Suki past two security men dressed as impeccably as Ken had been.

They arrived at a bank of six black elevators, whose doors were painted with a large gold ensō, except for one where the brush stroked circle was red. Suki stopped at this one and entered a code on a keypad. The doors opened. They were whisked to the fiftieth floor. The doors slid open to a large penthouse suite remodeled to look like a traditional Japanese home. Suki took her shoes off and placed them in a cubby next to the elevator. Akira did the same.

The furnishing was minimal but elegant. There was a butsudan, a tokonoma, and a low long table at the end of the room. If not for the windows overlooking Osaka Bay eight hundred feet below, anyone could have been forgiven for thinking they were in a villa on the hillside of the ancient city of Kyoto. Was this where Lady Kage lived?

"Ms. Akagi, let me know if you need anything." Suki handed Akira a cell phone. "My number is programmed. As is Ken's. I'll be next door on the same floor."

She bowed again, and Akira thanked her. Suki walked out of the room and into a hallway.

Akira went over to a window and took in the view. The residence was so quiet that Akira could hear her own heartbeat. Lady Kage had clearly taken drastic steps to ensure the noise of the outside world didn't penetrate this sanctuary. And yet there was a breeze and the aroma was unmistakable. Cherry blossom. Yet it couldn't be—the western hills of Kyoto's suburbs were thirty-eight-miles away.

The scent reminded her of her childhood days, before her family had moved to California. And inevitably thoughts of Mina surfaced. Tears pooled in her lower eyelids.

"Here, my child," a woman said in a low hoarse voice.

Akira turned. The woman held out a silk handkerchief.

"Mama," Akira said as she embraced Lady Kage.

She was seventy years old, trim, taller than Akira, with a chiseled jaw, gray eyes, and pale skin. Her long lavender-colored hair was pulled back by a red silk scarf. She wore a koi-fish-embroidered Kenzo pant suit, no shoes. The yellow varnish on her toenails gleamed, and a subtle fragrance enveloped her—azaleas, Akira thought.

Lady Kage ran her fingers through Akira's hair, then held her face with both hands and looked straight into her eyes.

"Look at you, my child from another mother. I missed you."

"I missed you too, Mama," Akira said, and wiped away her tears.

Lady Kage smiled and gestured around her. "You like what I did with the place?"

"I do. I guess if you're banned from Kyoto, you must bring Kyoto to you."

"It's the deal I made. If I stay away, I retain my status. Minus these." She smirked and displayed her left hand. Two fingers were missing. "Can't complain—I seldom used them."

"Talking of complaining, have you heard?" Akira asked.

"Yes." Lady Kage headed for a doorway. "Child, let's sit."

Akira followed her into a hallway that led to

a massive black door. It slid open automatically, and they entered a large garden with a cherry tree in full blossom. That smell. She reached the threshold, felt a breeze, and looked up.

For a moment, she thought she was falling. There was no ceiling. The opening in the top of tower was about forty feet wide. Akira staggered and used the door frame to brace herself.

"It's normal to experience vertigo. It happens to everyone the first time," Lady Kage said.

"Wow, that's something."

"I know. It is spectacular. Took my architect a full year just to draw the plans. I guess it's like the private beach you had. I have my private piece of the sky."

"You know about my home?" Akira asked.

"Child, I am a billionaire who can't leave her house. I have access to satellites. I can see it all. You left quite a statement on your beach."

"Did you see me in Greece?" Akira wasn't smiling now.

"No, child, after that, you were a hard act to follow. I can only see if I know where to look. I can't see what I don't know. That's why I was able to give permission for the yakuza to help your new friend, Robert."

"Bobby. He saved my life."

Lady Kage sat on a stone bench facing the cherry tree and overlooking a rock garden. In the center, next to the cherry tree, a twelve-foot black rock jutted out of an oval island surrounded by a gravel river. Akira sat down next to her.

"It's beautiful, isn't it?" Lady Kage said.

"Yes, it is." Akira smiled as her eyes filled with tears.

Lady Kage held her hand. "My child, tell me everything."

CHAPTER 36

Shadow

1986
KYOTO, JAPAN

After the death of Akira's mom, Uncle Busei had arranged for Akira's move to Kyoto, so she wouldn't be around during the investigation into William's death.

There, she was adopted by a dear friend and longtime client of Uncle Busei, a woman named Lady Kage—the most powerful crime boss in Kyoto's yakuza underworld. No one knew her real name, and those who had known weren't alive to tell. The name Kage, meaning Shadow in Japanese, had been earned because she could fight in pitch-black environments, a technique she'd mastered after years of practice with her grandfather, the boss of one of the most powerful and notorious yakuza clans in Japan.

The daughter of a yakuza, she was an only child who lived with her family in the hills overlooking Kyoto. They'd been slaughtered during a battle between rival gangs, leaving her as the only survivor of a long line of female warriors.

A brutal assassin, she'd quickly rebuilt her clan and regained control of the city she'd go on to reign for decades.

Akira's new home was surrounded by sakura trees and white azalea bushes. The view was astonishing. From the hilltop, she could see the Imperial Palace in the middle of the city.

She felt like a princess, living above the clouds.

But Lady Kage had different plans for Akira.

She would teach her the way of the warrior, mold her into an instrument of death, and embed in her a strict code of honor, loyal only to her clan.

Akira's training commenced. She honed her craft of multiple martial arts and how to handle military-grade weapons. Even at a young age, her kinetic scores were off the charts—a small warrior who packed power.

When Akira turned sixteen, Lady Kage tasked her with killing a man who'd betrayed the clan. And just like Yamano Ka'emon Nagahisa, the legendary sixteenth-century sword tester, Akira was to use her katana to slice the man in half with a single stroke.

Akira never forgot Lady Kage's words. "There will be no fear in you. You will respect death and the life that is before it. You will respect the failures that have made you the warrior you are. Your enemies will live in the agony of your blade, and you will respect and honor the blood that you spill."

Two years went by; training, learning, fighting, and slicing more enemies of the clan. One day, Akira was painting her face in the traditional kumadori style. Without warning, she was pulled aside, given her ancestors' sword, Itami, and told to meet Lady Kage in the garden.

In the courtyard she was greeted by the cheer of hundreds of yakuzas wearing their fundoshi, all gathered in a circle. This, Akira realized, would be her final test.

Lady Kage stood in the middle, dressed in a white hakama embroidered with lavender flowers and an ascending crane.

Akira, dressed in a black hakama, her face still marked by the white and red makeup, made her way down the steps. Many of the yakuzas snickered. At her side was the katana that had been in her family since the Edo period.

She stopped twenty feet away from Lady Kage. They stared at each other, eyes blazing. So she would fight the woman she now called Mother. Akira had watched previous bouts. No one had made it out unscathed.

"Didn't have time to wash up, child?" Lady Kage said, and bowed.

Akira bowed too.

Lady Kage attacked with a brutal roundhouse kick leaving Akira in no doubt that this was no training session; her mother was fighting to kill. Akira blocked the kick with her forearm.

Lady Kage threw a punch, then another. Akira blocked and parried. A third punch hit her in the face. Blood sprayed from the side of her mouth as she dropped to the ground.

Akira jumped up and wiped her mouth with her sleeve. Lady Kage took advantage of the movement and delivered a series of strikes, first to her liver, then to her chest and the face.

Akira rolled on the ground and knocked Lady Kage's legs out from under her. Lady Kage ended up sprawled on her back.

Akira pulled the katana out of her scabbard. Her eyes burned with fury.

Lady Kage unsheathed her blade. Akira's blade sliced the air an inch away from her Mother's face. Lady Kage pulled on Akira's hakama with her free hand and elbowed her under her chin.

Akira absorbed the pain and took a migi-jodan stance. Arms up, the blade diagonally pointing to her side. Then she attacked. Lady Kage parried with her sword. And as sparks of molten steel danced on the blades, she pulled a tanto dagger from her kimono and slashed at Akira, missing her by a hair but slicing through the fabric of her hakama.

Then Lady Kage retreated.

Akira moved forward; her katana ready to strike.

The hair on her arms stood up. Something wasn't right.

She looked down onto a wooden hatch.

What the fuck.

Lady Kage smirked and the hatch opened.

Akira fell sixteen feet. The hatch closed above her, and everything went black.

She waited for the dizziness to pass and for her eyes to adjust. There were rock formations, and other shapes she couldn't make out.

Then she heard the quiet whisper of breath.

Three shadowy figures surrounded her—each dressed in tactical military attire and black masks, and wielding a knife.

They attacked.

She swung her katana lightning fast. Two of the men were dead before they hit the ground, their heads severed. The whites of their terrified eyes glowed as they fell into the darkness. The third man lunged as she recovered from her swing, and stabbed her thigh. She grabbed his arm, and they both went down. Akira sunk her teeth into his face, then spat out gore.

He screamed and writhed.

She had bitten his nose clean off.

Akira pulled the knife out of her leg and stabbed the man in the neck ... until there was no neck left and the man's head tumbled from his shoulders.

A loud creak came from behind her—a second hatch opening. Water rushed in, flooding the chamber, sweeping her into an underground pipe where she was flushed away and spat into a koi pond at the foot of the hill.

———————

Several days later, Akira awoke. She was lying on a four-poster bed lacquered in red with gold leaf detail. On one side of the room, two elegant tansu chests flanked a butsudan.

The bedroom overlooked Kyoto. Outside, the wind drove clouds across a blue sky as if signposting the Imperial Palace below.

And then she realized.

She had passed the ultimate test.

Akira turned as Lady Kage entered the room.

"Good morning. I hope you had a pleasant sleep."

"Good morning," Akira said. "I did, but I have one question."

"You may ask me anything."

"Who were those men?"

"Enemies. Enemies whose freedom I promised if they could kill you."

"I see."

"Today is victory over yourself of yesterday," Lady Kage said.

"Tomorrow is your victory over lesser men," Akira added.

Lady Kage smiled. "Yes. You're now my true daughter."

CHAPTER 37
The Return

Akira, wearing a black Versace pantsuit and six-inch heels, stepped through the automatic doors of the busy terminal. It was the middle of summer, bright and sunny. She put on a pair of Black Flies. The city of angels. Hot and sexy. And she loved it.

The traffic outside the terminal was the usual shit show. A traffic cop gave a ticket to a foreigner who couldn't understand a word he was saying. A beep announced a small bus reversing into a parking spot by the curb. An airport worker drove luggage carts back to their hub. A patrol car came toward Akira and slowed as the driver gawked at her, his jaw hanging open. Akira smiled back and pointed at the car in front; he stood on the brakes just in time. The police officer shook his head and grinned. Akira chuckled and gave him a thumbs-up.

"You better get away from the curb or you're going to cause an accident."

Akira spun around. "Bobby!"

They hugged. Bobby had slimmed down and seemed more muscular than when she'd last seen him.

"Wow, you look great."

"I ... okay. Thank you." He smiled and pointed to a beat-up white Ford Explorer double-parked in front of several cars. "My car's right there. No more luggage?"

"I shipped it to the motel. I'll do anything not to carry my own shit."

He gestured to the back of the Explorer. "Hope it's not too funky for you."

She looked at the car and shook her head. "Thought you'd have a Mustang by now."

"Nah, but thank you for sending way too much money my way."

They got into the Explorer, and Akira said, "I thought about you, Bobby. All the time. That day, you saved two lives with one shot."

"I did? You're being enigmatic now."

"Kyle is not the only reason I'm back. We have lots to talk about. I'm just so glad to see you, my friend."

"Yeah, let's get the fuck out of here."

They took the 405 freeway south. The traffic got lighter, and the drive to Oceanside was better than it would have been driving to Ventura. Wilshire had burned her home to the ground. But not before Bobby and his friends had gotten to it. They'd retrieved her belongings and, of course, Kyle's body.

"We got most of what you wanted," Bobby said. "Computers, weapons, and the diamonds. As you instructed, I used them to buy the place on Oceanside and put my guys on salary. And most importantly, we got Kyle and I used my connections to get him cremated."

"Your guys?"

"Yakuzas. Apparently, they got some kind of approval from their clan's boss to stay here as long as I need them. Do you know anything about that?"

Akira nodded.

"After what you just told me, I guess it was the right call."

"And Oceanside?"

"I figured it was far enough from everything. You've never been?"

"Never been."

"You'll like it. So, what did you mean back at the airport about me saving two lives?"

"I was pregnant."

"*What the fuck?* Where's—"

"It's a girl, Mina. But they took her."

"No shit, That's why we're paying these people a visit?"

"Yes. Wilshire. And I have a plan."

CHAPTER 38

Ashes

Two hours later they arrived at the beachfront property. Bobby turned into a double-car garage and parked next to a brand-new black Lamborghini Murcielago. The garage door closed behind them.

Akira looked at the Lamborghini. "What the fuck? I thought you were happy with this piece of shit."

"I am," Bobby said. "That's for you."

"You got me a Lambo?" She smiled. "That was a stupid move."

"Was it though?" Bobby said as a smirk grew from the side of his mouth.

"Now I'll have to drive it. Wow, can I even see through those black-tinted windows?"

"Not from outside. That's the point."

"You're crazy," she said.

"Hell, yeah."

———————

The house had been built in the 1940s. Around the back, a patio led to a private sandy beach. The inside boasted vaulted ceilings and a stone fireplace. Akira eyed the mantel, where a black urn stood. Next to it were Akira's family's swords—the nodachi, the katana, and the tanto dagger.

She looked at Bobby. "I see you got my swords, but is that—"

"Yeah, it's Kyle." Bobby handed her the urn in which a dragon had been beautifully carved. "It's obsidian."

"It's beautiful," Akira said.

"This artist I know did it for me ... for you."

"Thank you."

"You sure don't want to stay here?" Bobby asked.

"No, I'm good. I need my own space for now. The motel is just fine."

"Let me know if you change your mind. It's small, but there are three bedrooms. One's already taken."

"You got a girl?" Akira said.

"No, I don't do girls. It's one of my guys, Bardot."

"Sorry, I didn't know."

"Nah, I'm not gay."

"Is he French?"

"No, he's yakuza. He's Japanese. What's with the questions? Wait, do I look gay to you?"

"No, Bobby, there isn't a look. And it's not a bad thing."

"Anyway, I'm not." He said in a serious tone.

She chuckled and tapped him on the shoulder. "I'm famished. Wanna order some food?"

———————

Akira looked over at the coastline. Catalina Island was to the right, another island to the left whose name she couldn't remember. She opened the window and the ocean breeze caressed her face like a refreshing shower. Her cell phone rang.

"You dressed?" Bobby asked.

"No, I'm not. You okay?"

"Get dressed. You won't believe it. I found them. I'll be there in five."

Akira put on a leather jacket, black jeans, and combat boots, then holstered a 9mm Glock. She flicked a five-inch butterfly knife open and shut a few times. Each time the blades came together, the image of a scorpion formed.

She pocketed it in her jeans, then headed downstairs using the motel's back exit. Bobby was waiting for her in the alleyway. She got in the Explorer.

"Can't believe we found these fuckers," Bobby said.

"No way, just a day after I came back?"

"I've been looking for three years. Had a good lead two months ago and it paid off big time."

"What's the plan?"

"Don't need a plan. My guys are there. They're just waiting for us."

"I'm impressed. You're running a good crew," Akira said.

"It's been hard trying to find those two fuckers without alerting Wool ... Will?"

"Wilshire."

Akira smiled as a hand grabbed the side of her seat.

"So, you're Akira?"

Akira almost jumped out of her skin. She pulled the Glock out and pointed it at the head of a young Japanese man.

"Whoa! You're a quick draw!" he said, snickering. "Sorry for startling you, boss. That was not my intent."

Akira withdrew the gun and glared at Bobby.

"Fuck. Sorry. This is Bardot—the guy I was telling you about."

"I could have shot him," Akira said, and unbuckled her seat belt. She turned around and looked at Bardot.

"Chill, boss. Yeah, I'm Bardot. Like Brigitte Bardot, I'm deadly but gorgeous. And I love your look, all dark and slick."

His voice was cool and elegant. He had shoulder-length black hair and wore a tight white T-shirt and orange plaid slim jeans. And like a typical yakuza gangster, besides the stunted pinkie, his muscular body was covered with tattoos. Strapped under his armpit was a Beretta in a leather holster.

"What's up, Bardot? So, are you two a couple?"

Akira smirked and Bobby rolled his eyes.

"Really?" Bobby asked.

Bardot chuckled. "Girl, I'm not much for crackers. If I have white bread, it better be Italian. And no disrespect, but Bobby is a keeper, and I ain't keeping anybody. Bitch, I'm a praying mantis. I eat and swallow the whole thing up. I'm a lover and a killer," he said, and licked his lips.

Bobby rolled his eyes again and floored the Explorer, taking it up to eighty. Akira cracked up.

"Okay, you two, stop busting my cracker balls for a sec, will you?" Bobby said, but couldn't hide a smile. "I need to focus, all right?"

A Cobra radar detector on the dashboard started beeping.

"What's up with that?" Akira said.

"No big deal. See those lines?" Bardot pointed at the readout. "It's like a volume. The closer the police cars are, the more volume you get, and the shorter the interval in the beeping. Right now, it's probably on the street and not on the freeway, about three miles away." He leaned closer to Akira. "Hey, boss, back in Japan I heard a story. They say you killed two men with a paperclip. Is it true?"

"No, Bardot, it was not a paperclip. I don't travel with office supplies."

"I knew it."

"It was a bobby pin."

Bardot's eyes widened, and he slouched back on the seat.

Akira turned to Bobby. "Where is this place?"

"Salton Sea. Stan and the woman have been living there for years. Her name's Jo."

"And the gang's waiting," Bardot said. "McQueen, Travolta and Poitier. And, of course, moi."

"What's with the names?" Akira said. "Is this going where I think it's going?"

"Yeah, once we started working with Bobby, we decided not to use our real names. So we borrowed from actors we relate with. So obviously I'm gorgeous so I'm Brigitte Bardot."

"You are gorgeous. Right, Bobby? Isn't he gorgeous?"

Bobby shook his head.

Bardot snickered. "Aren't you going to answer that?"

CHAPTER 39

Salton Sea

Two hours later, Bobby took a right past an abandoned mobile-home park. The landscape was desolate, the vast lake bending over the horizon vanished into a barrier of mountains that jutted through the Californian desert.

It reminded Akira of an apocalyptic movie she'd seen but couldn't remember the title of. A pelican skimmed the briny water under a glorious sky. But the lake was deceptive, its water oily. A pale-yellow slick shimmered on the deep turquoise, and thousands of dead fish floated next to mounds of urban junk. The morbid sight nauseated Akira. And then there were the beaches … hundreds of feathered carcasses—pelicans and other birds frozen as they'd tried to escape the poisonous waves that lapped at the shore.

To her right, the sagebrush was taking over abandoned buildings that had been left to rot, charred mid-century architectural skeletons declaring the end of the world ... another scene from that film she still couldn't remember the title of came to mind. A corner was crowded with telephone poles. Closer inspection revealed Akira's mistake. Not poles. Dead palm trees without their tops. Nothing could survive this environment. And yet some still wanted to live here. What the fuck was that about?

They continued south around the lake until they reached another abandoned town. A faded billboard with a woman in a red swimsuit, water skiing, welcomed tourists to a flourishing resort. The now-abandoned Bombay Beach.

Another sign read *Last Resort*. Akira's first thought was that she'd arrived in hell.

They drove past a pile of rusted cars and more animal carcasses as the road turned into a narrow lane. Akira examined the shoreline.

"First time here?" Bobby said.

"Yeah, I've heard about it, but in all these years I've never been."

Bardot awoke from a nap and leaned over. "Are we there yet?"

"Almost," Bobby said.

A short distance later the road became packed

dirt. Within a fenced lot stood a shiny Airstream.

"Is that it?" Akira asked.

Bobby nodded. "Yeah, that's it."

He drove through a broken chain-link gate. Drag marks in the dirt led to a black Chevy Suburban outfitted with a large brush guard, Under the SUV was the missing section of the gate.

Akira got out of the car, ripped off her jacket, and threw it into the vehicle. "It must be over a hundred out here. And what the heck is that stench?"

"Decay at the bottom of the lake," Bobby said. "Dead birds and fish on the shore. This place is fucked."

Akira spat on the ground, trying to get rid of the polluted dust she'd inhaled. She wiped her mouth with her forearm. "Why here?"

"Exactly the point." Bobby answered.

"Jesus. Smells like rotten eggs. And it's hot as hell," Bardot said and coughed.

Two young Japanese men emerged from the Airstream.

The first was tall, African Japanese, built like a middle-weight boxer. He had a shaved head and wore a pinstriped suit and tie over Chuck Taylors. The second was medium height, Japanese. Short blond hair poked out from under a vaquero's hat. He wore a short-sleeved blue mechanic's shirt with a Ford tag, khaki Dickies, and cowboy boots. Both had missing pinkies.

"This is Poitier," Bobby said, nodding toward the Black guy. He turned to the blond. "And this is McQueen. They all know who you are."

The two men bowed.

"Good meeting you, boys. From now on, no more bowing," Akira said. "I understand the respect you're showing but it takes time and attracts attention. Understood?"

"Understood, boss," they said in unison.

McQueen bowed again, then apologized. Poitier slapped the back of his head, making McQueen's hat fall off. McQueen caught it mid-air and put it right back on.

"Watch out with the hat, brah," McQueen said.

Poitier snickered. "Forgive him—he's old fashioned."

McQueen adjusted the angle of the hat, then glared at Poitier. "You're such an ass."

"Let's go in," Bobby said.

The Airstream was over thirty feet and forty years old, but had been remodeled and looked brand new. Piled up under it was desert sage brush turned into tumbleweed. Before Bobby could reach the door, it opened, and a tall Japanese man in his late twenties with a martial artist's physique emerged. He wore a white suit, black dress shirt and white patent leather shoes speckled with blood.

He stood on the fold-down stoop, and looked down at Akira.

"This," Bobby said, "is our weapons specialist. Akira, meet Travolta."

"It's a pleasure and an honor to meet you, boss," Travolta said, then combed his cherry-red hair back, and posed like Tony Manero in *Saturday Night Fever*. He jumped off the stoop and bowed.

"We'll tell him, boss," Poitier said.

"Tell me what?" Travolta asked.

Akira smiled. Bobby shook his head. They stepped into the trailer.

Inside was just as Akira had expected—clean and spacious.

In the kitchen area was a woman wearing a white tank top and short jeans. She was gagged and tied to a chair.

She was gorgeous, Akira said so before she could stop herself.

Bobby nodded. "That there is Jo. Even more beautiful than I remember. First time I've laid eyes on her since the night they drugged me."

Jo was trying to say something. Her eyes widened. Bobby slipped the gag off her mouth.

"What's going on? Do I know you?" Jo asked.

She was covered in powdery desert dirt. Her face was bruised and there was dried blood under her nose.

Bobby opened the trailer door and stuck his head out. "Hey, McQueen! What happened to her?"

"She ran, boss. Put up quite a fight."

"Yeah, watch out with that one." Travolta said.

Bobby ducked back in, grabbed the woman's head from under her chin, almost lifting her and the chair. He leaned in. She winced and clenched her teeth.

Akira could almost taste Bobby's anger. This woman was part of the team that Wilshire had sent to kill Sir Charles Barton. And one more reason why Lily was dead.

Bobby cocked his head, his face just inches away from hers. "You don't remember? We met in a bathroom three years ago. You almost got me killed, and you're the reason why my friend's dead."

Akira leaned on a countertop. Jo looked up at her. Akira pulled out the Glock, put one in the chamber, then peeked out from an open window. "Hey, Tony, you got a suppressor?"

"Coming right up," Travolta said.

"What's going on? What do you guys want?" Jo asked. Her left eye wept with a mixture of blood and aqueous humor.

"You sure you don't remember me?" Bobby asked again.

"No, I fucking don't."

"LAX, three years ago, Concourse Hotel. My name is Bobby." He let her go. Jo dropped on the chair, and whimpered and looked up at him.

"You look different. You got a haircut and lost weight."

"Where's Stan?" Bobby asked.

"He's on his way back from Palm Springs. Should be back any minute," Jo spat blood on the ground, "He's not going to like this."

Akira spotted Jo's cell phone, flipped it open, and searched the history. "She's telling the truth. Stan texted her about twenty minutes ago." She eyed a clock on a wall. "He should be here in a few."

Travolta came into the trailer and handed her the suppressor.

"Her man's on his way back. Park the cars behind the trailer and bring him in when he arrives. Don't let him see you," Bobby said.

Travolta stepped back out and called out instructions to Poitier and McQueen.

Akira looked out the window again, watching the guys moving the cars out of sight.

Bobby stared into Jo's face. "You know, Jo, I must give you the credit that you deserve. You're the reason I'm a killer."

He'd changed, for sure. Akira could see it. Not the man he'd been three years earlier. For better or for worse, something had snapped. Perhaps it was the moment he'd seen Lily's body, discarded in a roll of polyethylene, and Hassan's head flowering like a rose. Killing a man, no matter the evil, still made him a murderer, and twice if you included the man he'd killed during a boxing match that ended his career ten years earlier.

Akira twisted the silencer on the Glock. Jo watched intently, her body quivering, drops of sweat popping on her face.

"What can I do for you? What do you want? The money?" Jo said.

"Nah, we want to know if you heard something. That's all," Bobby said.

"Bobby, may I?" Akira asked.

"Yes, boss. She's all yours."

"You're the boss?" Jo asked with a glimmer of hope.

Maybe she believed that woman to woman, she could get out of this situation. Maybe she thought she could end this.

Maybe she didn't know Akira.

"Shut the fuck up," Akira spat, and placed the tip of the silencer on Jo's lips. "Shake your head either way to answer my questions. We are here for many reasons, but there is one, and only one, I care about. Understand?"

Jo nodded, sweat dripping from her forehead.

"Have you ever been to LA?"

Jo nodded.

Akira let out a tiny smile. "This is good."

She gave Bobby the Glock, then turned back to Jo, who seemed to relax now that the gun wasn't pointed at her mouth.

"Have you ever been to 5900 Wilshire, over there by Miracle Mile? It's a tall building. You can't miss it. Just past the old May Co. building."

Jo looked at Bobby on her left.

"Don't look at him. Look at me," Akira said, and grabbed Jo's head, twisting it like it was a marionette.

Jo shook her head—no.

Akira punched her nose, breaking it. Jo screamed and lowered her head.

"That wasn't smart," Akira said. She grabbed Jo's hair and pulled her chin up. Her nose was bleeding like an open faucet.

Bobby handed her a paper towel. "Should I get McQueen to pack her nose?"

"Nah, I've done it many times."

Akira cleaned the blood off the woman's face, tore the towel into small pieces and began stuffing the paper inside her nostrils with her thumbs. Jo winced and tried to move her head away, but Akira held her face vise-like.

Bobby handed her more paper, and Akira finished packing Jo's nose.

"Feeling better?"

Jo nodded as tears streamed down her face.

"Need some water?" Bobby asked.

Jo shook her head.

"Want a drink?" Akira asked.

Jo nodded.

Bobby looked around and grabbed a bottle of tequila, then filled a tumbler from the sink generously. He put the glass to Jo's lips and she gulped it down, then sighed.

"Good," Akira said. "Let's start again. You're a trained assassin just like me, right?"

Jo's eyes looked clearer. The alcohol had quelled some of the fear, no doubt. She looked at Akira and nodded.

Akira knew exactly what it was like being on the other side of it. But not this woman. Sweat, blood and tequila had collected at the top of her lip. Akira figured this was a first for her.

A knock came on the trailer wall signaled a warning from the boys. Stan had arrived at the property in a white Silverado.

Jo screamed, but Akira punched her hard in the stomach and pulled the gag up over her mouth.

Stan got out of the car and came through the front door. "Hey babe, what happened to the gate?"

A gun was pressed against his back. He was shoved inside the trailer, Bardot behind.

"Get in," Bardot barked.

Bobby knocked Stan to his knees, and the man

stared wide-eyed at Jo.

"You, okay? Jesus, what's happening?"

Akira yanked the gag down. Jo shook her head as Bardot jammed the cold barrel of his gun against the back of Stan's neck.

"Who are you?" Stan asked.

Bobby gave the Glock back to Akira, and she pointed it at Stan's head.

"I want you to shut the fuck up. Shake your head for a no; nod for a yes. Can you do that?" Akira said.

Stan looked defeated, and nodded repeatedly.

"First, let me take you back a few years. This is Bobby. You took money from his boss. His boss tried to kill him, then his best friend, Lily, was murdered. Your people then took my three-year-old daughter. Blah, blah, blah. We are fucking pissed. End of story," Akira said.

Stan looked at Bobby. His face blanched as he recognized him. He gasped, opened his mouth to speak, but Bobby just shook his head. Stan put his hands up, but Bardot twisted them behind his back and zipped-tied his wrists.

Akira turned to Jo, keeping the gun pointed at Stan. Bardot stepped out of the trailer, away from the line of fire.

Akira took a deep breath. Sweat dripped from Stan's forehead and pooled onto the floor.

"Jo, this is how it is. My daughter, Mina, is

three years old. She's everything to me. I would come back from the dead to save her. Some might say I already have."

"You did," Bobby added.

"Have you heard anything during your time freelancing for Wilshire about her, and where she could be?" Akira asked.

Jo trembled, blood dripping from her nose. She looked at Stan, who shook his head, warning her not to answer.

Akira depressed the trigger and shot Stan between the eyes. He dropped forward, and crumpled onto the floor. Blood and brain matter sprayed behind him and out of the trailer.

Jo screamed, "No! Motherfucker!"

Akira gave the gun back to Bobby, flicked open the butterfly knife, and cut the tie around Jo's right arm. She grabbed her wrist.

"I'm going to cut you right here, from below your elbow down to your wrist. You'll die slowly unless you answer my question. If you tell me the truth, I'll make it quick. Do I need to repeat myself?"

Jo shook her head.

"Speak."

"Yes. Fuck it. I did hear about your daughter ... chatter about a little girl ... and some guy. He was Italian, Alessio ... something like that. They were saying he took her to, um ... Rome? I'm pretty sure they said the Vatican."

"The Vatican?"

"Yes. They didn't know her name, so they were calling her the Vatican child."

"The Vatican child?"

"Yes, Wilshire had been involved helping the Vatican covering up sexual abuse by priests in Boston. And there's something going on in there in Rome. Something bigger's happening there."

"Fuck."

"Are you going to kill me?" Jo asked.

"No loose ends, right?" Akira said.

"That's fair, I guess. I'd do the same. I mean, I've done the same."

Jo tried to smile beneath her broken nose and the blood that had collected on her chin. She looked at Bobby. "Hey big dawg, it wasn't personal."

"I know. Just business," Bobby said.

Jo turned to Akira. "Let's get this over with."

Akira put her knife back in her pocket. Bobby handed her the Glock and walked out of the trailer.

———

Outside, Travolta, Bardot, and Poitier dowsed the Airstream with gasoline. McQueen slipped behind the wheel of the Suburban.

Then the quiet was broken by the unmistakable muffled pop of a pistol.

Akira came through the door, Glock in hand, the barrel still smoking. Then she got in the Explorer, Bobby at the wheel.

The guys lit the trailer on fire and got in the Suburban. They followed the Explorer as it exited the property. Behind them, the Airstream was engulfed in flames. It exploded, throwing debris everywhere. Yet more urban trash in the already fucked-up landscape.

CHAPTER 40

Stayin' Alive

Akira parked the Lamborghini in front of Denny's. The crew climbed out of the SUV and walked into the restaurant—Travolta in his signature white suit. Poitier, Bardot, and McQueen behind him.

Akira and Bobby stayed in the Lambo.

"How long we've been doing this?" she said. "Two weeks? I'm still surprised this isn't attracting too much attention. Especially Travolta."

"Nah, we've been making this stop for a while, and the worst we've had is people asking us for autographs. I mean we're like a mile from Disney and Warner Brothers' back lots. It kind of works like a disguise. It's Burbank. Nobody cares."

"I guess I'm a ball of nerves," Akira said.

"Well, today's D-day. And these guys are like

Gibraltar. It's good to be nervous. C'mon, Javier always gives us good seats."

They went into Denny's and the manager came over. "Hey, Prez. The guys are being seated. Same as usual."

"Prez? Is this a new thing?" Akira asked as they headed to the back of the restaurant.

"Yeah, the guys started calling me that. What can I say? I don't have a favorite actor."

They both chuckled.

The morning crowd hadn't arrived yet so the place wasn't too busy. A waitress approached their table. The nametag pinned to her uniform said *Norma*. She was a beautiful woman in her fifties, with a beauty mark above her lip.

"Hello, boys and girls. What can I get you started with?"

Everyone grinned.

"How's that TV show pilot going?" she said to Bobby.

"Very well. Hopefully they don't cancel it before it airs," he replied.

Norma took their order, gave them a wink, and headed back to the kitchen.

"She's so hot," Travolta said.

McQueen shook it head. "What's wrong with you? You say that every time."

"I never said that before," Travolta answered.

Everyone else laughed.

"What?" Travolta asked.

"Sounds like a love story to me, Tony," Akira said.

"Whatever." Travolta rolled his eyes.

An hour later their table had been cleared. In front of them was an empty glass with pieces of paper in it. Akira covered it with her hand, shook it, and placed it back down on the table next to a napkin with their names written on it. Bobby plucked a piece of paper from the glass and handed it to her. She held it for a few seconds.

"Boss, darling, the suspense is killing me," Bardot said.

Akira unfolded it. "And the winner is *Aladdin*."

"What do you mean, *Aladdin*? The cartoon?" Poitier asked.

"It's not a cartoon, idiot. It's an animated feature film," McQueen said.

"Exactly, as I said, a cartoon."

"Non-inclusive bullshit fable with racist overtones," Bardot said.

"Yeah, Bardot, but why is it wrong?" Akira said and put a check mark on the napkin next to Bardot's name.

"I said non-inclusive and racist. That's two points," Bardot said.

"You only get a point at a time—you know that," Akira said.

"Bardot, you know where you're going to be?"

Bobby asked.

"Yessir. I'm on the two guards by the elevator."

"And?" Akira asked.

"Yeah, got to do that before they cut me to shreds with their MP5s," Bardot added.

Travolta smirked and doodled on a napkin.

Akira smiled. "Back to the game. Okay, two more questions: Who directed it? Just the first names are enough to get the point."

"I know there were two—Don and Tom," Bardot said.

"I have no idea, but probably two old white guys. Tom and Jerry," Poitier said.

"She wasn't asking who's in charge of this country," McQueen said.

"It's Ron and John, the best directors in the whole world, if you ask me," Travolta said, his head down, focused on the doodle.

"Correct!" Akira said, and put a mark by Travolta's name.

"Great, that's the movie he picked," McQueen said, and sipped his coffee.

"Tony, who's your target?" Bobby asked.

"I'm on the guard at ten o'clock, closest to the receptionist. One blast to the head should do it," Travolta said without looking up.

"You haven't won the Benelli yet," Poitier said.

"Tony, don't kill the civilian. That's all I ask," Bobby said.

"Not my first rodeo, Prez." Travolta stopped drawing and held up both hands. "Still got my ten digits for a reason. I don't fuck up," he said with a big grin.

"Fucking show off," Bardot said.

Bobby tapped the table. "Back to Aladdin."

"This is bullshit. I don't watch kids' movies," Poitier said.

"We watched *Sleeping Beauty* together," Bardot said.

"Yeah? Who was sleeping, and who was the beauty? Do you have pictures?" Travolta snickered.

"You have to ask?" Bardot said.

"No, *you* watched *Sleeping Beauty*. I drank a six-pack," Poitier said. "Besides, *Sleeping Beauty* is an adult movie. I was watching to see which of the seven dwarfs looks like you."

"That's *Snow White*, you idiot," McQueen said.

Everyone chuckled.

"No, bitches. I'm the queen, the evil bitch that stomps on your ass and tears your heart out," Bardot said, moving his head cobra style.

"You should get a point just for that," Akira said.

"Actually, the queen dies in the end," Travolta said, still drawing.

"McQueen, what's your six in the lobby?" Bobby asked.

"I'm covering Tony and taking care of the civilian."

Bobby nodded. "Good man. Taking care of civilians."

"Another question," Akira said. "What's the name of Aladdin's magic carpet?"

"Damn, I have no idea what this is about," Poitier said.

"Carpet," Travolta said.

"Correct. One more point."

Akira drew a second mark next to Travolta's name.

"Carpet? Wow, those Disney writers had a chance to make something out of the magic carpet and named it Carpet?" Poitier said.

"Who picked this movie?" McQueen asked.

"Really? You have to ask?" Bobby said.

Akira sipped her tea. "Okay, what's the monkey's name?"

"How do you remember all these questions, boss?" Poitier asked.

"She has a photographic memory," Bobby said. "Don't interrupt the flow."

"Abu," Travolta said. "And as a bonus, he's a capuchin monkey, which is weird because they are native to Brazil, specifically the Amazon Forest. Not Aladdin-land."

"Well done, Professor Disney," Poitier said.

"Where are you, Poitier?" Bobby asked.

"I'm taking out the two mercs in the middle of the lobby."

"You got it. Just make sure you don't kill Tony."

"Yeah, don't kill me," Travolta said, still doodling.

"One more for Tony," Akira said. "Why is the genie blue?"

"Because of the way the gases the Genie is made of react with the atmosphere," Travolta said.

Everyone's jaws dropped.

"Yes!" Akira gave him a fourth mark.

"How in the fuck do you know this shit?" Bardot asked.

"Has anybody else seen this movie?" Akira said.

"I give up," McQueen said. "Just give him the fucking Benelli already."

Akira looked around the table. "You guys agree?"

Everybody nodded, except Bobby, who shook his head.

"No, we continue. We finish everything we start. Besides, I'm amused by how much Travolta knows about this movie," Bobby said.

"Okay, this is the last one. Why is Jasmine allowed to roam around without a hijab?" Akira asked.

Everyone turned to Travolta, waiting for an

answer. Travolta stopped drawing, looked up, and smirked.

"That's an easy one." He took a deep breath. "It's the future."

Akira winked at Bobby.

"As a gay man, I can't wait to get there myself," Bardot said.

"You mean, like a time-travel movie?" McQueen asked.

"Yeah, why not?" Travolta answered.

"Okay fuck it, he gets the Benelli M4," Bobby said.

"Great, he won the last time, too! Now this," Poitier whined.

"Gonna pump that M4 like a motherfucker!" Travolta said.

"This is not good; his ego is out of control. We can't continue feeding it like this," Poitier said.

Akira stood up. "So, are you ready?"

"Yes," Poitier said.

Bardot and McQueen nodded and smiled.

"Hell, yeah, let's do this," Travolta said, then stood up, swung his hips Tony Manero style, and began singing "Stayin' Alive," his Bee Gees impersonation pitch perfect.

The guys headed out of the restaurant. Akira put a hundred-dollar tip on the table and eyed Travolta's napkin. He'd drawn a close-to-perfect genie, only this one was armed with two machine guns, spraying at a group of men dressed in black. She pocketed the napkin and walked out to the parking lot and stood by the Lamborghini, taking a last look at everyone.

"Bobby," she said, "part two, one last time?"

Bobby nodded. "Part two. Bardot, you stay in the elevator. Once at the penthouse, you cover twelve o'clock. Take out everyone. Poitier, the CCTV in the elevator. You go to reception, wipe the drives and cloud storage. Tony and McQueen, you go to the offices. The boss and I go to Wilshire. Whatever you do, do not shoot the windows. Don't want glass falling onto the street. Last thing we need is law enforcement waiting for us when we're done." He took a deep breath. "Any questions?"

Everyone shook their heads.

"Hey, guys," Akira said. "Remember now, stayin' alive—that's all we need to do. Let's do this." She winked.

The Lambo's scissor door opened, and she slipped behind the wheel. Bobby got in the passenger seat. The engine roared like a T-Rex and she drove out of the lot, the crew in the Suburban behind her.

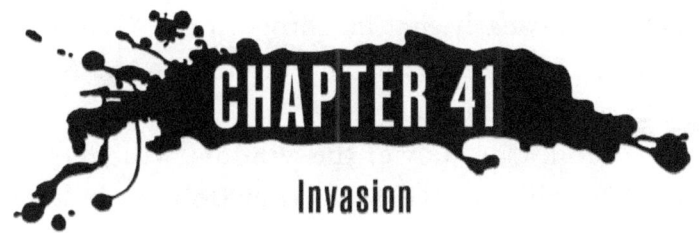

CHAPTER 41

Invasion

The crew in the Suburban had parked in front of the Wilshire building's entrance. Akira pulled up by the curb across the street and left the Lamborghini's engine idling. It sounded like a snoring dragon.

A black limousine drove up the parking ramp and into the street, merged with the traffic, and stopped right next to the Murcielago.

The limo's window began to descend. A voice called out, "Hey! Nice car. I'm buying one when I get back to Italy. Lower your window—I want to ask you something."

The familiarity of the voice niggled her, and she looked toward the now open window.

Adriano.

"Shit," Bobby hissed.

Adriano was supposed to have been on a flight back to Italy early that morning, not at Wilshire.

Adriano reached out and tapped on the Murcielago's blacked-out glass.

"C'mon, man. Lower the window, will you?"

Akira whipped a Glock from Bobby's holster and pointed it at Adriano, who was still gesturing for her to lower the window.

"Hey, I'm just saying it's a nice ride. Put the window down!" Adriano yelled.

Akira pulled the pistol's slide back loading the chamber.

"Don't do it," Bobby said.

She looked at her hand. It was trembling, the barrel tapping against the glass like a woodpecker. Her heart was racing.

"Stay calm. You kill him now, you'll never know where Mina is," Bobby said, and put his hand on the gun, lowering it.

"Don't look at him. Look away. Close your eyes and think."

"This motherfucker," Akira said, and took a deep breath.

Then she closed her eyes and Bobby pried the gun out of her hand.

"Vaffanculo!" Adriano yelled, then flipped her off and his limo drove away.

Bobby holstered the Glock. "Breathe in, my

friend. Focus on why we're here."

Akira gripped the steering wheel and let out an ear-piercing scream.

Then there was silence.

Bobby turned to her. "He must have changed his flight; he was supposed to be gone." He took a deep breath. "You good?"

"Yeah, I'm good," Akira said.

And suddenly, like she'd turned off a switch, she was all business. She revved the engine, made a U-turn, and drove down the parking garage ramp.

At the barrier gate, Bobby got out and used a screw gun to remove four large bolts from the arm blocking the entrance. He pulled it out of its housing and tossed it to one side. Akira drove through.

She parked by a lobby and Akira killed the engine. Bobby hid behind a column.

A security guard in full-on tactical gear emerged from the lobby, holding an MP5. He walked around to the driver's side of the Lamborghini's and Akira rolled down the black-tinted window. He leaned over and glanced into the car. Akira ignored him, instead yelling into her cell phone in Korean, like she was arguing with someone.

"Lady, you can't park here. We don't have valets. Do you—"

Akira jammed a taser under the man's chin, and fired off 75,000 volts.

The man crumpled onto the ground.

The scissor door opened with a sigh. Akira stepped out over the guard's body and took his MP5.

Bobby joined her and dragged the guard behind a parked car.

Then shot him twice in the head.

Akira twisted a suppressor into the MP5's barrel, checked the magazine, and loaded a round. Bobby pulled a walkie-talkie from his back pocket and set it to Channel One.

"McQueen, you good?" Bobby asked in Japanese.

"Yeah, we're in place."

"We're a go," Bobby said.

———————

McQueen, changed into a black Adidas tracksuit and white Adidas Superstar shoes, secured his walkie to his belt and joined the rest of the crew on the sidewalk—all similarly attired, except for Travolta in his signature Tony Manero ensemble. He handed Poitier and Bardot a gym bag each.

They slung the bags over their shoulders. Travolta tucked the Benelli M4 tactical shotgun under his jacket and grinned.

A few cars drove by, but it was clear except for a young delivery man who paid no attention to them. He held a large box of donuts and was going up the wide sandstone steps leading to the building's lobby.

"We're on," McQueen said.

He pulled a silenced H&K pistol from under his tracksuit, and they quickened their pace up the same steps, catching up to the delivery man as he entered the building.

They scanned the interior through the glass windows.

"Four enemies, one civilian. Two in the lobby and two by the elevators. Receptionist at the desk on the left," McQueen said.

Poitier and Bardot dropped their bags. Poitier pulled out a silenced AR-15. Bardot grabbed a silenced Kel-Tec Sub2000 with an armor-piercing 50-round drum.

They pushed the delivery man aside.

Then they fired.

Travolta blasted a guard's armored chest, knocking him off his feet. McQueen finished him with two pops to the head. The receptionist screamed and ducked under the sandstone desk.

Two more guards returned fire, but it was too late. Poitier sprayed one in the head and the other in the neck as Bardot was cutting the two guards by the elevators to shreds with the Kel-

Tec. Travolta blasted one more shot that blew the head off one of them. Bardot sprayed the remaining guard, hitting a sixth man behind him who'd emerged from a hallway beyond the elevators.

Then everything went quiet.

The smoke settled, and the smell of black powder hung in the air.

"Anybody hit?" McQueen asked.

Bardot lay on the ground in a pool of blood.

Poitier rushed over and turned him over. "Shit! Bardot!"

"I knew you loved me," Bardot said with a smile on his face.

Donuts lay squashed on the floor next to him. And by the mush, the delivery man's body.

The blood was his. Poitier shook his head, and grinned.

Bardot stood up, unzipped his jacket, and tossed it on the floor, revealing a Kevlar vest with two rounds embedded right in the middle. A tattoo of a two-headed dragon wrapped around his neck and trailed down to his wrists, his hands emerging from the dragons' mouths.

He wiped blood spatter off his face, plucked the bullets out of the vest and tossed them. "One of those fuckers shot me in the chest."

McQueen headed over to the reception desk. "Miss, are you okay?"

The young woman stared glacially at him,

clearly in shock. McQueen zip-tied her wrists and ankles and gagged her with duct tape from a roll tethered to his belt.

"Don't move," he said. "This is not your fight, understand?"

She nodded, terrified and compliant. McQueen pressed a button marked *ENTRY*. There was a beep as the glass doors locked.

An elevator chimed, the doors opened, and Bobby and Akira stepped out.

"All good?" Akira asked.

"Yeah, all good, smooth, on schedule," McQueen said.

"What's that?" Akira pointed at the delivery man's body.

"Shit, my bad. We'll clean it up," Poitier said.

He took a roll of plastic from his gym bag, then he and Bardot wrapped up the delivery guy and the guards and dragged them into to a side hallway, away from public view. Meanwhile, McQueen and Travolta cleaned the blood off the floor.

They regrouped at the elevators. Bardot pressed the call button. A few seconds later, the door marked with a P opened, and they all stepped in. Bobby eyed a CCTV camera in the corner of the ceiling.

"I'll take care of it," Poitier said, and bashed it with the stock of his AR-15 until it disconnected from its mount and fell on the floor.

Bobby pressed the button to the penthouse, and they were swept upward.

"Haven't been in the penthouse in over ten years," Akira said. "Last time I was here, I was about to kill a redhead bitch."

"What happened?" Bobby asked.

"Kyle talked me out of it."

"Oh."

"Funny or not, he ended up killing her three years ago, the day before he died. I'm still angry about it."

"About which part?" Bardot asked.

"Both."

"Why didn't he want you to kill her?" Travolta said.

"He said it was bad for business."

"But he killed her?" Travolta said.

"Yeah, it's confusing, isn't it?" Akira said.

"I don't remind you of her, do I?" Travolta asked, running his finger through his bright-red hair.

"No, Tony. Your hair is a different shade of red. I love your hair," she said, and winked at him.

He smiled awkwardly.

The elevator reached the thirty-first floor. The doors opened.

Two guards were standing by the reception desk, talking with the receptionist, their backs to the elevator. One was drinking from a paper cup; the other was laughing at something the receptionist had said.

The receptionist's eyes widened.

Bardot stood in the middle of the car. The rest of the crew moved to the side walls. Then he unleashed his Kel-Tec, firing his 50-round mag roll.

The two guards died on the spot. The receptionist ducked under her desk.

"How about the civilian?" Bardot asked.

Bobby shook his head. "She's not a civ—"

The receptionist emerged from one side of the massive stone desk, holding a pistol. She fired two rounds that missed Bardot by an inch, then ducked back behind it.

"Fucking-A," Bardot said.

He dropped to a knee and sprayed the desk with the armor-piercing rounds, punching through the sandstone like Swiss cheese. A spatter of blood painted the wall behind the desk, and he stopped firing. A chair spun around a few times, then collapsed.

All was quiet, the smoke settled, and powder burn hung in the air.

Akira and McQueen flanked Bardot, pointing their weapons and covering the group.

Bardot ejected his spent 50-round drum as Poitier handed him another.

Akira and McQueen ducked as two men armed

with MP5s emerged from a hallway.

Bardot fired and killed them both. Then he covered them from the elevator while Poitier headed for the reception desk where he'd wipe the CCTV footage and disable the alarms. McQueen and Travolta took a right. Akira and Bobby went left down a hallway she knew all too well—it led straight to the executive offices.

To her former boss.

Bobby followed, covering her six. To their right, a wall of glass provided a stunning view of Los Angeles, past the Dodger Stadium, Downtown LA, and beyond to the San Bernardino National Forest.

Today, she would tear this place apart.

A man bolted out of an office, one hand up, the other holding a pistol. "Don't shoot!"

Akira fired a burst from the silenced MP5, the sound reminding her of popcorn flowering. Part of the man's head was blown off, brain matter trailing away as he collapsed.

"Fuck you," she said.

As they stalked past the man, Bobby flipped the pistol from the dead man's hand, ejected the magazine, and threw it back into the hallway behind him. Then he expelled the chambered round and tossed the pistol into an open office. Bobby had never been part of an invasion, but knew enough not to leave a loaded weapon behind.

Akira popped her head into another office, but no one was there. Suppressed gunfire came from behind. Akira froze, her MP5 trained ahead into the hallway. Bobby spun around and looked back. Poitier had engaged a young man wielding a hammer but had cut him down to shreds with his AR-15. Poitier looked at Bobby and gave him a thumbs-up.

"Enemy down. Let's move," Bobby whispered to Akira.

They inched forward toward the main office. Toward Wilshire.

CHAPTER 42

The Son

Travolta and McQueen found the kitchen with a glass door. Inside was a young man in a faded Fe-dEx uniform, making coffee. He was listening to a Walkman plugged into a headset. There was a dead-bolt on the door, unlocked. Strange, McQueen thought. Why have a deadbolt on the outside of a kitchen door? He locked it. Travolta pointed the shotgun at the kid through the glass, his index fin-ger caressing the trigger, but McQueen reached out and lowered the barrel.

Travolta looked at him.

"He's neutral," McQueen whispered.

"Gotcha."

They continued past the kitchen.

A guard came out of a room up ahead, saw

them, reached for his pistol. McQueen squeezed off two silenced shots into his face. Travolta took the man's pistol and slipped it into the back of his pants.

Then McQueen tapped Travolta's shoulder and took the lead. He took a few steps, then held out his hand. They stopped behind a square pillar jutting from the wall next to a conference room.

To the right, floor-to-ceiling glass offered a view of Wilshire Boulevard and the Hollywood hills in the distance.

Travolta's eyes narrowed. "Damn," he whispered. "I can see the Hollywood sign from here."

McQueen shook his head. "Great, we'll visit Madame Tussauds later to see if they made a wax figure of your dead ass."

Travolta shrugged. McQueen popped his head around the pillar. Inside the conference room were three men, two in black suits and ties, the other man wearing a shiny gray suit over a white shirt.

He raised three fingers and checked his weapon as Travolta added two more shells to the M4.

They fired. The glass doors shattered and they busted into the room. Travolta shot the two black suits in the head and the gray in the chest. All dead.

"Dude! That was something," McQueen said.

"You think the kitchen heard us?"

"Nah."

They both took a deep breath and exited the conference room.

"How did you know the gray suit wasn't wearing a vest?" McQueen asked.

"You don't wear Vanquish II garments over a Kevlar," Travolta said.

"Whatever. Let's move on."

Travolta smirked and reloaded the shotgun. "Did you know that silkworms feel pain?" Travolta said.

McQueen let out a long sigh "There you go again. Is this the onset of dementia?"

They continued past the bathroom and back to the kitchen. The kid was still making coffee.

McQueen turned to Travolta. "Watch out!" he yelled.

A massive man, over seven feet tall, emerged from a bathroom. A black ballistic face shield covered his head. Like Darth Vader on steroids. In his right hand was a tactical Bowie-style gutting knife.

"Hey, Tim, what do you think about this knife? ... Tim?"

He looked around, adjusted his mask, and headed toward the body lying in the middle of the hallway.

"Tim?"

McQueen shot him in the head twice.

The mask didn't budge. Instead, the man swung the knife toward Travolta. Travolta backed up and shot him in the chest and the face. The guy charged him, knocking Travolta to the floor as if he wasn't there. McQueen got two more shots out of his pistol, hit the guy square in the chest, but the guy kept coming.

He leveled McQueen to the floor, straddled him, raised the huge Bowie.

———————

Travolta came from behind, tried to pull the guy's mask off, but the man reached around and grabbed him, launching him upward and hurtling him ten feet into the hallway.

Bardot watched them from the elevator, ejected a clip, and grabbed another magazine from the gym bag. It was marked with red tape. Travolta made eye contact and nailed Bardot with a glare—red tape meant incendiary rounds. Yes, they'd pierce a bulletproof vest and kill this fucker, but they'd blow up on impact like a small grenade. The hallway would turn into an inferno.

Fuck, he doesn't realize. He'll kill us both.

Bardot loaded the mag and aimed.

Travolta stretched his hand out and yelled, "No!"

Bardot took a deep breath, scoping his prey,

waiting for the moment.

"Stop!" Travolta yelled. "You loaded a red one!"

Bardot looked down at the clip, dropped the submachine gun. A few feet away, the large man was still on McQueen. And McQueen was losing the fight, the blade an inch from his face.

Bardot grabbed a taser from the gym bag and slid it like a hockey puck over to Travolta.

Travolta grabbed it and jammed it against the guy's hand, sending 75,000 volts through him and McQueen. Both men began to spasm and foam at the mouth. Travolta tossed the taser and picked up the Benelli.

The large man dropped the knife but was still conscious. He punched McQueen in the face. Travolta vaulted over him, jammed the shotgun under the mask at the base of his neck, and fired.

———

McQueen came to, stars and black specks floating in his vision. Then everything turned crimson. His face felt hot and wet.

He could taste blood.

He wiped his eyes and took in the carnage. It was grotesque. The large man had collapsed on the floor at McQueen's side, his head in bits. The shotgun's barrel had brain matter on it, and crackled from the heat, like the sound eggs made when being fried. Travolta let out a guttural scream. McQueen gave him a thumbs-up and laughed.

Travolta's once-white suit had turned into a Jackson Pollock painting. Stuck to the lapel was an ear. Travolta flicked it away in disgust.

Then they heard gunfire.

———————

Akira and Bobby had cleared all the rooms leading to the CEO's suite. In the hallway, a guard lay in a pool of blood, still holding onto a Glock. Bobby pried the gun away from him, ejected the magazine and pocketed it, then ejected the round in the chamber and tossed the pistol in a trashcan.

"You hit?" Akira asked, her eyes on the hallway ahead of them.

"Yeah, my left arm. Through and through. I'm peachy."

Travolta and McQueen caught up with them.

"You okay, Prez?" Travolta asked.

Bobby's eyes widened. "What the fuck happened to you?"

"We argued with a large man," McQueen said.

"Motherfucker ruined my suit," Travolta said.

Akira nodded toward an eight-foot door at the end of the hallway—the CEO's suite. "Take down that door, Tony, and I'll get you a new one."

Travolta stepped up to the door and blasted it with four rounds, one at each hinge. Akira aimed the MP5. Bobby and McQueen did the same with their pistols.

The door teetered, then slammed down onto the office floor, kicking up dust. Bobby threw a flash-bang inside, and they all turned away, shielding their ears.

Two seconds later, there was a boom. The aftershock blew ceiling tiles, sheets of paper and other debris back into the hallway. The air was filled with the unmistakable smell of magnesium.

Travolta entered first, followed by Akira.

The room was empty.

Akira pointed the MP5 at the desk and yelled, "Get the fuck out. Now."

She nodded at Travolta, who fired two slugs at a massive glass cabinet behind the desk. Nazi memorabilia, corporate awards, and framed war mementos exploded and shattered.

"Is the desk bulletproof?" Akira yelled.

Two hands emerged.

"Don't shoot!" a male voice with a hint of a German accent said.

A man stood up from behind the desk.

Thomas Wilshire.

The German was in his mid-sixties, medium build, with slicked-back silver-gray hair. He wore a tailored Brioni Vanquish II suit made of the rarest silk thread. His blue eyes skimmed the desk. If he was looking for an advantage, he didn't find it. The confusion on his face turned into disdain as he glanced from Akira's MP5 to Travolta's Benelli M4, and finally to Bobby's and McQueen's pistols.

All pointing at him.

"You think you can get out of this, Thomas?" Akira said.

"You should be dead," Wilshire said. "You're dead."

"Can I shoot him, please?" Travolta asked.

"No, we are not shooting him," Bobby replied.

"That's true," Wilshire said, and came around the desk, his hand still up. "I can help you. I can get all of you out of this mess."

"Can you?" Akira asked.

"May I?" Wilshire pointed at a bottle of Kors vodka on top of a bar counter.

"Sure, have a drink, Thomas," Akira said.

Wilshire grabbed the bottle, looked at it for a moment. The crystal bottle was decorated with platinum and gold leaf. His hands shook as he twisted the cap off.

"Beautiful, isn't it?" He poured a healthy measure into a square tumbler. "It's a bit like you, I guess."

Akira lowered the MP5. "How so?"

"Oh, fuck, is he going to tell a story?" Mc-

Queen said.

Travolta nodded. "Yep."

"This vodka is legendary," Wilshire said. "Like you. This was a gift from Czar Nicholas II of Russia to his cousin, George V, the king of England. But the shipment was lost and never arrived."

"For fuck's sake, are we really going to let him finish?" McQueen said.

Travolta nodded again. "Yep."

"For reasons unknown," Wilshire said, "it remained hidden for almost a century and was recently rediscovered. So yes, it's a bit like you. And it came back worth much more than when it left. This bottle cost me $25,000." Wilshire slammed the vodka and refilled the glass. "So, yes, I can do a lot for you. All of you. So how much are you worth? That's the question, no?"

Akira drove her fist into Wilshire's stomach so hard that he was momentarily lifted from the ground. Then he dropped to his knees, the wind knocked out of him. He opened his mouth, gasping for air, and vomited up the Kors.

Akira walked over to the bar, grabbed the vodka bottle, and smashed it against the wall. "You know why I'm here, right?"

"Yes, but I don't know where ... where she is." Wilshire staggered to his feet.

Travolta and McQueen flanked him and held him fast while Akira forced one of his hands onto the desk and splayed the fingers. A swastika tat-too peeked from under his cuff. Akira flicked open her butterfly knife, looked Wilshire in the eyes, and severed his pinky.

Wilshire screamed, then vomited more of his precious vodka onto the desk.

"Where is she?" Akira said.

Tears rolled down Wilshire's cheeks. "The b-black folder."

Travolta snickered. "He's yakuza now."

McQueen couldn't hold in a chuckle.

Akira eyed a folder on the desk. She opened it. Inside was a dossier. She scanned it and, aston-ished, handed it to Bobby.

His eyes widened as he looked at the content. "Motherfuckers."

Akira plunged the knife into Wilshire's neck and twisted.

He screamed and collapsed.

Dead.

Bobby searched the desk drawers, and held up a PalmPilot.

"Bingo, here's the 411 on these fuckers."

Akira rummaged in Wilshire's pocket, found his cell phone, and handed it to Bobby.

"We're done," she said.

They headed for the elevator, where Poitier and Bardot were stationed.

Bobby handed Wilshire's cell phone and

PalmPilot to Poitier. "Need to scrub through these."

"You got it, Prez," Poitier said.

Bobby pulled the walkie-talkie from his back pocket, "We're good to go?" Bobby asked.

"All quiet at the elevator, Prez." Bardot said.

"We're on our way." Bobby added.

"How about FedEx guy?" McQueen asked.

"What FedEx guy?" Bobby said.

"Shit, we forgot. We have a civilian locked up in the kitchen," Travolta said.

"Show me," Akira said.

McQueen led the way and unlocked the kitchen door. They stepped inside, weapons pointed. The kid had his back to them. Three thermoses were lined up on a counter. He placed the carafe back on the coffeemaker.

Akira tapped him on his shoulder. The kid almost jumped out of his skin as he turned to face her and McQueen, then removed the headset from his ears.

"What's happening?" he asked. "Oh, my God, did my mom send you?" He sighed as tears formed in his eyes. "They've had me trapped here for three years. Oh my God, thank you." His hands went to his face and he began to sob.

"Who are you?" Akira asked as she put a hand on his shoulder.

"I'm Rigo. My mom's Vera. She sent you,

right?" His eyes gleamed with hope.

"Vera?" Akira asked.

She remembered the woman's last words, mumbled through a gag: *Save him, save my son.* And now here he was. Holy shit.

"Yes, call her," Rigo said. "She'll vouch for me."

Akira nodded. "Okay, Rigo, let's go. Let's get out of this tomb."

CHAPTER 43

Rome

Akira exited the terminal and headed toward a freelance limo driver parked at the curb. She tossed the suitcase into the backseat and got in. "Castel Sant'Angelo, per favore."

"Si, signora."

Her cell phone rang and she picked up.

"Ms. Winter? It's Giorgio." He spoke in English with a heavy Italian accent.

"Ciao, Giorgio. Is it ready?"

"Yes. Are you coming?"

"Sure, I'm on my way."

Akira flipped her phone shut and said to the driver, "Sorry about this, but I'm changing itinerary. We're going to Cinecittá."

She handed him a card with Giorgio's address

on it. "Right here."

"No problem."

The driver made a sharp right at an intersection. Several cars honked their horns, and another driver cursed him out.

"Sorry, signora."

Akira chuckled.

Forty minutes later, the cab pulled through the gates of Cinecittá Studios and followed a sign that read *Set Design & Build DPT*.

"Right there, signora—that small building on the right," the driver said.

She entered. It was smaller inside than she'd expected—a cramped desk in a corner and curtains covering a section of the back wall.

Akira moved the drapes aside, revealing a doorway. It led to a carpenter's shop inside a back warehouse attached to the same building.

Giorgio, a skilled prop master, was stocky and looked every bit of his fifty-eight years. He was standing on a Carrara marble platform two feet deep, two feet tall, and three feet wide. He jumped off it, landing awkwardly on his dusty brown loafers, and winced as he straightened, holding his side.

"That's going to hurt tomorrow. Hello, Ms. Winter," he said, his generous smile accentuated by a large silver mustache.

They shook hands.

"Buongiorno," Akira said, and appraised the platform. "It looks great. I can't tell it's fake. Is it wood?"

Giorgio smirked proudly. "No, no wood. But it is stronger than wood. Carbon fiber. Light and super strong. I learned how to work with this material back in Modena."

"How does it open?"

"I hid a small latch in the inside. Same on the outside. See here?" He pointed at a tiny indentation. "You press here."

Giorgio pressed a small recessed button and the side of the marble base opened. Inside was hollow, the space large enough for a person.

"It's not too large to transport?" Akira asked.

"No, signora. It folds, like origami. It weighs only ten pounds." Giorgio picked up the box, then twisted it. The box clicked four times and folded into a single flat panel. "Good, right?"

Then he twisted the panel again and the box reverted to its original box shape.

"Great work, Giorgio. Bobby will pick it up later today."

Akira got back into the limo and headed to the Grand Olympic, a hotel conveniently located only half a mile from the Vatican.

———

Adriano rode through the Vatican gates, his red MV-Agusta F4's headlight beam sweeping across the two guards at each side of the entrance. He slowed the motorbike down to a crawl.

The guards waved him through and he drove a few blocks, then turned into a small alleyway and parked next to an old green double door.

He turned the lights off and killed the engine, pulled the kickstand down with the heel of one of his Prada hi-tops, then removed the helmet. He stuffed his gloves inside and hung it on the handlebar, then smoothed his black Valentino suit and checked his blood-red tie.

Inside the building, he passed by a line of mailboxes on a wall to his right, then limped up the staircase. His kneecap had never recovered from the parting gift he'd received from Akira back in Greece. He stopped at apartment A, unlocked the door and flicked a light switch.

The hair on the back of his neck bristled as tiny black dots floated in front of his eyes.

The room was suddenly enveloped by a sparkling vortex, and a crackling sound invaded his head. At first, he thought he was having a seizure, then the smell of hair burning told him otherwise. Someone had jammed a taser into the back of his neck.

Everything went black ...

Then he was sitting up in the middle of his living room, his limbs bound. His jacket, shirt, and tie had been removed.

What the hell? What kind of coward used a taser?

Akira's pale face emerged from the shadows across the room.

Adriano blinked through the gloom. Was he having a seizure after all? How could this woman be standing in front of him? It wasn't possible. She was dead for sure. He'd killed her. Did she have a twin?

"You're probably thinking this isn't fair game, right? Me ambushing you like this? Using this?" Akira waved the taser.

Adriano tried to focus as his kaleidoscopic vision adjusted. As the woman came nearer, the image came together.

She turned the lights on.

Reached into a long duffle bag to her right.

Placed a katana on the table. The blade shimmered as she pulled it out of its sheath.

"How?" Adriano asked. "How is this p-possible?"

Akira turned her head and pushed a clump of hair back. Part of her scalp had been shaved, revealing a long C-shaped scar.

"Pretty bad ass, right? I had a titanium plate. That's what saved me."

"Cazzo. I should have shot you."

"Where is she?" Akira asked.

"May I have my Bible?" Adriano said. "It's over there on the table."

"No, you may not."

"Okay. I understand."

Akira placed the blade on his shoulder. "Where is she?"

"Fine, right to the point. Believe it or not, she's not too far. She's with a cardinal, Leo Müller."

"Where?"

"At a museum. It's his hideout from the pope. The Museum of the Saints. It's–"

"I know where that is."

Adriano smiled, surrendering to whatever was coming next.

"You know," Akira said, "I could have shot you with this." She gestured toward her holstered Glock. "Instead, you're dying by the sword."

"I figured. Why bring a sword to a gun fight?"

"Right."

"Precious in the sight of the Lord is the death of his saints." Adriano stared at her. "They ordered me to kill your little Mina, did you know that? But I didn't, so am I a saint?"

"No, you're not."

She extended her arm and placed the tip of the katana in front of Adriano's mouth. "Open your mouth, or I'll open it for you."

"You think I'm scared?" Adriano hissed, his

mouth wide open.

Akira inserted the sharp blade.

It sliced through his tongue and the inside side of his cheek.

Adriano gagged, tried to move his head away, but he had nowhere to go.

And then she lunged.

———————

Akira pulled the blade out of Adriano's head. She put the katana into the bag and speed-dialed Bobby.

"You okay?" he asked.

"Yes, all good. He's done."

"Great." Bobby let out a sigh. "You got Mina?"

"No, we have a slight issue. She's with ... How should I put it? She's with a cardinal. They're holding her in some fucking museum."

"What? There's over a hundred of them."

"Yes, but I got a name. Leo Müller."

She killed the line.

———————

Akira fired up the MV-Agusta and rode toward the Vatican gates. The guards were busy with an incoming vehicle and waved her through. She made a right into Via di Porta Angelica, and a few blocks later turned into a tight alleyway. She stopped behind a box truck, revved and drove up its ramp, dumped the bike and helmet, then hopped into the passenger seat of the truck's cab.

Bobby was already at the wheel.

"A cardinal, huh?" he said as he drove off.

"Yes."

"Well, Giorgio's box is in place. I guess we need it after all."

"That's why it's good to have Plan B," Akira said.

CHAPTER 44

Supernova

The museum was in a palazzo not far from the Vatican. It had once belonged to the Borgias family, and it was a four-story structure the size of a football field. On the fourth-floor hall, Akira had found the perfect time to slip into Giorgio's box, and now sat in darkness. Even from inside she could hear the tourists' chatter coming from the Hall of the Dead. Giorgio had built it with such precision that the only light leaking in came from tiny vent holes that provided air. She pulled Mina's pink pacifier from her pocket and kissed it. Then she tethered it to the katana's hilt.

"... and this is the reason Pope Alexander VI commissioned Pinturicchio to paint this beautiful fresco," a guide said. "This is the last stop for today."

There was a collective murmur, and voices expressed their astonishment in multiple languages.

"Well, it's closing time, everyone. It's time for us to head for the exit. Please follow me. Tomorrow, we'll continue our tour with the Chapel of the Saints. Thank you all."

As people passed her, Akira heard the patter of soft shoes and boots, and the occasional clip-clop of high heels. Someone bumped the box, kicking it hard. The thump echoed in the hallway like a timpani drum. Akira pushed at the sides of the box, deadening the sound.

There was silence for a moment, then a woman's voice hissed, "I've told you not to touch anything. Come on!"

Akira exhaled, and wiped at the sweat on her forehead. Fucking kids.

———————

Much planning had gone into finding the perfect spot for the box and placing it in position. Bobby had pretended to be an artist delivering an ancient canvas that needed restoration. Once away from security cameras, he'd unwrapped and unfolded the box and left Giorgio's astonishing trompe l'oeil next to a marble wall of the same texture and color.

No one would be able to tell that the faux marble pedestal didn't belong there, no matter how close they got. Unless they touched it.

That fucking kid.

Akira felt for her weapons, checking their position. A silenced Beretta holstered to her Kevlar vest. A tactical claw knife in a sheath fastened to her belt. And her katana, Itami. It lay diagonally on the floor beneath her.

She looked at her wristwatch. Half an hour past closing time.

It's now or never.

She removed a small plug that Giorgio had built in the box's front. Through it hole she could see both sides of the hallway. No one there.

She unlatched the hinges, opened the front panel, and emerged holding the katana. She sheathed the sword and took out the claw knife, her free hand ready to grab the pistol if needed.

She closed the panel and stole toward the Hall of the Dead.

She'd studied the floor plan, could navigate every corner of the museum, and knew precisely where the cardinal was.

Two armed guards turned a corner and faced her. They looked surprised, fumbled for their guns, and were met with the muted spit of Akira's silenced Beretta. Both slumped down onto the marble floor.

Akira turned another corner, heading for the museum office without breaking stride. The office door swung open. A priest stepped out, stopped, confusion washing over his face.

He opened his mouth, but Akira slashed his throat with the claw knife before he could make a sound. Blood spewed from the wound as he dropped down dead.

She peeked into the room, but it was empty, and continued forward along the corridor until she arrived at another exhibit.

Seven priests stepped out of the massive doorway and she almost bumped into them.

"Chi sei? Fermati! Stop!" one yelled as he reached for her.

Akira turned, but two of them grabbed her and slammed her against the wall. A third man launched a sidekick toward her stomach, but she blocked it with her left leg and twisted her body at an odd angle. The two priests holding her lost their grip. Akira swung the claw knife across their necks, once ... twice ... three times. They fell as the third man grabbed her from behind. Akira walked her legs up the wall, flipped her body over, wrapped her thighs around the man's neck, tensing and pulling until his neck snapped.

Another priest shoved his fist toward her face. She parried the punch and she slashed his face, cutting him from lip to cheek. He screamed and tried to stem the blood gushing from his mouth with his hands. Akira punched him in the sternum, grabbed her pistol and shot him in the head.

Four down, three to go.

Akira bolted forward, jump-kicked one man in the face, knocking his teeth in; slashed at another man's face with the claw knife at the same time. She landed as the third priest pulled a knife from under his cloak and threw it at her.

It missed and landed in a wooden door behind her.

The priest with the cut face grabbed her arm. She slashed his wrist, and he began to bleed out, screaming as he tried to stop the blood flow. Akira aimed her Beretta and popped him twice in the head.

Five down.

The man who'd thrown the knife pulled his pistol out, but not quick enough. She launched the claw knife toward him, stabbing him in the eye, then kicked him in the face.

She took a deep breath and stared into the eyes of the last priest standing.

He was tall and muscular with a shaved head. He pulled off his collar and tossed it, revealing a swastika tattoo on his neck. He reached behind his cloak and produced two tactical tomahawks with handle straps that he tethered to his wrists, then swirled the axes in the air like helicopter blades.

Akira pointed the Beretta and depressed the trigger, but it jammed. *Shit*.

She unsheathed her sword and took the waki no kamae fighting stance—the katana in both hands, blade pointing down toward her back.

The pacifier dangled from the hilt. The man's glanced at it, his eyes narrowed. A perplexed look washed over his face.

He blinked twice, then spun the tomahawks downward, shearing the air.

Akira struck.

The axes flew up and over, landing into the hallway behind her, the man's severed hands still gripping them.

He shrieked, fell to his knees, blood spurting from the stumps of his arms. Akira brought down the ancient carbon steel blade, and sliced him from head to crotch.

She'd re-sheathed the sword before the two halves of the man's body had separated.

Akira stepped around the pool of carnage and headed further into the hall.

The building was vast, with over three-hundred rooms, including an exquisite library stacked with books floor to ceiling—books the public would never be allowed to see. Akira moved down the hallway passed several administrative offices, then ducked into a room where an armed guard dressed in tactical gear stood by a chair. As he turned, she fired the Beretta—a double tap to the head. He collapsed into the chair. Akira inspected the rest of the room, then headed back into the hallway.

At a corner, she turned left. Around her was a magnificent collection of frescoes and artifacts dating back centuries. And ahead, down the hall, was the cardinal's secret office. A long green rug embroidered with gold braid covered the floor. She followed it, passing an empty dining room and kitchen to her right and a private office to her left.

There was no one in sight, but she could hear voices ahead. They came from the cardinal's private chambers.

Akira closed in on the sound and approached a junction. To the right was a short hallway where the cardinal's room was located.

Instead of entering, she turned left down another corridor. The cardinal could wait. She needed to find Mina.

There was a bathroom, a bedroom, and at the end of the corridor the TV room where his closest friend, the chief of security—Dirk Matthias Frei—watched the news.

Akira stopped at the bedroom door. Inside was a woman who oversaw cleaning duties—Maria, fifty-five, tall, hair pulled back in a bun. She usually worked with two other women, but they shift had ended.

It was the cardinal's private secretary Akira had to look out for. Luciano Giordano, ex-Italian Special Forces, in charge of security, and one of Adriano's peers. He would be standing behind the door, armed with an Uzi.

The ancient green door was solid but not thick enough to stop a bullet. Akira looked down at the crack between the door and the floor. Saw a tell-tale shadow.

Her muscles tightened.

She unsheathed her katana.

And lunged.

The door swung open. Akira entered the room and let the door slide back. Luciano hung there, impaled on her blade. His dead eyes stared ahead.

Maria gestured to the bed. "Right there. She's okay."

Tears welled as Akira walked over to her daughter. She picked her up, hugged her, and kissed her forehead. "My baby, momma's here. You're coming home."

Maria spoke into her cell phone. "We're almost done, Bobby. I'm coming out with Mina. We'll meet you at the hotel." She ended the call and turned to Akira. "We need to move. I'll take her. She won't wake up for another hour."

"Where is he?" Akira asked.

"In his chamber with two assistants. But Frei is alone in the TV room. We'll see you at the hotel. You take care."

Maria had worked at the museum for two years and had been preparing for this moment since Bobby, her old friend, had contacted her, asking for her help.

Maria carried Mina into the hallway.

Akira braced herself. Then pulled the katana out of the door. There was a thump as Luciano's body dropped to the floor.

Akira headed to the TV room first. Dirk Matthias Frei was staring at the monitor where Italian Prime Minister Silvio Berlusconi was discussing his new public-works program. Akira double tapped him in the back of the head. Then she shot the TV screen.

Now for the cardinal.

The two assistants—bodyguards—were Piero Battaglia and Antonio Ferrazza. Both special ops, late twenties, and armed with Berettas.

She walked down the hallway to the chamber and picked the lock on the door, then entered a foyer that led into the cardinal's chamber. Piero and Antonio were on their knees in front of Cardinal Leo Müller. His eyes were closed and he was reciting something in Latin she couldn't make out.

Akira shot Piero and Antonio in the head,

spraying blood over the cardinal's cassock. His eyes widened as they slumped onto the floor. Akira holstered the pistol and unsheathed the katana. The cardinal's expression changed, and he regained his composure. Cold as the marble he was surrounded by.

"Who are you? What have you done? Get out. This is a sacred place," he said, his tone so sharp it could have cracked a mirror.

He reached for a phone on a table, but Akira swung the katana, slicing through the cord. The cardinal stepped back and dropped the receiver.

"You don't know what's going on, do you?" Akira said.

"No, I ..."

She inched forward, pointing the katana at him. He edged back until his back was against the windowsill.

"Wait, are you a believer?" he asked.

"I believe you've betrayed those who serve you. So, yes."

"Why are you here? What do you think you're going to achieve?" Müller said, clutching his gold crucifix. "You can't kill me."

"Your boy Adriano is no longer with us, and your god isn't coming for you either."

"You're crazy. You have no idea what you're up against."

"I know about the girls you raped and tortured here. Charles Barton is dead. And just in case you're thinking that your god's banker got away with the money scam, we've siphoned every penny of the two-hundred million you held in the Bahamas. I have it all."

"You are the devil." the cardinal whispered.

"The devil? I don't think that even you believe it exists. And if you dig deep, under all of that pretense, I don't think you believe in the alternative."

The cardinal's face tensed. "I have no fear of moving into the unknown. But you, you shall fear your judgment, woman."

"There, see? Not the devil, but a woman and a mother."

His eyes narrowed, and his tight lips parted, baring his teeth. "You, bitch," he hissed.

"There you are. So easy when you peel back the layers."

"Who are you?"

"I'll tell you what I am not. I'm not a pedophile, and I don't wish to control billions of people with your lies."

"Fuck you."

"There you are again."

"Who sent you?"

"It's like physics, Müller. We have traveled through space and time just to get to this moment. We began as two independent particles ...

until we were entangled—the moment you took my daughter."

He seemed confused for a moment. "The child? That's why you're here?"

"We've been on a collision course, you and I, since the beginning of time. Some things can't be explained until you get to the last fucking second. And this is that second. Now you'll have your answer."

Akira took a step forward.

The cardinal looked from side to side, but he'd run out of space. The confusion turned to defiance, but fear lurked in the depth of his eyes.

"Are you the mother?"

"I am the song."

"What?"

"I am the song at the center of her universe. I am the planet off its course. The unexpected."

"Nothing is unexpected. Everything is ordained by God."

Akira raised the sword, Mina's pacifier dangling from its hilt.

"You have strayed from the light, forsaken it," Müller said.

Akira gripped the handle, her knuckles white. "I am the supernova. I am the light."

The cardinal swatted at the air in front of him. His gold Rolex peeked from under his sleeve. "You'll burn in hell for your insignificant hopeless justice."

"You unholy motherfucker," she hissed, and swung Itami.

The blade severed his head. It hurtled out of the open window behind him, and blood streaked the moon crimson red.

CHAPTER 45

Water

ONE WEEK LATER
HOLLYWOOD BEACH, OXNARD, CALIFORNIA

Ahead, the Anacapas looked like a dragon's crest poking out of the water in the blinding five o'clock sun. Mina clutched three white orchids. Bobby stood next to a surfboard planted in the sand. And Akira traced her fingers over the dragon carved into the urn containing Kyle's ashes. By the shore, forty surfers had gathered with their boards to honor him, to say goodbye to an old friend. They wore Hawaiian leis and chatted, remembering him as they burned sage. These were the people who'd known Kyle since his teens, when he was a lifeguard. Most hadn't seen him since he'd joined the military.

Ron, a tall, trim man in his forties, was the master of ceremonies. He turned to the small crowd and waved his paddle. Everyone got quiet.

"Before we paddle out to form the floating memorial and say goodbye to our brother Kyle, I want you to know that we are bound to this earth, so please pick up some trash. We want to leave this beach a better place than it was before we got here. Thank you."

Akira hugged him. "Thank you, Ron, for organizing this. And thank you all for being here. I know some of you have traveled a great distance to say goodbye. After this, you're invited up at Ron's house to celebrate Kyle, eat and drink. I'm sure we all have some fun stories to share."

"Kyle is in our hearts," Ron said, "and as Kyle would say, let's tape this bitch up like Van Halen's guitar."

Everyone laughed.

"And remember, the ocean brings us together," she added.

Bobby brought the surfboard to her and they kissed. Akira got into the water and straddled the board. Bobby picked up Mina, kissed her forehead, and placed her on the surfboard between her mother's legs.

"The ocean brings us together," the surfers repeated in unison.

They paddled a mile out, gathered in a circle, and held hands. Akira and Ron paddled into the center as a Coast Guard rescue vessel approached and idled nearby.

Akira and Ron said a few words, and the surfers again chanted, "The ocean brings us together," and threw their flowers into the circle. Akira opened the urn. It had been three long years since she'd lost Kyle, but she had Mina, and she would never let her go.

She tipped the urn spilling the ashes into the ocean.

Mina looked up at her. Akira kissed the top of her head, then looked up at the sky and closed her eyes. The chanting swirled in her mind. *The ocean brings us together. The ocean brings us together.*

Then the Coast Guard sprayed a stream of water toward the floating memorial.

Mina giggled as a dolphin swam right under the flowers, then disappeared into the deep blue below. Akira felt the warmth of her daughter's body against her. Another chance, another life. And on the shore, Bobby waited for them. And with him, the beginning of a new day.

EPILOGUE

SEVERAL DAYS LATER
HOLLYWOOD, CALIFORNIA

Amber was behind the wheel of a brand-new, white Corvette Z06. Her shiny red mane caught in the wind through the open window, revealing a long neck, flawless but for the scars from two bullet wounds. She liked her music loud. Enough so that anyone in the next car would know that she had refined taste. At a time when most people listened to pop, she played "Birdland" by Weather Report.

Once parked, she turned to the rear-view mirror. Lipstick, check. Eyebrows, mascara, check. She emerged from the Corvette, Prada heels preceding long legs and what some said was a magnificent behind. The Versace hot pants weren't doing any harm.

She stood there for a couple of seconds, taking it in, then looked down at the sticky urine-stained sidewalk.

She gagged. For fuck's sake, what was that stench? She blinked a few times, like it might shake away the sensation. Fucking people. Couldn't they piss in a bush rather than on the sidewalk?

The silk of her blouse rippled in the breeze, caressing her nipples. She adjusted her Gucci shades and picked up her pace, leaving behind the urine fest, heading east for her favorite coffee house. Coffee—that would help.

She strutted down Melrose Avenue as if she owned the funky two-mile cluster of stores selling everything from used clothes to couture-wanna-bee designer labels and a few tailor-owned boutiques. Sprinkled with the best restaurants and coffee houses, it was the perfect street, second only to Rodeo Drive, her go-to place for shopping and dining.

After eighteen-months in a coma and two years rehabilitating from the nine bullets she'd taken from Kyle three years earlier, this was exactly what the doctor ordered. Relax, eat, shop, party.

And one more thing—revenge.

Begun on February 2022
Completed on July 2023

Thank you for reading *Killher*!

I hope you enjoyed the ride, and if you did, please don't forget to tell your friends. For independent authors, exposure is everything. You are the first line of assassins, so please leave a review.

ALSO AVAILABLE FROM THE AUTHORS

PALE WITCH, a horror novella.

A condemned man. A cursed witch. A pact that defies time. From 1931 New York to Los Angeles decades later, an ancient evil resurfaces—and a final reckoning awaits.

ACKNOWLEDGMENTS

I am grateful to the following people
for all their support.
No one writes a book alone.

To my wife, Gay, my partner in crime, for
art directing the cover, tolerating my obsession,
and giving me strength throughout.

To Larry, for helping me keep the first seedling alive.
To my brother-in-law, David, the only one that read the whole
manuscript when I needed it, and for all the advice.
To Ennio, my childhood pal, for all the helpful comments.
To my friend Rob for being so supportive.
To Mitch, for your encouragement—your
words of support meant so much.
To Russell, Amy, and Zia for listening.
To Martin, my 90's computer wiz.
To my neurosurgeon, Dr. Westra—well, I'm alive.
To Tina and CTN Studio for being so supportive.
To my friend and EMT Jesus for being an awesome consultant.
To Fox Mulder, for your inspiration
to start writing at 4:30 a.m. everyday.

And finally, to my editor Louise, for your guidance
and for sharing your mad katana skills.

Valerio Ventura is a multi-award-winning artist, and a 2014 Prime-Time Emmy award recipient with more than thirty years of experience in the film industry.

Born in Rome, Italy, Valerio grew up on the stressed-out and crime-ridden streets of the Quadraro neighborhood, near the Cinecitta Film Studios where Fellini and Sergio Leone made cinematic history.

As a teen, Valerio dreamed of coming to the US. After moving to California and becoming a US citizen, he devoted himself to art directing animated shows, and writing and directing television commercials and music videos. Now he's decided to write and publish his own books.

In this first novel in the Akira series, Valerio explores the world of assassins with razor-sharp action, hyperviolence, sex, dark humor, and urban poetry.

MORE BOOKS AVAILABLE FROM THE AUTHORS

ECHOES IN THE WALLS
Horror Poems by G.A. Lawrence

More books by Valerio Ventura:

GRAFFITI DREAMIN'
Urban Art

WE ZOIX!
Fine Art

NOVA
Hell in the Machine
A Sci-Fi Noir Thriller

Visit these websites for more information

www.ValerioVentura.com
www.GA-Lawrence.com

www.Zomvoos.com
The art of G.A. Lawrence